"So, will I live?"

Erik growled, watching the nurse through narrowed eyes. He shifted to his side and swore again as pain ripped through him.

Her tone softened, and Marybeth almost smiled as she made some notations on his chart. "I'm afraid so," she replied. "Unless our hospital food kills you or your own sweet disposition does you in."

Before Erik could speak again, she turned away. "I'll send the doctor."

"Wait," he demanded. But she was gone.

Great going, he told himself. She was only being nice. Why had he jumped on her like that?

Erik raked a hand over his face. He knew damned well why. Because Marybeth *was* nice. And the last thing he needed was some sweet-faced angel of mercy making him comfortable. Making him feel good. Making him want what he, of all people, had no right to want...

Dear Reader,

Each month, Silhouette **Special Edition** publishes six novels with you in mind—stories of love and life, tales that you can identify with—romance with that little "something special" added in.

August is a month for dreams . . . for hot, sunny days and warm, sultry nights. And with that in mind, don't miss these six sizzling Silhouette **Special Edition** novels! Curtiss Ann Matlock has given us *Last of the Good Guys*—Jesse Breen's story. You met him in *Annie in the Morning* (SE#695). And the duo BEYOND THE THRESHOLD from Linda Lael Miller continues with the book *Here and Then*—Rue's story.

Rounding out this month are more stories by some of your favorite authors: Laurey Bright, Ada Steward, Pamela Toth and Pat Warren.

In each Silhouette **Special Edition** novel, we're dedicated to bringing you stories that will delight as well as bring a tear to the eye. For me, good romance novels have always contained an element of hope, of optimism that life can be, and often is, very beautiful. I find a great deal of inspiration in that thought.

What do you consider essential in a good romance? I'd really like to hear your opinions on the books that we publish and on the romance genre in general. Please write to me c/o Silhouette Books, 300 East 42nd Street, 6th floor, New York, NY 10017.

I hope that you enjoy this book and all of the stories to come. I'm looking forward to hearing from you!

Sincerely,

Tara Gavin
Senior Editor
Silhouette Books

PAMELA TOTH
A Warming Trend

Silhouette Special Edition

Published by Silhouette Books New York

America's Publisher of Contemporary Romance

This book is dedicated with love to Wilma Patterson,
a special lady and a terrific mom-in-law,
who made me feel welcome from the start

SILHOUETTE BOOKS
300 East 42nd St., New York, N.Y. 10017

A WARMING TREND

Copyright © 1992 by Pamela Toth

ISBN: 0-373-09760-3

First Silhouette Books printing August 1992

Printed in the U.S.A.

Books by Pamela Toth

Silhouette Special Edition

Thunderstruck #411
Dark Angel #515
Old Enough To Know Better #624
Two Sets of Footprints #729
A Warming Trend #760

Silhouette Romance

Kissing Games #500
The Ladybug Lady #595

PAMELA TOTH

was born in Wisconsin, but grew up in Seattle, where she attended the University of Washington and majored in art. She still lives in the Pacific Northwest with her husband, two teenage daughters, a boxer named Jackson, two Siamese cats and several tanks of tropical fish. Relationships have always fascinated her, especially relationships between parent and child, friends and lovers, husband and wife. Writing romances gives her the chance to explore the courtship between men and women, and the potential for love that exists in all of us. When she isn't sitting at her computer, she likes to read, travel and spend time with her family and pets.

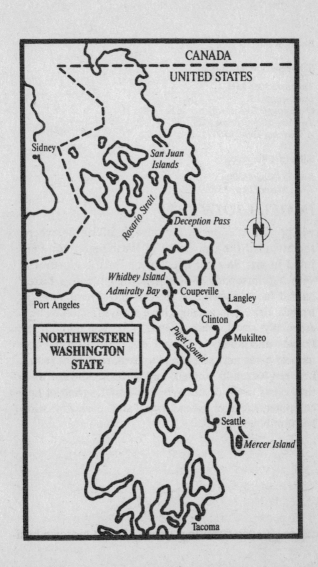

CANADA

UNITED STATES

Sidney

San Juan
Islands

Rosario Strait

Deception Pass

Whidbey Island
Admiralty Bay · Coupeville

Langley

Port Angeles

Clinton

**NORTHWESTERN
WASHINGTON
STATE**

Mukilteo

Puget Sound

Seattle

Mercer Island

Tacoma

Chapter One

Marybeth waited impatiently in line, wishing she were somewhere else. There were still two people ahead of her, and only two tellers. She glanced around. Four more customers stood behind her in the afternoon sun that poured through the window.

Her eyes met the piercing blue gaze of a man with silver-blond hair. Something flickered briefly between them before she looked away. She had seen him before in the small town of Coupeville but wasn't sure when. Perhaps he had come into the hospital where she was a nurse.

"May I help you?" One of the tellers smiled expectantly. An older man in front of Marybeth, wearing baggy jeans and a blue work shirt, stepped forward. Overhead, the lazy ceiling fan stirred the warm air as she double-checked her deposit slip.

Two people behind her, Erik Snow fought down his impatience. He hated waiting. Usually he did his town business in the middle of the week, in the morning when the stores weren't busy and the bank was deserted. Or he sent his hired man, Trevor. Even studying the feminine curves of the woman farther up in line, her legs slim in white hose that matched her uniform, her caramel curls glinting in the sunlight, wasn't enough to divert Erik's mind from the time he was wasting.

He forced himself to take in a deep breath while he looked around slowly at the muted blue and rose of the bank lobby's walls and carpeting. Restful colors. Erik felt anything but restful. Too much work awaited him at the ranch. Idly he examined the bank's layout, brightened by the sunlight coming through the windows and the glass front doors, and then, falling back on old habits, he began studying the other people in the lobby.

A tall, gaunt man with dark hair and a pockmarked face partly obliterated by a bushy mustache stood at a side table where blank forms were kept for the customers' convenience, but he wasn't filling anything out. As Erik watched, the man nodded toward the end of the line. Curious, Erik followed his gaze to an older bearded man wearing a bulky windbreaker despite the day's warmth.

As the second man nodded back, patting the front of his jacket, Erik's instincts came alive, screaming *danger*.

Too late.

The bearded man turned, stepping away from the ragged line of people. His hand dived into the front of his jacket. Erik cursed beneath his breath, shifting slightly forward to shield the pregnant woman ahead of him.

The holdup man whipped out a gun. "Nobody move!"

His younger accomplice did the same as he came around the side table. The pregnant woman began to scream. The bearded robber whirled to level his gun at the tellers, frozen behind the counter. "Touch anything, and you're dead. Step back slowly." Both women obeyed, hands up.

Erik wondered if either teller had been able to press an alarm button. He glanced around, but there was no bank guard. The pregnant woman next to him was still screaming.

"Shut up," the younger gunman shouted, waving his weapon. "Now."

She shut up. Erik could still hear her muffled sobs.

The older robber circled behind the counter and tossed a cloth sack to one of the tellers. "Fill this. C'mon, baby, *move!*" She immediately complied, working quickly.

Good, Erik thought. Let's all cooperate and maybe no one will get hurt.

A man at the front of the line lunged suddenly, grabbing for the young robber's arm. He pulled free and crashed his gun down on the man's bald head, cursing.

Erik watched the heavyset body crumple. Fool, he thought. You could have gotten us all killed.

Behind him, the pregnant woman screamed again. The woman in the white uniform turned slowly and looked back at her. One part of Erik's brain registered that she was attractive in an uncomplicated way. Her skin was smooth and clear, her eyes dark with concern. On her uniform was pinned a name tag: Marybeth MacNamara, RN, it said. Again Erik's gaze snagged hers. He was tempted to smile, just to reassure her. Stay calm, he willed silently instead.

"Stand still and shut up!" the gunman who had hit the old man shouted. "Or somebody's gonna get shot." He gestured with the pistol, and someone gasped. "Hurry up," he screamed at the teller. She was shoving handfuls of bills into the bag under the watchful eye of the bearded robber, who kept glancing at the front doors.

Erik moved slowly, turning to the pregnant woman beside him. He tried to calm her with his eyes but she wouldn't look up.

"Shh," he whispered. "You're only upsetting him."

"No talking!" The younger gunman moved closer, his hand trembling with nerves. "You her old man?"

Erik shook his head. "Just someone who wants to stay alive."

"You might not if she keeps screaming." He grinned, showing an uneven row of discolored teeth below the ragged mustache. Erik memorized his narrow face.

Someone moved, and the robber leaped back, swearing. "Dammit, lady!" he shouted at the nurse. "I almost blew your damned head off."

She paled but her expression remained determined. "Let me help her," she said, indicating the pregnant woman between her and Erik. "She'd be better off sitting down. And calmer. Wouldn't that be easier for you?"

Erik watched closely as the gunman studied the young woman in white. She stood before him as if she were in a doctor's office talking to a patient. She had guts, Erik thought appreciatively.

The younger robber scratched at his scarred cheek as his gaze raked her. Erik went tense.

"Okay," he said finally. "Drop your purse and move slow." He looked around warily.

Not taking her eyes off the gun, the nurse walked past Erik, taking the woman's arm gently. The scent of flowers caught him off guard.

"Come on," the nurse coaxed. "Let's sit down right over there." They moved a few feet away, to where two rose-colored chairs were positioned together.

"Okay, okay," the older robber told the teller. "That's enough." He grabbed the bag of money and hurried out from behind the counter. "Let's go."

As they headed toward the glass front doors, a local police car pulled up. Erik groaned to himself.

"Damn!" The bearded man carrying the money, whom Erik assumed was the boss, crouched and wheeled around, facing the room. His eyes shifted wildly. He reminded Erik of a rat looking for a hole. Outside, through the glass, Erik could see the policeman emerge slowly from the car, bending to say something to his partner and then laughing. They had no idea what was going on in the bank.

"Everybody down! On the floor, *now!*" Both gunmen circled the little group and then ducked down at the ends of the counter where they could see the people inside the bank and also watch the front doors.

"Over with the others," one said to the tellers, who were still behind the counter. "Quick! You, too." He gestured to the two women who were sitting down. "Hit the floor!"

They all got to their knees and then stretched flat. The man who'd been hit on the head groaned and stirred.

Outside, the officer straightened and pulled out his wallet, walking toward the bank. Two steps away from the doors he finally peered inside as one robber stood and waved his gun.

"Get back! We have hostages!"

The policeman gave one disbelieving look and then dived for the open door of the patrol car. Erik could see his partner grab the mike as he hunched down.

"Be brave and you're dead!" The gunman's voice cracked with fear. He hadn't counted on this, Erik could tell. A nervous man with a gun was doubly dangerous.

"Over here!" the older robber shouted at him. "Stay down, or they'll pick you off."

Erik didn't think the police would fire into the building with civilians inside. At least not until they got some sharpshooters or a SWAT team at the scene. He doubted that Whidbey Island had either, and he wondered how much experience the local officers had with hostage situations. Help would have to come from the mainland, maybe Seattle. They were *all* in for a long wait.

The boss glanced around, spotting one of the tellers lying facedown on the carpet. "You!" he said, nudging her with his foot, "go lock the front door. Is there another entrance?"

She got to her hands and knees, and nodded. "Yes, through there." She indicated with an inclination of her head.

"Lock it, too. I'll go with you."

While they were gone, the younger man waved his gun at the rest of them. "Nobody get cute," he growled, "or you're dead." He caught Erik's gaze and grinned. "You first if you don't put your head down."

Erik complied. He had seen beads of sweat on the robber's forehead, between his dark, lanky hair and his thick eyebrows. Maybe he was strung out. The other one was still in control despite this new twist, one they obviously hadn't counted on. He probably had more experience. Might have killed before. Erik's blood chilled, and he wondered if any of them would still be alive when this was over. He found himself thinking of the pregnant woman and the nurse with her quiet courage, hoping that *they*, at least, would be spared.

Several feet away, Marybeth reached out slowly and grasped the wrist of the woman who lay awkwardly beside her, shaking with fear. She had said she was five months along.

"It's okay," Marybeth whispered. "Just do what they say."

"No talking!" the scar-faced gunman screamed.

"Police!" the officer shouted from outside. "Come out with your hands up."

The boss was back from locking the rear door. "No way," he yelled back. "We have several hostages—we want to deal."

There was no reply. Marybeth hung on to the other woman's wrist, feeling the racing pulse and wishing she dared look up to see what was happening. The carpet beneath her face was dusty, and she fought back a sneeze.

By the time a half hour had crawled by, there were more squad cars out front, from the county sheriff's department and state patrol, as well as local police. A telephone hookup had been established. The older robber picked up the receiver when it rang after shouted instructions from outside.

"We want a helicopter and a pilot," he yelled, "and we want it yesterday." He listened for a moment, uttered a curse, and slammed down the phone. Everyone was getting more nervous.

"I have to go to the bathroom," the pregnant woman, who'd told Marybeth her name was Susan, said in a low voice.

The younger gunman whipped around. "What did you say?"

"She needs to use the rest room," Marybeth told him, raising her head.

"Forget it," he snarled. "Nobody moves."

"Please," she continued, making herself look into his crazed eyes. "I'll go with her."

He sneered, about to speak, but before he could, his partner did.

"Take them both. Stay with them."

"Thank you." Marybeth helped Susan to her feet. Her face was pale and her eyes were wide with fear. One hand rested protectively across her stomach.

"I'll be right behind you. No talking." The younger man followed them right into the rest room, waiting there while both women went into the stalls. Marybeth decided it would be a good idea to take advantage of the opportunity, ignoring the indignity of the man's presence as best she could.

When she followed Susan back to the lobby, she saw the customer with the light blond hair turn his head and look up at her. Something on his face compelled her to move closer before she knelt back down. When she stretched out, she was next to him.

"Marybeth, will you help?" he breathed so quietly she barely heard him.

Surprised, she turned her head slightly, then remembered the name tag she had forgotten to remove. "Yes."

"Later," he whispered. "When they separate."

"Yes," she murmured again, then turned slowly away. She had no idea why she trusted this man instantly, but she did. There was something about him, an air of quiet confidence, of danger met and dealt with, that inspired trust. She didn't know why, but she suddenly felt safer, even though she had probably just agreed to risk her life. This man would protect her, of that she was positive.

Beside her, Erik shifted toward the person on his other side, a thickset young man in a college letterman's jacket. "Tom" was embroidered on the chest.

"If one leaves..." Erik muttered to him, "you, around other side...we distract, you jump him...I'll help...must get gun." He said each word slowly, without haste, waiting each time until the nervous younger gunman was distracted by something outside before speaking.

Beside him, Tom whispered, "Okay." Now they could do nothing but wait.

It was later, dark outside except for street lamps and the flashing lights atop the now large group of police cars. There had been several more impatient phone calls. Again the boss argued, swore over delays and his demands for a chopper. He didn't believe there was nothing available. Erik assumed it was a stall while the cops tried to decide what to do. Everyone must be getting uncomfortable. Even Erik, who had sometimes waited for hours without shifting a muscle, was finding the floor unyielding despite its layer of plush carpeting.

"You could have brought a chopper clear from Seattle by now!" the boss shouted into the receiver. "You'd better do something fast, or we start shooting hostages."

There was silence while he listened, then he swore again. "Fifteen minutes!" he screamed. "Then we off the first one."

The man who'd been hit on the head groaned. The pregnant woman began to whimper. Erik turned his head, looking up at the gunman who'd slammed down the phone. "I gotta use the bathroom," he said. "We all do. It's been a long time."

"Tough," the younger robber said. "Go in your pants."

"No," the boss intervened, raking a hand over his face above his full beard. "It's okay. Take them one at a time. I'll stay here."

Disappointment chilled Erik. He'd hoped the older, more experienced one would go, leaving his younger accomplice to the mercy of Tom. While the two gunmen conferred, Erik looked quickly at Marybeth.

"Whenever I signal, you distract," he whispered. "Understand?"

Her gaze was steady. He wondered what she was thinking behind those gray-green eyes. After all he'd been through, situations so dangerous it had been a miracle he'd escaped, the irony of facing death in a small-town bank on a sprawling island in Washington state almost brought a grin to his mouth. Well, he wasn't going to die without a fight.

Beside him, Marybeth nodded cautiously. "Understood."

"Shut the hell up over here!" the boss screamed, standing over them and kicking at Erik.

"I'm sorry," Marybeth whimpered, the fear in her voice surprising him until he figured out what she was doing. "I'm sorry. I was afraid, so I was just talking. Don't hurt him. I'll be quiet."

The gunman's small eyes narrowed. "You better," he sneered, "or I'll have to keep you with me." He straightened, staring pointedly down her body, then raised his gun to indicate that Erik get up and go to the rest room.

You're a dead man, Erik vowed silently, all his protective instincts aroused when he saw Marybeth's face go white. Then he forced himself to relax. The only way to survive was on nerve and brains, not emotion. Waiting for a chance to catch the younger one off guard, he steeled himself to what he would have to do, feelings forced aside, every sense alerted as he walked slowly toward the men's room, knowing the gun was pointed directly at his back.

The chance didn't present itself until after the two of them returned to the bank lobby. After one teller had closed all the blinds, they had been allowed to stand and stretch while they were taken one at a time down the hall.

When they were all back, the boss glanced at the other gunman, who had escorted each of them.

"I'm going to the head. Keep an eye on things."

After he went down the hallway, Erik glanced at Tom. Catching the younger man's eye, he blinked slowly, then shifted away. He looked to make sure that Marybeth was watching. She was.

"Hey," Erik said to their captor, "that's some gun you've got. Can I see it?"

The young robber looked surprised, and then he stepped closer, in front of Tom, who had been inching aside. "Sure." He aimed right at Erik's head. "You wanta see a bullet close up, too?"

Erik gave him a sheepish grin, hands outspread and palms up. "Sorry," he said haltingly. "I didn't mean anything."

The gunman leaned closer. "Shut up, or you'll be dead sorry."

As soon as his attention shifted away, Erik glanced at Marybeth and lowered his head slowly. She blinked back, then clutched her stomach and doubled over.

"Ooh," she groaned loudly. "Help me!"

The gunman turned away from Tom, who immediately lunged, hand chopping downward. The gun skittered across the carpet. Erik dived for it as the other two struggled.

"Frank! Frank!" the robber shouted as Erik grabbed the gun. He couldn't risk a shot—he might hit Tom. As he rose to one knee, Frank raced in, gun pointed directly at Erik. Even as a burning explosion filled his chest, Erik's finger squeezed the trigger. He saw Frank go down. Someone screamed as Erik plummeted headlong into darkness.

* * *

When Erik woke up, he was in a hospital bed, in a cool room with blue walls and flowered curtains. His chest and shoulder were sore as hell, and he groaned when he tried to move. With a curse, he stabbed at the bell to summon a nurse, wondering what had happened at the bank after he'd been shot.

To his pleased surprise, it was Marybeth who answered his call. "You're awake!" she exclaimed. "How are you feeling?"

He ignored the burst of pleasure he felt at her presence, ignored her question.

"How long have I been out? What happened back there? And why are *you* here?" His tone was unfriendly, to say the least.

Her smile faded. "You've been here since yesterday," she said brusquely as she began to check his vital signs. "You shot one gunman, and Tom subdued the other until the police came in, and I'm here because I work here. Anything else you'd like to know, Mr. Snow?" Her tone was now as chilly as his.

"Yeah. How's Susan?" He thought of the pregnant woman Marybeth had tried so hard to protect.

"She's doing fine. Her doctor checked her over."

Marybeth's tone had softened slightly. Erik watched her through narrowed eyes. "So, will I live?"

She almost smiled as she made notations on his chart. "I'm afraid so," she replied. "Unless our hospital food kills you, or your own sweet disposition does you in."

Before he could speak again, she had turned away. "I'll send the doctor."

"Wait a minute," he demanded, but she was gone. Great going, pal. Why had he jumped her like that? She was only being nice. Erik raked his good hand over his face. He knew damned well why he'd acted the way he had.

Because she *was* nice, and the last thing he needed was some sweet-faced do-gooder hovering over him. Making him feel good. Making him comfortable. Making him want what he of all people had no right to want.

Erik turned to his side, away from the door, swearing again when the pain ripped through him.

"Sounds like you're beginning to recover," said a voice behind him. "I'm Dr. Hamilton, the one who dug the bullet out of your chest. Luckily it didn't hit anything too vital."

Erik didn't bother to look. The doctor circled the bed until they were face-to-face. "Nurse MacNamara tells me you're awake and asking questions," he said in a friendly tone. "Anything I can tell you?"

"Yeah, when can I get out of here?" Erik tried to move his arm again and the pain almost made him cry out.

"When you're well enough that we don't have to worry about you," the doctor said. "A few more days at least."

"Great," Erik grumbled. "What about my ranch, my cattle?"

The doctor frowned thoughtfully. "I believe someone called your assistant. He was in yesterday, if I'm not mistaken. Nurse MacNamara talked to him. If you like, I'll send her back in?"

"No. Thanks." Erik shifted again, gritting his teeth, and reached for the phone on the bedside table. "I can call him myself."

"You can do anything you want," the doctor agreed, turning toward the door. "But if you don't lie still you'll start to bleed again. And then you'll be our guest for another week."

Marybeth caught herself glancing in a small mirror hung behind the nurses' station and smoothing down one undisciplined curl before she went back into Erik Snow's room. Realizing what she'd been doing, she lowered her hand as if it had been burned, frowned, and walked briskly to room 216. When she entered quietly, she saw that his eyes were closed. Taking the opportunity to study his face, she found herself wondering again about this complicated mixture of courage and crankiness.

Seeing Erik made her think of the attempted robbery, and how it could have ended if he hadn't taken charge. He'd put his own safety on the line. She shuddered at the thought and stepped closer to his bed.

His lashes were several shades darker than his short, light blond hair, and lay thickly against the weathered skin of his lean cheeks. His nose was straight except for a bump on the bridge. Broken at least once, she thought. There was a faint, thin scar on one cheek, in front of his ear. Another, pinker scar on his temple below the soft fringe of his hair. His jaw was solid below a mouth that was closed in a tight line. A mouth that made her feel funny, staring as she was.

His arms and chest were bare and deeply tanned except for the white dressing on his wound. Needing to do something, Marybeth leaned forward and smoothed the blanket.

Erik's eyes blinked open.

"How are you feeling?" she asked automatically. "Can I get you something?"

"You could break me out of here." He shifted and groaned.

"I don't think so. You've lost a lot of blood, and you need to get your strength back." Marybeth could see from the wide shoulders and muscular arms that he was very fit. That would help him heal more quickly.

"I have to make a call," he muttered, trying to pull himself up. His face paled, but he managed while Marybeth watched, curbing her instincts to help.

"You have family that I could contact for you?" she asked.

A shadow crossed his face. "Not really. I want to call my hand and make sure he can manage without me."

"Oh, yes. Your ranch." Marybeth's curiosity was peaked when she spoke with his assistant yesterday.

"Yeah. Beef cattle."

She wondered if his was the spread that locals still called the Morton Place. It had a reputation for raising the best beef around, and the steak house in Coupeville was one of its regular customers.

Marybeth handed him the phone.

"Thanks." He sat looking at her with his hand on the receiver until she colored and turned away.

"The sheriff wanted to talk to you as soon as he could. I'll let him know you're awake," she said, slipping through the door. She had already submitted to an interview with the police and one with a reporter from the local newspaper. If the case went to trial she might have to testify.

Behind her, Erik cursed softly. Why did she bring out the mean in him? His conversation with Trevor was hardly confidential. He was just going to ask if the man's brother could help out until Erik was back on his feet.

"It's all taken care of," Trevor said before Erik could ask the question. "Jethro will come over in the mornings to help me, then go back to his place at suppertime to finish his own chores. I figured you'd want me to ask him."

"Good," Erik said. "If anyone calls, just put them off. I'll be home in a couple of days."

"That's not what the doctor said yesterday," Trevor replied in a drawl. "He thought you'd be there for a week and home in bed for another."

Erik thought of the work that had to be done. "Care to make a wager on that?"

Trevor laughed. "No way, boss. Them's poor odds. Shall I bring Tina in to see you?"

Erik thought a minute. "I'll let you know. But bring me the books and the bills." After a few more minutes, Erik hung up, surprised at how drained he felt. Well, he'd been in worse shape before. He would just have to overcome it.

The door swung open and a short, heavy man in a uniform entered. "Mr. Snow, I'm Sheriff Johnson. If you're up to it, I have some questions about the incident at the bank yesterday."

"And if I'm not?" The last thing Erik wanted was to talk to the police, to call attention to himself.

The sheriff grinned, a purely automatic movement of his facial muscles, and pulled up a chair. "I'm afraid we need to get this settled as soon as possible." He opened his notebook and licked the point of his pencil. After he'd taken Erik through the whole thing twice, the sheriff gave him a piercing look. "Pretty handy under fire, aren't you?"

Erik shrugged, then sucked in a breath at the pain. "Just lucky, I guess."

Sheriff Johnson pointed his pencil. "Lucky you aren't as dead as Frank Skinner."

Erik stiffened. "I killed him?"

"Yup. Didn't I mention that?"

Erik eyed him carefully. The sheriff was no fool. "No. Guess you forgot."

"All those hostages are lucky you knew what to do with that gun."

Erik kept his face expressionless. "I guess."

The sheriff hesitated and then, when Erik remained silent, he rose and thanked him. "The younger guy's name was Harcourt. They both were wearing wigs, and one had a fake beard while the other had a fake mustache," he said. "Seems they had a speedboat hidden down by the water. Figured they'd never be spotted with all the boat traffic around here." He cleared his throat. "They were probably right. Well, I'll drop back by," he added. "In case you think of anything else you want to tell me. Obviously, there won't be any charges brought against you, but we may need your testimony later."

When he left, Erik realized he was sweating heavily. Forcing himself to relax, he let his eyes drift shut.

When Marybeth came back in to check on him, he was sitting on the edge of the bed, bracing himself with his hands. She glared into his pale face, beaded with perspiration.

"What do you think you're doing, trying to finish the job the bank robber started?" She circled the bed and gripped his shoulders with her hands.

Erik looked up and swayed. The determination in his blue eyes shocked her. "Help me up."

"No way! You'd fall on your face, and I'd have to call a male nurse to help me haul you back into bed." She flipped the covers out of the way so he could lie down. Below the bandages, he was stark naked. For an instant, Marybeth reacted to his raw maleness. Then he swayed again, and the nurse in her took over. When he was finally lying against the pillow, she began to scold.

Erik raised one hand. "Spare me the lecture."

Marybeth stopped, sputtering. Why did she bother? "If you want to get out of here early, this isn't the way to accomplish it," she said finally.

"I know what I'm capable of." His jaw was set in a stubborn line, his eyes chilling.

"And I know what the human body can withstand," she answered. "You need rest."

He shifted restlessly, and she wondered what devils drove him. She glanced at her watch and made a decision. "I'll be back in forty-five minutes," she told him. "And I don't want you to move until then, unless it's to push the call button. Understood?"

She backed away from the bed, wondering what misguided impulse had made her offer to return when her shift was over. Erik Snow might have one of the most compelling bodies she'd ever seen in or out of medicine, but every instinct told her to keep her distance. There were things about him that she didn't want to know.

He stared hard, frowning. Then, as she watched, his features relaxed slightly. He didn't smile, but the line of his mouth gentled, giving her a glimpse of what a smile from him would be like. "Are you married?"

"No. I'm a widow."

For a moment the frown was back. Then he said, "No wonder."

She couldn't resist. "No wonder what?"

A flicker of what could have been humor crossed his hard face. "You don't have anyone to henpeck at home, so you're taking it out on me."

"How do you know I don't have anyone to henpeck?" Marybeth asked him flippantly. "I only said I wasn't married. Now, are you going to behave or not?"

Chapter Two

"Yes, ma'am," Erik drawled, looking up at Marybeth with his piercing blue eyes. "I won't do anything I'm not supposed to."

Surprise at his sudden capitulation kept her silent for a moment. "Okay," she agreed finally. "I'll see you soon."

Turning, Marybeth left the room, ignoring the urge to glance back. Anything she could do to help a patient to get well, she silently reassured herself, was part of her job. She had stayed after her shift and come in on her days off before. So what if the other patients she had visited on her own time had always been children, usually scared and homesick? If Erik was scared he kept it well hidden. Some instinct told Marybeth that he'd had a lot of practice keeping fear under wraps. And other emotions as well.

"I thought you'd left," Dr. Hamilton said to her, when he came into Erik's room an hour later.

Marybeth's smile was sheepish as she rose from her chair. "I'm just about to. I wanted to stop by Helen Dempsey's room first and see how she's doing."

She had been talking to Erik for almost fifteen minutes without making much headway. It seemed that his supply of idle chatter was severely limited, and he chose to either turn aside or completely ignore any question of a personal nature. Finally she had resorted to war stories about her experiences as a nurse. One humorous tale actually brought an intriguing ghost of a smile to Erik's hard mouth.

She hesitated by the side of the bed. "Thanks for coming," he said, without looking up.

Annoyance hit Marybeth like a slap. "No bother," she said coolly, then smiled at Dr. Hamilton. "I'll see you tomorrow."

All the way home she argued with herself, burning with embarrassment at Erik's indifferent dismissal after she had tried so hard to draw him out, to share a little human warmth with a man who seemed so alone. The elderly neighbor she had stopped to visit on her way out of the hospital wasn't showing the improvement Marybeth had hoped to see, either. Now her normally cheerful spirits were mired in depression. Helen Dempsey had been a friend since Marybeth moved to Whidbey Island two years before.

Finally, as she turned into the long gravel driveway that led to her small house above the rocky beach, she vowed to leave Erik Snow strictly alone except for the necessary nurse-patient contact. She sternly banished the image of his shadowed eyes from her thoughts.

When she parked her red Ford Escort beside the house, her two dogs, Arthur and Annabelle, appeared, barking happily. Marybeth's mood lifted as she got out of her car.

Instantly Arthur jumped up while Annabelle licked her hand, plumy tail wagging.

"Hello, hello," Marybeth greeted them, patting blond heads as she pushed past the furry bodies. Both dogs were large indiscriminate mixtures. Marybeth's friend Sandy McPherson, who worked at the local animal shelter, insisted she could see German shepherd blood in Arthur and golden retriever in Annabelle. Marybeth was sure it had just been part of the sales pitch aimed toward persuading her to take the abandoned animals in.

"The sooner you let me by, the sooner you get fed," she told Arthur, who seemed determined to block her way up the stairs to the small front porch of her rental house. She'd been lucky to find it on lease from the owners, who were teaching in Japan for a year.

Arthur's bark boomed out, and Annabelle's sharper, higher voice joined his. The commotion summoned two of the three cats that also shared Marybeth's quarters and generous portions of her affection.

"Mugsy," she exclaimed, "how are you? Sassy, are you hungry?" She glanced around as both cats, one orange and the other black with white feet, leaped to the porch railings, out of the way of the dogs' wet tongues.

Marybeth glanced around. "Where's Tiger?" The third cat was nowhere in sight. She shrugged. He would undoubtedly show up. Although all of her animals had been neutered, Tiger didn't seem to realize he wasn't supposed to roam, and sometimes disappeared for days.

Marybeth opened the door to the green-and-white house, then stood back as the animals crowded in ahead of her. She left them out while she was at work but they all stayed in at night. Now, as they clamored impatiently to be fed, she set the mail she'd been carrying on the small kitchen table and opened a cupboard door. At the sound of the can opener, the meows and barks increased both in frequency and volume.

It was the kind of enthusiastic greeting that she looked forward to every evening.

The next morning, as Marybeth was making her rounds, she hesitated outside the door of 216 and took a deep breath. She had ignored the impulse to look in on Erik as soon as she got to work, submerging herself in other patients' charts instead. Now, even though she had every right to be there, she felt ridiculously self-conscious. He's only a patient, she reminded herself. Attractive, intriguing, with the personality of a rattlesnake forced from his hole, but a patient nonetheless. Convinced that all she felt toward him was gratitude for his role in overcoming the robbers who had held them hostage, she pushed the door to his room open and entered.

Erik's bed was empty.

Marybeth was standing in the doorway, wondering if someone had taken him downstairs for X rays, when she heard a voice from the bathroom. It was Erik, and he was cursing.

As she watched, the door swung open. Clad in nothing but light blue pajama bottoms that rode dangerously low on his hips and a bandage that contrasted starkly with the tan of his broad chest, Erik was holding on to the door frame, face pale, knuckles white with strain. Marybeth's first impulse was to rush over and help him back to bed. One look at his black expression and she stayed put.

"Good morning." She hoped her tone was friendly but impersonal. "I don't suppose you want any help?"

"You suppose right." His voice was gritty with frustration. "But what I want and what I need don't seem to be even remotely connected." He took a step forward, hand tightening on the door frame. Then he let go, and for a moment Marybeth thought he was going to fall on his face, taking the portable IV stand with him.

When he caught himself, she moved quickly. "Put your arm around my waist," she said in a no-nonsense tone.

He complied, and she could feel his dormant strength. The warmth of his body soaked through the thin nylon of her uniform like hot water through coffee grounds.

After a couple of moments and several slow steps, he let go of her and sank onto the side of the bed. "Thanks," he growled.

"All part of the service," Marybeth replied as she looked beneath his bandage. "I'll be back to check your vital signs. I don't think I'd get an accurate reading right now."

Erik's gaze clashed with hers, and his expression was wry. "I'll be here."

His sarcastic tone wiped away her smile and added even more color to her face. "Somehow I don't think I'd be surprised if you weren't," she retorted, glancing at the window. "After all, we're only on the second floor."

Her comment surprised a bark of laughter from Erik, but before he could say anything more, she was gone, leaving him grinning at her caustic remark.

On the other side of his door, Marybeth did her best to fight her uncharacteristic annoyance. It was *her* vital signs that were jumping. From the moment she'd seen him clinging to the side of the doorjamb, his face pale and damp, she had overreacted. Didn't the man have a lick of sense? He could have reopened his wound, fallen, remained on the floor bleeding if she hadn't come along when she did. What on earth was wrong with him that he had to keep pushing himself so hard?

Sighing, she raked her fingers through her curly hair. Her hand still tingled where it had inadvertently touched the heated skin at his taut waist. Then she remembered his unexpected laugh at her jibe and a smile twitched her lips. Apparently there was more to him than the coldness he would like her to think made up his entire personality. He possessed a sense of humor even if it was a reluctant one.

During her break, Marybeth went to check on Helen. The eighty-three-year-old woman had been having trouble with her heart. Despite Marybeth's training and her knowledge of the case, she kept looking for signs of improvement.

Helen was such a good soul, friend to many around Coupeville. It was hard to remember that she was in the twilight years of what Marybeth knew to be a rewarding but sometimes painful life. They had exchanged stories one dreary afternoon. Marybeth often recalled the sadness and the pride in the old woman's voice when she had described the son, her youngest, who had been killed in Vietnam. Helen had survived the loss, could even smile when she spoke his name. The thought encouraged Marybeth when memories of her own late husband's brutal murder threatened to overwhelm her with regret and unanswered questions.

"Hello, dear," Helen said faintly when Marybeth entered her room. Marybeth glanced at the chart, keeping her reaction to Helen's lack of color from showing.

"How are you feeling today, sweetie?" She pulled up a chair and sat down.

"Okay, I guess. My daughter was here."

Marybeth knew that Helen's daughter lived with her family in Oak Harbor, at the northern tip of the island near the bridge that joined it with the mainland of Washington State. They were frequent visitors. Marybeth's own

heart had ached at their tight-lipped worry when they left
Helen's room. She worried, too.

"Think you could sleep for a while?" Marybeth asked
when she saw Helen's eyelids droop.

The woman nodded. "I guess so."

Marybeth stood and forced a smile past her worry. "I'll
try to come by later, okay?"

Helen didn't answer. She was already asleep.

The last time Marybeth checked on Erik before her shift
ended, she thought he was sleeping, too. Ignoring her
vague feeling of disappointment, she refilled his water jug
and fiddled with his IV. The other times she had come into
his room that day they had both been unfailingly polite.
Despite his unwise trip to the john he was getting better,
and at a surprisingly rapid rate. Marybeth attributed his
quick healing to the obvious fitness of that tall, muscular
body.

Now, as she looked into his sleeping face and then
straightened, oddly reluctant to leave the hospital without
telling him goodbye, he opened his eyes.

For a moment, Erik looked pleased before the familiar
mask dropped over his features.

"Are you back again?"

"I'm just making sure you're still alive," she said
crisply. "Part of my job, you know."

"I'm too ornery to die," he responded with a faint
chuckle, watching her as she straightened the sheets.

For a moment she was tempted to make a definitely unprofessional remark, but as she turned her attention back
to him, the words died unspoken. A curious awareness
passed between them. She was certain, from Erik's sudden frown of displeasure, that he had felt it, too.

"Have a good evening," she said.

"Aren't you going to come by when you get off?" He looked as surprised by the question as she was.

Her composure temporarily routed by the unexpected glimpse of vulnerability and her own warm response, Marybeth shook her head. "I have an appointment," she improvised, thinking that her daily arrival at home to feed her four-legged dependents could very loosely be called an appointment.

Erik's face closed completely. "Good," he said firmly. "I just wanted to know if you'd be interrupting the movie I'm going to watch." He reached for the television control and turned on the set opposite his bed, holding one finger on the volume button until it was easy to hear even from where Marybeth stood.

Without another word, she turned and left.

Marybeth had the next two days off, and spent them doing laundry, housecleaning and marketing. She took long walks down the beach both days. The dogs ran happily ahead of her to investigate dead crabs, piles of seaweed, and every piece of driftwood that was small enough to fetch. Marybeth found pleasure in the ordinary things that filled her life, and the aftereffects of the bank robbery faded even more.

When she asked an older neighbor who lived down the road if he needed anything from the store, he invited her in for a chat and some of the coffee he had sent up from a specialty store down in Bellevue, separated from Seattle by Lake Washington and a floating bridge. Sensing that Mr. Isaacson was lonely and enjoyed her company, Marybeth had gotten to know him fairly well over the past few months. Her friend Sandy had placed a dog from the animal shelter with him, too. The miniature dachshund had been just hours away from being put to sleep.

The only things that marred Marybeth's well-deserved break from the hospital were her concern for Helen Dempsey, and the mingled hope and dread that Erik would have been released before she went back.

Erik shifted restlessly, trying his best not to snap at the nurse who hovered over him like an irritating fly.

"I can take my own sponge bath," he told her. "You don't need to wait." He hadn't seen Nurse MacNamara for two days and couldn't help but wonder if she had been transferred to a different part of the hospital. Did they rotate assignments? Every time he found himself on the verge of asking one of the other nurses, he clamped his jaws shut and glared at whoever was attending him at the time.

"I thought you'd like to see a copy of the Seattle newspaper," this particular Florence Nightingale said when she came back a while later to collect the basin and damp towels. She held the paper out to him. "There's a follow-up story to the bank robbery you managed to disrupt. Imagine our little community being written up in the *Times.*"

Erik grabbed the paper, mumbling a distracted thanks as he unfolded it. He'd seen the local front-page story that ran the day after the aborted robbery and had convinced himself that an unsuccessful bank holdup was hardly newsworthy enough to be picked up by the wire service.

"The story's on page two," the nurse told him helpfully. "You enjoy it. I have to go."

He didn't even hear her leave. His eyes narrowed, and he groaned with dismay. His name wasn't likely to set off any alarms, but the story was accompanied by several pictures. One of them was the very shot he'd hoped would fade into oblivion after gracing the front page of the *Whidbey Island Examiner.*

Chicago Cop Killer Shot During Robbery in Washington State, read the headline. Erik scanned the wire service write-up anxiously. Frank Skinner had been on the FBI's most-wanted list for several years, ever since he had killed a bank guard and a local policeman during a robbery in Illinois. The story was straightforward, containing nothing to raise unwanted suspicion.

Now the only thing Erik had to concern himself with was his picture. It was next to Skinner's mug shot, and showed a couple of the other hostages, the younger robber being taken away in handcuffs, and Erik on a stretcher.

Wondering if anyone else would be able to identify him from the grainy photo, he spent a lot of time staring at it while debating his options. By the time one of the hospital staff brought in his lunch tray, Erik had managed to convince himself that no one from his past would recognize him, that his new life was not in jeopardy and that he didn't have to pull up stakes yet again and disappear.

While Erik was busy convincing himself, a thin man in a dark suit came into the room.

"Erik Snow?" he asked, consulting a folder he had brought with him.

"Yeah," Erik answered cautiously. "Who're you?"

"Deputy Prosecutor Turner," he said, extending a hand that Erik shook briefly. "I need to ask you a few questions about the bank robbery. If Harcourt's case goes to trial, you'll probably have to testify."

Erik just looked at him. We'll see about that, he thought. As soon as Turner was done with his questions and had left, Erik reached for the phone.

"You've been here for several days. I thought you might like a back rub with this lotion so you don't get a rash."

Nurse MacNamara's eyes were practically shooting fire as she waited by the bed. Erik had the impression that if he so much as grinned, she would empty the bottle of lotion over his head.

"A back rub sounds good," he drawled, sitting up. He felt stronger all the time. Perhaps he'd be released tomorrow. Trevor had come in the evening before to tell him that everything at home was fine, but Erik wanted to see for himself. The habit of not relying on anyone else was deeply ingrained, and he didn't question it.

Now he shifted slightly to expose his bare back to Nurse MacNamara. In another life he might have expected her to sink a knife into his flesh; now he just hoped the lotion wasn't ice-cold.

It wasn't. She must have warmed it in her hands before she spread it across his skin. As she kneaded his aching muscles, Erik suppressed the sigh that threatened to slip out.

"Anyone ever tell you that you have the touch of an angel?" he asked instead as his knotted muscles turned to mush beneath her competent touch.

He felt her hesitate, then rub more briskly with her hand.

"All the time."

Behind him, Marybeth did her best to ignore the wide slope of his shoulders and the curve of his spine. She bit her lip to keep back her question about the scar that could have been another gunshot wound. If she asked, he probably wouldn't tell her, anyway.

Working in the lotion, enjoying the feel of his warm skin beneath her hands, she wished she could ask why the only visitors Erik had had were his farmhand, Sheriff Johnson and the deputy prosecutor. Erik had told her he didn't have family to speak of, but surely he had friends. A man who looked like him and was single, which she knew Erik was from reading his chart, could have as many girlfriends as he wanted. Devilishly attractive bachelors were as scarce as cheap waterfront property on Whidbey Island.

Finally she finished and silently worked the excess lotion into her own hands. "All done," she said briskly as she came around the bed.

His stare was intense, searching. Then he blinked and the spell was broken. "Thanks," he said, rolling first one shoulder and then the other as Marybeth watched in helpless fascination. "You really took care of the knots."

"Good. Anything else you need?"

Something flashed in his eyes, and she could feel the heat climbing her cheeks.

"Could you come by when you get off, or do you have another appointment?"

Her defenses rose like hackles at his tone. "Didn't you believe me the other day?"

He shrugged. "Sure, I did. If you want to call a date an appointment, I guess that's up to you."

"What do you mean?"

His eyes narrowed as he changed direction. "You said you were a widow. How did he die? Car accident?"

Marybeth saw genuine interest in his hard face. She absently tightened the top on the lotion bottle. "Mike was a policeman in Seattle, a detective. He was investigating a drug ring. There was a leak, and he got shot." She was glad that her voice hadn't wavered. Perhaps she was finally getting used to Mike's pointless death.

"That's tough. I'm sorry."

She studied Erik's lean face. He looked as though he meant it. "Thank you."

"How long ago did it happen?" he asked, fiddling with the bed control.

"Two years." Marybeth hesitated. "And that wasn't a date I had the other day."

"Oh." Erik ignored the warm spot of pleasure her words created. He had no business asking about her personal life.

"What about you?" She turned her back as she folded an extra blanket that had been at the foot of his bed. "All I know is that you raise beef cattle at the old Morton spread."

"That's about all there is to tell." Served him right for being nosy. Now she would ask him questions he didn't want to answer.

"Did you grow up around here?" She put the blanket into the closet and faced him, her smile making him react in a way he would have thought his body still too weak to manage.

Erik shook his head and wondered if her hair was as soft as it looked.

Marybeth waited for him to elaborate, then shrugged. "You're so closemouthed that anyone would think you were hiding from a questionable past," she mused. "I was only making conversation."

Erik glanced down at his fingers, which were twisted into the sheet. How much did she suspect? Was she teasing him, trying to get him to admit something, or had her remark only been a shot in the dark?

The cliché made him shudder. Perhaps he'd been overconfident to think he could stay hidden forever.

"I was born in St. Louis," he said, using the background story he had long since memorized. "I came out here four years ago to look for something I couldn't find back there."

"What?" she asked, stopping at the foot of his bed.

"Space. Peace. Somewhere to be left alone."

Marybeth's face reddened. She had the kind of complexion that was a barometer of her emotions. "I'm sorry," she said rather shortly. "I didn't mean to pry."

Erik looked away. His shoulders stiffened and then, abruptly, relaxed. "No, I'm sorry," he said, thoroughly surprising himself. "I guess I've been alone on the ranch too long. I've forgotten how to make polite conversation."

He shifted and hoped to see that the discomfort he'd caused her was gone from her expressive face.

Marybeth's smile was tentative. "I guess I don't always know when to stop," she said apologetically.

Erik's heart twisted at her smile, and he waved a dismissive hand. "No problem. Just overlook my spells of bad temper."

Her eyes began to twinkle. "I'll do my best, but I have to come in here sometimes, you know."

Erik found himself responding to her smile with one of his own. "I'll try to be on my best behavior when you come around, okay?"

"Fine. Sounds like you're getting better. You should be out of here any day now." Marybeth knew the words were ones he wanted to hear, so why did his unexpected smile fade? He'd been talking about being released practically since he'd been admitted.

"The sooner the better," he said gruffly, wondering if he would ever see her again after he'd checked out. At forty-five miles, Whidbey Island might be the longest island in the United States, but Coupeville was still a small town. Even so, he didn't remember ever noticing her before the robbery. Perhaps it was just as well. Thinking about all the things he would like to do to Marybeth's tempting body had kept him awake the night before, and he needed his sleep to recover.

"I'm tired," he said abruptly, turning away. Behind him there was silence. Then the sharp slap of her hand against the door as she left told him how upset she'd been by his sudden dismissal.

Erik sighed and punched his pillow. The sooner he got out of here, away from temptation, the better off they would both be.

"I'm sorry we couldn't do something more to save her," Dr. Okimoto said, giving Marybeth's shoulder a hard squeeze. "Her heart finally gave up, and she went in her sleep. I know that you were especially fond of Helen."

"It's always so hard to lose a friend." Marybeth's voice came out strained and scratchy, and she cleared her throat. "But I'll be okay. It's her family that's been through a hard time. Are they still here?"

Dr. Okimoto took off his glasses and polished the lenses with his handkerchief. "They're making arrangements." His name came over the PA system, and he reached for the phone.

"Thank you for coming to tell me," Marybeth told him. She made herself square her shoulders and return to the medication she'd been dispensing.

Helen had been ready to go, Marybeth knew that. She had seen patients die many times, but it always hit her hard, especially if the person was someone she knew. She blinked back the moisture that threatened to fill her eyes and concentrated fiercely on the medications.

Later, when she entered Erik's room, he was sitting in a chair by the window. He took one look at her pale face and rose slowly to his feet, hitching up his pajama bottoms.

"What's wrong?"

Marybeth glanced at him and then ducked into the bathroom. "Nothing," she said over her shoulder. "I'm just very busy today."

He walked slowly to the doorway, where he stood watching her back. Tension radiated from her slim form like sunlight off a mirror.

"I don't believe you." He reached out to touch her hair, then reconsidered and let it drop to his side. Why should she confide in him? He'd hardly opened up to her during his stay in the hospital. And why should he care? He only knew that seeing her in such obvious turmoil twisted his gut.

While he stood in the doorway, debating what to do, a sniffle so soft he almost missed it whispered in the confined space. Then he saw a faint tremor go through Marybeth's slim white form.

"Tell me," he coaxed, touching her arm. "What's wrong?"

To his utter shock, she whirled around and pinned him with a watery stare, her hazel eyes brimming with sadness. Before Erik could allow himself to debate the wisdom of it, he pulled her unresisting body into his arms. He braced himself to take her weight as she sagged against him, and he held her tightly, one hand caressing the bronzed curls that were as soft as he'd imagined them to be. Her hot tears wet the bare skin of his chest, each drop burning him like acid.

"It's okay, it's okay," he repeated like a litany, ignoring his body's clamoring response to her scent and warmth. When her sobs finally began to lessen, he reached behind her and got a tissue from the box on the back of the toilet. Lifting her chin with one finger, he dabbed gently at her eyes, doing his best to blot up the excess moisture.

"I'm sorry," she gasped, and scrambled from his loose embrace as if they had been doing something shameful. "You must think I'm awfully unprofessional."

His fingers closed around one delicate wrist and measured her galloping pulse. "Maybe just awfully human."

A smile trembled on her lips. "I can't believe I lost control like that!" Her voice was shaky.

Erik thought grimly that he could tell her a few things about losing control. He released her and curled his hands into fists to keep from pulling her back against him. His body had its own ideas about how to respond to her nearness. Years of strict self-discipline were being summarily ignored by his roiling hormones and rigid flesh.

"It's okay," he said gruffly as she followed him from the bathroom and leaned against the wall. He placed a protective palm flat on either side of her. "You're a human being before you're a nurse."

Marybeth blinked, baffled by his rough attempts to comfort her. Of all places to let the sorrow over Helen's death hit her! She had planned to take a long walk down the beach with the dogs when she got home, keeping her thoughts and feelings firmly under control until she was alone. Instead she had done her best to drown a patient with her tears. And not just any patient!

Swallowing, she met Erik's grave stare and noticed that his eyes were dark with emotion. For once he'd allowed his feelings to show. She found the concession oddly comforting.

"You should sit down," she told him, realizing for the first time that he was standing over her as if being out of bed didn't tax his strength in the least.

"Quit fussing, and tell me what's got you so upset," he said in a chiding tone, "or we'll both stand here until our legs wobble."

As briefly as she could, Marybeth told him about Helen and their friendship. "We knew it was only a matter of time," she finished. "But I hoped, perhaps selfishly, that she wouldn't die yet. Sometimes I really hate death."

Standing before her, Erik felt himself go cold as he pictured a certain little girl's shy smile and sparkling black eyes. What would Marybeth think of him if she knew his past? Would she agree that for Tina, losing him might be an even worse tragedy than losing her mother? And how long would the pain from that one accident continue to torment him before he could put it behind him and forgive himself?

"Anyway," Marybeth continued, "I appreciate your being here." She made a futile gesture with her hand as her gaze shifted away from his. "I'd better get back to work. Thank you again."

She waited, but Erik didn't back away. Instead he moved one hand so that his fingers tangled in her hair. "I'm getting out tomorrow," he murmured. "Dr. Hamilton told me when he came in earlier."

Marybeth felt a lurch of disappointment. They hadn't exactly become friends, but there was a quiet strength inside him. It was probably one reason she had unconsciously chosen his room for her temporary loss of control. "We'll miss you," she said.

Her eyes widened as he stared down at her with a grim expression. Then, before she could frame a question, he swooped, covering her mouth with his.

Without a thought, she responded to the fierce heat of his kiss. She realized faintly that his hands were biting into her waist and her own were splayed flat against his hard chest, below the small bandage that still covered his incision. It was only for a moment that his mouth caressed hers before he pulled away, but in that tiny fragment of time, the world shrank to contain just the two of them.

Then Erik lifted his head and glared at Marybeth as if *she* had been the one to initiate the kiss. Unable to bear his censure after the understanding and comfort he had shown, she pushed abruptly past him, fleeing the room as if the hounds of hell were snapping at her heels.

The last thing she heard before the door swung shut behind her was his angry curse.

Chapter Three

When Marybeth appeared for work the next day to fill in on second shift, Erik was gone. He'd been released early that afternoon. Debbie Brennan, the nurse who passed on the news, eyed Marybeth curiously. She had probably heard about the postshift visits to his room.

"Is Mr. Snow a friend of yours?" Debbie asked. "He's sure cute."

"I never met him before the bank holdup, but what he did for the rest of us there was pretty brave." Marybeth found herself being just a little defensive. She softened her tone. "I'm glad he got to go home. That's what he wanted."

She would have liked to ask if he'd left any kind of message for her, but she knew he hadn't or someone would have mentioned it. After the way Marybeth had run out of his room when he had kissed her, she wouldn't blame him for thinking she wanted nothing more to do with him.

The middle-aged man who now occupied that bed while recuperating from gall bladder surgery was pleasant enough, but Marybeth couldn't help comparing his weak jokes to the sexual attraction that Erik exuded from every pore. The pang she felt each time she crossed the threshold of room 216 was enough to thoroughly irritate her.

During her dinner break that same evening, Marybeth was joined by her friend Sandy in the hospital cafeteria. Setting down her tray, Sandy began bemoaning the endless parade of kittens and puppies the animal shelter had to deal with each week.

"They're all so cute," she grumbled, toying with her grilled cheese sandwich. "People never think about their fates when they're left at the shelter and no one adopts them."

"My place is full up," Marybeth said. "You know I'd take more if I possibly could, but I'm lucky my landlords let me keep the menagerie I already have."

"So what are you going to do about Erik Snow?" Sandy asked, changing directions abruptly.

Marybeth had told her about him being released while she was gone. "Do?" she echoed while she poked at her chef's salad with her fork. "What do you mean?" She hadn't confided what had happened the last time she had been in Erik's room. The memory of her unprofessional conduct was humiliating, and her reaction to Erik's kiss wasn't something she wanted to think about, let alone discuss.

Sandy leaned forward across the Formica table. "Yes, what are you going to do? You've talked about nothing but Erik Snow since the robbery. You don't really intend to let him get away without a struggle, do you? From what you said, he's one handsome hunk."

Marybeth frowned, picturing his silver-blond hair and tanned skin. "I don't remember using those words." She hadn't realized she had revealed so much about Erik.

When it came to the opposite sex, Sandy wasn't bashful. She had a pixie-cute face and more curves than a winding road. Most men didn't seem to mind her less-than-shy personality, either.

She waved a dismissive hand. "Whatever," she said, eyeing Marybeth's flushed cheeks, "but I happen to know you're interested. Don't bother to deny it, not to good ol' Sandy. And I know it's the first time since you moved up here that you've been more than indifferent to a male of your species. This Erik must be some guy, and I'm dying to meet him."

"What's stopping you?" Marybeth had no trouble picturing Sandy on Erik's doorstep, introducing herself as a friend of his former nurse. The sharp jab of jealousy she experienced at the idea came as rather a shock.

"I'm not about to poach on your territory," Sandy exclaimed, looking offended.

Marybeth took a long drink of her iced tea, wondering for a moment if her friend could read minds. "He's not *in* my territory. My interest in Erik is—was—purely professional. Anything beyond that is a figment of your imagination." She ignored Sandy's inelegant snort. "Maybe *you've* been without a man for too long."

Sandy accepted the dig with good spirits, grinning. "You're the one who's grumpy here." Her eyes sparkled. "He's a bachelor, isn't he? Take him a casserole."

Marybeth stared. In her place, Sandy would probably do just that. And invite herself to dinner. Sometimes Marybeth wished she had her friend's nerve.

* * *

This is crazy, Marybeth kept telling herself two days later as she stopped to check a road sign. Beside her on the floor of the car sat a covered white casserole dish filled with spaghetti and homemade sauce. Next to it was a foil-wrapped loaf of garlic bread. The only thing Marybeth hadn't brought was wine.

She glanced around warily, half expecting her mother to jump out of the bushes and scold her for being forward. There was silence all around except for the sound of her Escort and the drone of traffic back on the main road. She had gotten directions to the old Morton place from the butcher in Coupeville. Her excuse had been ready in case he asked why she wanted to go there, but he hadn't. Feeling guilty, Marybeth had bought two packages of bone-less chicken breasts before leaving his shop. Now she was less than a mile away from Erik's, and wondering not for the first time what she thought she was doing.

He would think she was desperate, following him home like this. Marybeth was tempted to turn back and take the spaghetti to her neighbor, Mr. Isaacson. Then she remembered that air of solitude that surrounded Erik, and how much she owed him for saving her life and the lives of the other bank hostages. That in itself was enough to spur her on.

The memory of the way his mouth had moved against hers was hastily banished as she drove along a fence that separated the road from a pasture scattered with coal-black cattle. A few glanced up curiously as she passed, but most of them kept grazing. She couldn't help but notice how big and sleek they were. One of the other nurses had told her that Erik's beef was famous all over the state for its tenderness and flavor. There was a persistent rumor that he used a secret feeding formula.

A few minutes later, Marybeth came to an open gate. A small sign gave the address. She swallowed nervously, glanced at the food she had brought, and popped a breath mint into her mouth. Then she turned onto Erik's property and drove down the gravel road to the blue-and-white rambler-style farmhouse the butcher had described earlier.

Before she could shut off the engine, a young man wearing a ponytail and faded overalls came out of a nearby white building, followed by a little girl with shiny black hair.

"Help you?" the man asked as he bent to peer through Marybeth's open window.

How she wished she had never listened to Sandy's bean-brained idea. "I'm looking for Erik Snow."

The man's grin was friendly, but when Marybeth turned an answering smile toward the little girl, she crowded behind his long legs and peeked around him with big, dark eyes. She was pretty with her straight hair and dark skin. Marybeth wondered if her mother was Mexican.

"I think Erik's in the house, making some phone calls." The man hesitated. "Why don't you wait here, and we'll see if we can find him." He glanced down. "Come on, Tina."

"Thank you." Marybeth shut off the ignition, feeling more foolish all the time. She gathered her courage as the mismatched pair disappeared into the house. While she waited, she admired the flower boxes at the front windows, painted a neat blue to match the house's trim, and filled to overflowing with pink and white petunias, blue lobelia and yellow marigolds. She had to remind herself why she was there when the door opened again and Erik strode out.

For a moment Marybeth's pulse went wild as she gaped at him. He was tanned and fit in his blue work shirt and tight, worn jeans. The sunlight turned his hair to gold and warmed his burnished skin. Fumbling with the door handle, she got out of the car.

"You!" he exclaimed when he got close enough that she could see the blue glinting through his narrowed eyes. His expression was wary. The other man was walking back to the building he'd come from, but the little girl stayed with Erik.

He stopped in front of where Marybeth stood and shoved his hands into the waistband of his jeans. Then he rocked back on the heels of his worn boots and studied her boldly. The silence lengthened.

"How are you doing?" Marybeth asked. She felt horribly awkward.

"Fine. I didn't expect to see you again. Do nurses make house calls?"

His question brought the heat to her cheeks. "I'm sorry to barge in on you like this," she began. She had been crazy to come.

Erik's expression relaxed slightly, and he shook his head. "No, don't worry about it." He hesitated. "It's nice to see you." The words came out slowly, as if he were testing them. "Look, why don't you come in the house? Mrs. O'Reilly just made cookies, and I'm sure there's some iced tea in the fridge."

Marybeth was surprised by his sudden burst of hospitality. She glanced back toward the car. "I didn't realize you had a housekeeper," she said, feeling more embarrassed by the minute. "I brought you some spaghetti."

Erik made no effort to hide his surprise. "You did?" For the first time since he had come out the door, a smile curved his hard mouth, and his voice warmed by several degrees. "That's nice." He turned to the little girl hovering behind him. "Tina, go tell Mrs. O we have company."

Her dark eyes flickered toward Marybeth and then, wordlessly, she ran toward the house.

"She's darling," Marybeth said. "How old is she?"

"Six." Erik's attention didn't waver from Marybeth's face.

"Well," she said after a moment, "I hope I can get a smile out of her before I leave."

"She can be shy with strangers," he said, gently moving her out of the way so he could lift the covered casserole she was reaching for. Beside him, Marybeth glanced down at the bare arm he'd touched. She almost expected to see charred marks from where his fingers had burned her skin.

He held the casserole with one hand, raising its lid with the other. "Looks good," he said as he straightened. "I love spaghetti."

When he moved away from her car, Marybeth let out the breath she had been holding and reached for the foil package of bread. Erik preceded her toward the house.

"This your day off?" he asked, pulling open the screen door for her.

"No, I have to work second shift." She stepped into the kitchen and glanced around. It was spotless and homey, with a vinyl floor in a red brick pattern and blue checkered curtains at the windows. The housekeeper had left a plate of cookies and a pitcher of tea on the tile counter, but she was nowhere in sight.

Behind Marybeth, Erik had to suppress a grin at Mrs. O'Reilly's lack of subtlety. She would have married him off to the first single woman she could find if she had her way, and she told him all the time that living by himself wasn't natural. She and her husband of forty-some years lived down the road. She went home each night after dinner was served and she had cleaned up, then returned each morning.

Beside him, Marybeth was looking around curiously. "This is a lovely room," she said after a moment. "A real cook's kitchen."

"My housekeeper advised me when we remodeled." He set the covered dish on the counter. "I can cook if I have to, but I avoid it whenever possible."

Marybeth grinned. "I didn't picture you as being that domesticated," she teased.

Erik glanced around, but Tina had disappeared. "Survival has nothing to do with domestication," he said in a low voice.

When Marybeth didn't reply, he indicated the round maple table, surrounded by matching chairs. "Have a seat." Quickly he brought the plate of cookies and the tea, and sat across from her, his booted feet stretched before him. He wondered why she had really come. After the way she had run out of his room after he kissed her, having her turn up here was the last thing he had expected.

Maybe she had decided she had liked the kiss after all and had come looking for more. The thought sizzled for a moment as he poured them both some iced tea, but one glance at her expression told him he was way off base. If anything, she looked distinctly uncomfortable, like someone performing a distasteful duty.

"Thank you again for saving all of us at the bank," she said. Then he understood. The food was a payback, her visit just good manners. Erik handed her a glass of tea and shoved the plate of cookies across the table. "Eat some, or Mrs. O'Reilly's feelings will be hurt."

Marybeth's eyes widened slightly at his clipped tone. Silently Erik cursed himself, and bit into a cookie as if it were his enemy. Why did this woman affect him the way she did? She slipped past his defenses like a wisp of smoke. He wanted nothing more than to either pull her into his lap or run her off his place. Instead, he was forcing himself to play the polite host, and doing it so clumsily that all he was accomplishing was hurting her feelings. Washing down the cookie with a swallow of tea, he rose, scraping back his chair. Marybeth seemed to shrink away. Then her chin jutted out in a gesture he remembered from the holdup.

"I'm keeping you from your work," she said as she stood stiffly. "I'd better go."

Erik surprised himself by laying a hand on her shoulder. It tensed beneath his fingers. "Please," he said in a quieter tone, "finish your iced tea, and tell me how you've been."

He waited while her gray-green gaze searched his face. Then she nodded to herself as if she had come to a decision and sat back down. Erik followed her example and dragged his chair back to the round table.

What followed was a conversation that was slightly awkward and riddled with underlying currents. Finally the talk began to flow easier. Marybeth asked several questions about the farm that Erik answered patiently. He asked her in turn about her work, and about some of the other hospital staff who had taken care of him.

"I should go," Marybeth told him. She drained the last of her tea. "I feel that I'm keeping you from things. You must have a lot of catching up to do."

Erik shrugged, standing again when she did. "Trevor and his brother did pretty well while I was gone."

"How's your shoulder?"

Erik rolled it experimentally. "Not bad." A wicked expression came over his face and one hand went to the buttons of his shirt. "Want to see?"

Marybeth colored and glanced away. "I'm sure you have a follow-up visit scheduled with Dr. Hamilton."

"I do, but he's not nearly as interesting as you." He watched added color sweep across her cheeks. Then he moved closer. His fingers reached out to cup her chin, lifting it so her eyes were gazing directly into his.

"Would you like to look around?" he asked.

Marybeth swallowed, almost giving in to the temptation to stay longer. "Perhaps some other time. I have a few errands I need to run before work."

If he was disappointed, he hid it well. "Sure," he said, dropping his hand. "Thanks again for the food. Mrs. O will appreciate the evening off tomorrow night to spend with her husband. Trevor and Tina and I will sure enjoy that spaghetti and garlic bread."

"What about Trevor's wife?" Marybeth asked. "Do they live here on the farm?"

Erik looked puzzled. "Trevor isn't married."

"Oh," Marybeth said, confused. "I guess I assumed that the little girl was his."

Erik frowned. "Tina?" he asked as she came into the kitchen and ran over to wrap her tiny hands around his leg. "Tina's my daughter."

The silence that followed his startling announcement seemed to grow long and heavy, but Marybeth couldn't think of anything to break it. She was sure the blood had drained from her head, slowing her thought processes to a crawl.

The idea of Erik with a child was totally unexpected, and surprisingly difficult to accept. He had said he didn't have family, so what had happened to Tina's mother? Were they divorced? If he was widowed, why hadn't he said so when Marybeth told him about Mike? The questions crowded her brain and danced on her tongue, but when she looked at Erik's closed expression, she couldn't force them out.

She should be glad he had been close to someone; instead she felt something dangerously similar to jealousy.

"Daddy, who is this?" It was Tina's light voice that finally broke the awkward silence.

Erik tore his attention from the parade of expressions that had crossed Marybeth's face. He glanced at his daughter.

"Daddy," she said again impatiently, patting his leg with her hand. "Who is this lady?"

Erik knew from experience that Tina was perfectly capable of repeating the question until he answered her. She had come full circle from the silent, fearful waif he had brought back with him from South America over two years before. What had begun as a duty on Erik's part had turned into all-encompassing love almost without his knowledge, and most certainly without his consent.

Love brought pain, disappointment, and desertion; that was a hard lesson he had learned well. But with Tina, love was returned tenfold. Only occasionally now did he ask himself what she would feel for him when she learned the truth, about both her mother and the man she called "Daddy" with so much trust.

"Daddy," she said again.

Before she could repeat her question, Erik squatted down beside her. "This is a nurse from the hospital," he said while he looked directly into Tina's dark eyes. "You remember me telling you about Mrs. MacNamara?"

Tina's head bobbed and her black hair danced. She followed his gaze to where Marybeth stood over them. Quickly she, too, squatted down. Tina immediately moved behind Erik.

"This is Mrs. MacNamara," he said, bringing Tina gently but firmly back around to his side. "She brought us some spaghetti and garlic bread for our dinner tomorrow evening."

"Why?" Tina studied Marybeth gravely, while Marybeth's gaze flickered back between Erik and the little girl.

"Because I thought you might like it," Marybeth said before he could speak again. "Your daddy was hurt, and I didn't know if he was strong enough to cook."

"Mrs. O'Reilly cooks," Tina said bluntly.

"I know that now," Marybeth replied. She settled a glance of reproach on Erik.

He straightened and cupped her elbow to pull her up with him. Then he bent down and lifted Tina, setting her on his shoulders. When one of her heels touched the small bandage on his chest, he winced.

"I forgot about that," he said.

Marybeth smiled. "Not as tough as you like to think?" she asked.

He didn't reply, just lowered Tina to the floor. "Piggyback rides will have to wait a little longer," he told her.

She looked back at Marybeth. "Thank you for the spaghetti," she said politely. "I'm sure it's very good."

"You're welcome." Marybeth's smile broadened.

Tina's dark eyes blinked, and then she smiled ever so slightly. The movement brought a dimple to one round cheek. "Do you like my daddy?"

Marybeth glanced hastily at Erik. A spark of laughter glowed in his eyes. "Yes," she said to the child. "Of course I do."

"Good," Tina replied gravely. "I bet he likes you, too. He told me that before he found me a mommy, he had to like her and she had to like him."

Tina turned to Erik, and he found himself tensing, wondering what outrage the child might come out with next. "Can I go watch television?"

"Yes, for a little while." He watched as she ran from the room. She pulled up short and turned to wave to Marybeth, then whirled away again, straight hair flying around her face.

"She's precious." Marybeth's cheeks were a fiery pink, her face alive with unspoken questions.

Erik debated briefly how much to tell her, then sighed as she turned away.

"I have to be going," she said again.

"Marybeth." He liked the way her name felt on his tongue. Feminine. Soft.

She kept walking, and he muttered a curse under his breath. Damned stubborn female.

"Marybeth!" He followed her out the door, catching it before it could bang shut behind her.

She kept going toward the car. "Thank your housekeeper for the iced tea and cookies."

He sucked in an angry breath, ready to shout, and then glanced toward the outbuilding where Trevor had disappeared. He might be watching them, or at least listening. Erik couldn't fault his curiosity. It wasn't often—hell, it was never—that a woman came to the house to see the boss. Maybe that was why Tina had spoken the way she had. Clearly Erik needed to have a talk with her.

He swallowed the loud words he had been about to shout and walked faster instead. Marybeth opened her car door and glanced around. Before she could slide inside, he was beside her. His hand fastened itself around her wrist.

"Just a minute."

Her pulse raced beneath his fingers. She glared, and he released her.

"Please," he added. He remembered that her trip out had probably been motivated by the type of unselfish, uncomplicated kindness he'd seen in her more than once back at the hospital.

She turned toward him more fully, but she left the car door open. "Yes?" Her voice was cool. It bordered on frigid.

Erik raked the hand that had grabbed her wrist over his short hair and tried to think what to say. He wasn't often in the position of owing someone an explanation. He found he didn't like it.

"Hell," he muttered, searching the ground between them for clues.

Marybeth took a deep breath and willed her galloping heartbeat to slow. If this maddening man wasn't shutting her out or shocking her with offspring she hadn't even guessed at, he was royally ticking her off with his high-handed orders and strong-arm tactics. She didn't know why she put up with him for even a moment, let alone got herself into these situations voluntarily.

She looked into his face and remembered immediately why she had come back for more. The shadows were in his eyes again. The shadows of loneliness and distrust.

She touched his arm. "What is it?" she coaxed.

Erik glanced down at her hand and then back into her face, confusion in his blue gaze. "You must have some questions about Tina's mother." His tone was guarded.

Marybeth felt herself relaxing. "Your little girl is certainly a sweetheart," she said. "And outspoken, too."

Erik returned her wry grin with one of his own. Marybeth decided she would rather enjoy the suddenly peaceful feeling between them instead of spoiling it with her curiosity.

"My questions will keep, I expect. Is there anything you wanted to tell me? You don't have to, you know."

For a long moment he studied her face. "Damn, if you aren't full of surprises," he said softly, touching her cheek with the tips of his fingers.

For a moment, Marybeth thought he was going to kiss her. Forgetting all about Tina and the hired hand, she swayed toward him. Then she caught herself and straightened, reddening as Erik's mouth curved upward.

"Tina's adopted," he said without preamble. "Her mother's..." his voice stumbled. "Her mother's dead. I'm not sure about her real father. It's complicated."

"I'm sorry." Some of the sympathy Marybeth felt soaked into her words. "Did you know them?"

Erik's expression turned grim. "Yeah. I knew them." He didn't add anything more.

"Well," Marybeth said briskly, while she yanked the car door open wider, "thank you for letting me meet her. I'm sorry I couldn't stay and look around, but I appreciate your offer."

"My turn to thank you," Erik said, stilling her movements with his hands curving at her waist. He leaned forward. "My way," he said huskily.

Marybeth was helpless to do anything except watch his descending mouth. Rational thought fled. Right before his lips touched hers, she closed her eyes and leaned into him, letting her hands settle lightly against the hard muscles of his upper arms.

This kiss was like nothing she had ever experienced. It heated the moment his mouth covered hers. His arms shifted, closing around her, and she melted against the broad wall of his chest. After a moment Erik broke away, but when she pulled in a ragged breath, his arms tightened.

Again he swooped. His lips demanded even more of a response. Marybeth gave it to him as he dragged her closer, muttering something dark and unintelligible. She knew she should protest. What about Tina? And the hired man had to be around somewhere. Any remnants of logic disintegrated in the passion of Erik's embrace.

After a moment suspended in time he loosened his hold reluctantly and let his hands slide down to her elbows while his mouth was still fused with hers. He half expected her to pull back, but she didn't. The part of his brain that was still functional insisted he free her mouth before he found himself tossing her over his shoulder and heading for the first flat, private place he could find.

Her eyelids flickered open as he watched her, willing his shallow breath and pounding heart to slow. All Erik's blood seemed to have settled in his groin, and he resisted the urge to rearrange the suddenly uncomfortable fit of his jeans. Even though she was a nurse, he'd bet she embarrassed easy.

Marybeth's lips parted, and then she turned without speaking, sliding behind the wheel of her car. Erik's grin was reluctant as he bent down to look in the window. If she could have read his mind, she'd bolt like a startled rabbit.

"Thanks again for the food," he said.

She killed the engine once before she got it into reverse, and he heard her mutter a pungent curse. For a moment her clouded gaze locked with his. A faint smile trembled on her lips, and Erik had to fight the impulse to lean down and take her mouth again.

"Drive carefully," he said instead.

She dragged her gaze from his. He stepped back and watched her through narrowed eyes until her car was out

the gate. When he turned back to the house, Tina came
bounding down the steps like an exuberant puppy, bringing with her a reminder of all the reasons he didn't dare see
Marybeth MacNamara again.

Chapter Four

Marybeth put down the chart she had been working on and allowed herself a moment to stare off into space. It had been four days since she'd seen Erik out at his farm. Every time she thought about the kiss they had shared or the way she lit out of there afterward, she became embarrassed all over again. What was it about Erik Snow that twitched her hormones so she barely knew her own mind?

No matter, she thought, and returned her attention to the chart she had set aside. Erik had a daughter and too many secrets. Hadn't Marybeth learned anything from her husband? A man with secrets was a good man to avoid. Surely a grown woman, smart enough to be a nurse and stubborn enough to make her own way in the world, could put one man from her mind, even if he was a four-star kisser.

Marybeth had just finished her personal pep talk and begun working on another chart when a small sound made her glance up. Her gaze settled unerringly on a worn brass belt buckle that dissected a distinctly masculine torso—flat middle in a plaid cotton shirt above, and well-worn, tight denim below. Thoroughly rattled, Marybeth pushed back her steno chair and rose to look Erik Snow full in the face.

She had no time to speculate on how long he had been standing there. His first words put her on the defensive.

"Working hard?"

Marybeth detected an underlying sneer in his tone, and her hackles rose accordingly. "Yes, as a matter of fact I was. The information that goes on patients' charts is crucial, sometimes life or death, and interruptions can cause errors."

For a moment Erik looked taken aback. Marybeth was horrified at her own rudeness. Lord, but the man brought out the nasty in her.

"I'm sorry," she said hastily. "I didn't mean to sound so cantankerous."

Erik shrugged, as if her moods meant nothing. Then he set a brown paper bag on the counter between them. It clunked heavily. "Your casserole dish."

"Oh. Thank you." That was why he had come. Not to see her, but to return her dish. She ignored the disappointment that shivered through her and set the bag behind the counter.

Erik jammed his hands into his pockets, straining denim that was already stretched tight. Marybeth averted her eyes and finally worked her way back to his face. It bore a slightly hostile expression.

"The spaghetti was good. It was thoughtful of you to bring it." His tone was gruff.

Matching his tone, she said, "No problem."

A light began to gleam in his blue eyes. Was it humor she saw there? His lips twitched, and she was sure. An answering smile pulled at her mouth.

"Look," he said, shifting his weight, "could we start over? I guess my social skills are rustier than I thought."

She tipped her head slightly, eyeing him with more warmth. "As long as one of my patients doesn't press his call button. You know how *demanding* some patients can be."

Erik's smile widened to a genuine grin. "I've heard tell. Run you off your feet?"

"Some try to." She relaxed, beginning to enjoy herself.

"We did appreciate the meal you brought," he said, reminding her of his daughter, Tina. Marybeth wondered about her but now wasn't the time to ask.

"I'm glad," she said instead. "Of course I didn't realize you had a housekeeper—"

"Or you wouldn't have brought it," he finished for her. "Our gain that you didn't know."

A bell sounded. Marybeth glanced down at the board. "Not mine," she said, "but it probably won't be long now. Thanks for stopping by."

His eyes narrowed. "Wait a minute. Let me return the favor. A meal, I mean."

"You cook?" she asked, smiling again.

"Some, but that isn't what I had in mind. How about going to dinner with me?" For a moment he looked as surprised as Marybeth felt at the sudden invitation. Perhaps he hadn't really meant it.

"I don't know." She hesitated, trying to give him an out. "I have a crazy schedule this week."

"I can work around it." His gaze was steady.

She thought a moment, but her earlier resolve not to see him again had dissolved like foam on the tide.

"What about tomorrow evening?" he asked.

"I start graveyard tomorrow."

"I wasn't asking to spend the night."

A sizzling retort danced on her tongue, but she saw the challenging gleam in his eyes and decided to swallow it. "How about a picnic?" she asked in a mild tone, pleased with his momentary look of confusion. "You could bring something out early, and we could eat on the beach." Somehow being outside with him didn't sound as intimidating as facing him across the intimacy of a dinner table.

"A picnic?" He sounded doubtful.

"Sure. It would be fun."

He shrugged. "Okay, if that's what you want. How early?"

They settled on a time as another bell sounded. "That one is mine." Marybeth gave him quick directions. "My house is at the end of the road," she finished. "Can't miss it."

"See you then." Erik turned to go and, for a moment, she stood and watched the way his long legs moved and his nicely rounded buttocks shifted in the tight jeans. Then she remembered her patient. Putting Erik firmly from her thoughts, she turned in the opposite direction from the one he had taken, a silly grin still on her face.

Erik wasn't sure what he had expected when he pulled up in front of a small, neat green-and-white beach house. He hadn't planned to see Marybeth again, but with her his careful plans seemed to go out the window, followed closely by his better sense. He had no business getting involved with her and yet here he was, picnic basket in hand. Leaving it on the seat of his pickup, he got out and walked up the steps to the porch. As he crossed the worn floor, he heard barking from inside. Before he could knock, the door opened and two light-colored dogs of indiscriminate breeding pushed out, tails wagging.

For a moment, Erik eyed them watchfully. Then he saw Marybeth in the doorway. She was smiling, and he was suddenly glad he'd come.

"Don't worry about the dogs," she said. "They're friendly to anyone who doesn't sneak up in the night."

He found himself returning her easy smile. "Is that a warning?" To his delight, she blushed.

"Well," she said briskly, "come on in." She stood aside, pulling the door open wider. As he moved past her, Erik glanced down at her trim jeans and short-sleeved sweater. Beneath the soft knit, her breasts rose and fell enticingly. He caught her scent, part wildflower and part pure Marybeth.

The dogs began to follow him back in. She spoke firmly. "Arthur, Annabelle, go outside."

When she shut the front door, Erik glanced around at the open living and dining areas. A couple of rag rugs lay on the wood floor and dried flowers in a glazed clay pot graced the table. The furniture was worn but the room looked friendly, inviting. It made him curious about her bedroom. Would it be warm and comfortable, like the rest of the house? Frilly and feminine or tailored and neat, like Marybeth herself?

She said something, and he shook the speculations from his head. "I'm sorry—what?" He turned to look at her.

"I asked if you wanted the five-cent tour?" she asked, her eyes more green than gray. They almost matched the mossy tone of her sweater. "There isn't much else to see."

Erik stuck his hands into his pockets, trying to relax. "Sure. This is nice."

"Thanks. I was lucky that it came furnished." She walked toward the back of the house, through an open doorway. The kitchen had tiled counters, oak cabinets and older white appliances.

She led the way to two more doors, pushing open the first as she gestured inside. "Bathroom." Erik stuck his head in. The usual fixtures, plus a fluffy blue rug and a ruffled shower curtain.

"Bedroom." She pointed toward the open door and stepped back. Erik sensed that he was only intended to give the room a cursory glance. Perversely he stepped inside and turned in a slow circle. Double bed covered with a quilt, plain curtains at the window, older wooden dresser and a chest by the bed holding a table lamp, a clock radio and a photograph of a man in a brass frame. Curious, Erik picked it up.

He studied the dark-haired, smiling image. "This is your husband?"

Marybeth came forward and took the picture from him, her movement uncharacteristically jerky. "Yes," she said. She glanced at it for a moment and then set it back on the chest.

"I'm sorry."

She nodded without looking at him.

"You over him?" he asked.

Now she did look up. "As much as a person gets, I guess," she replied after a moment.

Her answer raised more questions. Before he could voice one, she whirled away.

"Well," she said brightly, "are you ready to eat? I'm starved." She took a folded blanket off the foot of the bed. "Pretend this is a tablecloth."

Erik took his cue from her. "Sure. The food's in my truck." He followed her back outside. When she opened the front door, a black cat squeezed in past her feet.

"That's Sassy," she said. An orange cat followed the black one inside. "And Mugsy."

"Any more?" Two dogs and two cats. He should have known she'd collect strays. So what did that make him?

"One more cat, named Tiger, who still thinks he's a tom," she said as they went down the front steps. "He roams." She glanced back at Erik, and there was laughter in her eyes. "Typical single male, spreads himself too thin."

Erik wasn't sure how to respond to her teasing. He brushed past her to open the truck door. "I bet his ladies don't mind."

"No ladies," she corrected. "Tiger just *thinks* he's still a tom. He's been fixed."

Erik made a sympathetic noise. "Poor guy." He got out the hamper.

Marybeth's eyes widened. "How many are we feeding tonight, General?"

Erik glanced at her, saw she was smiling. "What can I say? Mrs. O'Reilly thinks I'm still a growing boy."

"If you eat all that, you will be."

"About poor Tiger—" Erik began.

"He's from the animal shelter," Marybeth explained as she led the way down to the beach. The two dogs came running up to follow her. "You get an animal from there, you agree to have it altered."

"That's a descriptive term," Erik muttered as he stepped over a driftwood log and set the basket down on a sandy stretch of beach. "How about here? We can use the log for a backrest."

Marybeth turned. "Perfect." She spread out the blanket, then straightened and looked at him, raising her brows. "Something wrong?"

He shook his head and set down the basket. He opened it while he collected his thoughts. For a moment, she had looked so appealing with the breeze stirring her honey-brown curls and the diffused sunlight warming her skin that he had wanted to kiss her.

"We've got turkey sandwiches, macaroni salad, pickles, carrot sticks..." He took out another container and examined it. "Chocolate cookies. One of Mrs. O's specialties."

"Bless Mrs. O," Marybeth murmured when she saw the size of them.

Erik arched a brow. "What kind of wine goes with chocolate chips?" He unearthed a slim bottle.

Marybeth laughed, and something tightened inside him at the musical sound. "I have no idea."

"Doesn't matter. This is pear wine, made locally." He tore his gaze from hers and pulled out two glasses. Then he closed the basket and set them on its flat top.

Marybeth sat down, crossing her legs Indian fashion. "I've never tasted pear wine." She hesitated. "I do have to work later, but I guess a few sips wouldn't hurt."

Erik sank beside her, his back against the log and his long legs stretched out before him. He handed her a partially full glass and waited while she took a sip.

"Mmm," she said. "It's good."

Erik gave her a paper plate and a napkin, then began reexamining the pile of food. Soon they were eating as the dogs raced up and down the beach in front of them, nosing into things and splashing through the shallow water as they alternately explored and chased each other.

"They were from the shelter?" Erik asked, to break the silence. He pointed at the canines with a carrot stick.

"Yup. I have a friend who works there, Sandy McPherson. For a while, whenever they had an animal due for a shot she'd call me. My place filled up pretty fast. So far my landlords have been extremely understanding, but I've got all the animals I can handle."

"Due for a shot?" Erik echoed, puzzled.

She frowned at the half sandwich in her hand. "Due to be put to sleep," she said quietly. "You can't imagine the numbers of unwanted cats and dogs they have to euthanatize every month. It's monstrous."

Erik didn't know what to say. "How does your friend handle it?"

Tears filled Marybeth's eyes. The sight of them made him feel helpless. "She says she gives each one a hug first, in case it's the only kindness the poor thing's had." She shook her head, dabbing at her eyes with her paper napkin. "I'm sorry. You'll think I'm a complete idiot."

"No," he said as he caught her chin with his finger and tilted her head back up to his. "I think you're a tender-hearted woman with a lot of love in her heart." A woman who got hurt easily, he thought as he wiped away her tears with his thumb.

What the hell was he doing here?

Marybeth blinked and then turned her face away. Erik finished his sandwich in silence, feeling uncomfortable with the emotionally charged scene he'd just been a part of.

"Want to take a walk down the beach before we have our cookies?" Marybeth asked when he put his empty plate aside. "The basket will be okay here if we take Arthur and Annabelle with us."

Erik stood up and then held out his hand. She put hers into it and he pulled her up, but he misjudged the distance and tugged a little too hard. She put her free hand out as she bumped his chest. Erik's arm went around her waist and, for a moment, he held her protectively.

"Sorry," he murmured into her hair. The wildflower aroma filled his head.

"It's okay," she said. "I guess you don't know your own . . ." Her voice trailed off as Erik stared deep into her eyes. He leaned closer, unable to stop himself.

Abruptly Marybeth stepped back out of his loose hold. "I think we'd better take that walk and burn off some of this great food," she said, turning away.

Erik heard the breathless catch in her voice. She wasn't immune, any more than he was. "Sure, let's go," he said, following her across several big rocks as she called to the dogs. He caught up with her as she stepped down onto the sand, and enfolded her hand in his. "Don't worry so much," he found himself saying when she turned a frowning gaze his way. "We'll be okay."

"Will we?" she asked, but she didn't seem to expect an answer. The dogs ran on ahead, stopping every few minutes to make sure the humans were still following. The lack of conversation didn't seem to bother Marybeth, and Erik found himself soaking up the peace of the setting, with the sounds of the wind in the trees along the edge of the beach, and the gentle slap of the waves. In the distance, a ferry crossed the wide sound. By mutual consent, they stopped to watch its progress.

"You like living on an island?" Erik asked as they began walking again.

"Yes," she said. "I like the small-town atmosphere of Coupeville. What about you? Is an island somehow symbolic?"

"Symbolic of what?" He didn't like being analyzed.

"Solitude?" she asked. "Peace?"

"But no man is an island," he quoted, then grinned to break the serious mood that had fallen over them.

Marybeth batted at him playfully, laughing. "Don't be a ninny."

Erik pretended to be offended. It had been a long time since he had participated in such lighthearted teasing. "A ninny! I don't think I've ever been called that."

"You have now. Come on, time to turn around." She called the dogs again and began to head back the way they came. "So what happened in between St. Louis and here?" she asked. "You can fill in a few blanks for me, can't you?"

Erik pulled at her hand, dropping a kiss on its back.

She yanked it away. "Quit trying to distract me!"

"Is that what I was doing?" He tried to look innocent.

"Undoubtedly! Is your past so black?" she asked.

Erik shook his head, for once strangely reluctant to keep from telling her some of the things he always kept private. "Just dull," he said finally.

Marybeth slowed her steps and studied him for a moment. The silence stretched awkwardly between them, but Erik couldn't think of anything to fill it.

"Okay," she sighed, and he sensed her disappointment. "Be a mystery man. But it makes small talk more difficult."

Suddenly Erik bent his head, surprising both of them. He planted a swift, hard kiss on her upturned mouth and then stepped back before she could react.

"Maybe we don't need small talk," he said, taking her hand again as he started walking toward the basket and blanket he could see around the next curve of beach. He realized almost immediately that kissing her had been a mistake. Now there was no way he was leaving without kissing her again, and thoroughly.

Beside him, Marybeth walked silently, her attention on the rocky ground before them. Her pulse was beating faster than normal, and she had to concentrate to keep her breathing steady. Erik was full of secrets and surprises. If he thought a kiss could distract her for long he was wrong. No way was she going to repeat the same mistakes she had made with Mike. Somehow she had to either topple the protective wall Erik had built around himself and discover what put the shadows in his eyes, or find the strength to stop seeing him. That settled, she waited while he stowed the hamper in his truck. He didn't say anything, so she led the way back inside.

"How about a cup of coffee? I have some special beans my neighbor had sent from Seattle."

He paused halfway up the front steps. "If it's no trouble."

"No trouble." She glanced at the two dogs who were watching them expectantly. Arthur's tongue lolled out, and Annabelle was thumping her bushy tail.

Erik moved closer. "Then I'd like some coffee."

When it was done perking and she had filled two mugs, Marybeth led the way back to the porch and sat down on the top step, leaving room for Erik to sit beside her. Dusk had fallen. The water looked dark and mysterious.

Erik took a sip of his coffee. "It's good."

"Thanks. Mr. Isaacson insists it's the best-tasting blend in the world."

"Who's Mr. Isaacson?" Erik sounded annoyed.

Marybeth sampled her own coffee before she answered. The idea of Erik feeling jealous on her behalf had a certain appeal to it. "He's my neighbor." She hesitated, then confessed, "Mr. Isaacson must be in his seventies."

Erik lifted his hand and stroked the hair framing her cheek. "That's okay, then," he said abruptly.

With mixed feelings toward his sudden possessiveness, Marybeth set down her mug and rose. She went down the steps to stop at the bottom, folding her arms across her chest as she gazed at the water.

Erik got up and followed her. "What's wrong?" he asked.

His closeness set off alarms across her skin. "I don't know."

He put his arms around her and eased her closer, cradling her in his embrace. "Sure?"

Agitated by her reaction to the warmth of his body, Marybeth pulled away. "It's us." She didn't bother to censor her words. "We're wrong."

Erik remained still. "How do you know that?"

She shrugged, feeling slightly foolish for her outburst. "It's just a feeling," she murmured.

He faced her, sliding his fingers through her hair, capturing her head and holding it still while his gaze burned into hers. "I've told myself the same thing," he muttered, voice rough. "But it doesn't help."

Marybeth stared up at him in the lengthening twilight. Behind him, the lamp she had left on in the house glowed softly through the window. "Doesn't help what?" she asked.

His fingers tightened on her scalp and he bent over her. "This," he whispered, right before his mouth settled firmly on hers.

His kiss was demanding and passionate, as if he had been waiting impatiently to claim her mouth. Marybeth met his urgency with hunger of her own. She parted her lips so his tongue could thrust deep and tangle with hers. He released his hold on her head to wrap his arms around her body, pulling her close to his hard contours. Marybeth melted beneath the intensity of his desire and molded herself even closer.

For a moment, he lifted his head. His eyes glittered in the gathering darkness. Then he bent to her again, and even before his lips touched hers, she was reaching up to meet his descent.

The kiss was rougher, wilder. Erik's hands stroked down her sides to settle on her hips; his fingers splayed as he brought her tight against him. Marybeth moaned, and his body shuddered. Then he tore his mouth from hers and buried his face in her hair.

She had to stop this madness before they both lost control.

"Let's go inside," Erik groaned, the grip of his hands harder as he rubbed himself against her.

Marybeth froze, reality intruding. What was she doing? The way she was acting, she couldn't blame Erik for making assumptions.

He must have sensed her withdrawal, because he loosened his hold and moved back to peer into her face.

"What's wrong?"

She shook her head and turned away. Another moment in his embrace and she might have . . .

"Nothing. I'm sorry that I gave you the wrong impression."

She felt his hand on her shoulder. "Oh, you didn't give me any wrong impression. You were as caught up in it as I was."

"I'm sorry," she repeated. "I didn't mean for things to get out of hand." She didn't look at him as the silence lengthened.

Finally he sighed, and she did look. He was running a hand over his short hair. His face was all harsh angles and his mouth was pulled into a grim line.

"You don't have to be sorry," he said. "I was moving too fast."

His sudden about-face surprised her. "*We're* moving too fast," she corrected him, compelled to be honest. "You were right—it wasn't all just you." She paused and licked her lips. "I'm not ready for anything complicated."

Her words brought home to Erik his own situation and limitations. He had no business hustling her into bed no matter how good he knew it would be.

"Yeah," he said, touching her cheek with his finger. "Good thing one of us has some sense." He managed a grin and saw the relief on her face.

"Thanks," she said.

Erik knew that he had to get out of here, before his shaky control was strained any further. "Look," he said. "I'd better go. Got a lot of things to do tomorrow."

Marybeth turned her watch toward the light from the house. "Oh, my," she said. "I have to get ready for work pretty soon."

Erik's hand wrapped around her upper arm and he bent to give her a quick kiss on the cheek. "I'll see you," he said, before he turned toward his truck.

"Thanks for supper," Marybeth called after him.

He didn't dare look again, or he might end up right back where he'd started. He waved but didn't risk a glance until he was in the truck with the door safely shut. Then he forced a smile as the engine fired up.

Damn, but he still wanted to go back and wrap his arms around her, kiss her one more time. Ten more times. Waving again, he threw the truck into reverse and backed around.

Marybeth stood on the porch until the taillights had disappeared down the road. Part of her wished that he had stayed, that she had called in sick, something she never did. But the sensible, grown-up, dependable side of her was relieved that he had left. The part that reminded her how much she could be hurt by a man like Erik, another man with secrets.

She had tried hard to be the perfect policeman's wife when she had been married to Mike, to be warm and loving yet respectful of his privacy. She'd let him keep his secrets about his work after he made detective, let him go his way without question. He had shut her out of an important part of his life and she had gone along with it, but never again. Better not to love than to love and lose, totally ignorant of and unprepared for the danger until it was too late. Too damned late.

That night, as she walked the almost silent halls of the sleeping hospital and tried to acclimate herself to the late shift, that sensible part of her was cold comfort while she thought about what she was missing.

Back at his ranch, Erik thanked Mrs. O'Reilly for staying and taking care of Tina for him. Then, after the housekeeper had driven away, he peeked into the little girl's room. He stood in the doorway for a long time, watching Tina sleep and wondering what she dreamed. Did she remember anything of her life in Argentina, before he had brought her with him to the States? She said not, but every once in a while she would ask him a question about something that must have flashed across her consciousness or come to her in a dream. If Erik could have his way, she would never remember, never know of the events that had brought the two of them together.

Eventually he shut the door quietly and moved into the den where he kept the ranch's books. As always, there was a stack of paperwork waiting for him on his desk. Erik looked through it for a moment without anything registering, then tossed the papers down with a muttered oath and crossed to the liquor cabinet. Pouring himself a brandy, he went into the empty living room. After a moment, he flicked on the television to a late-night talk show. Even as the voices droned around him, his thoughts went back to Marybeth and the way she had melted in his arms. The memory immediately affected his body, barely cooled from their shared passion, and he shifted uncomfortably in the chair.

What business had he lusting after her? She wanted to know all about him, and he couldn't fault her curiosity. It was normal. But *nothing* about him was normal.

He couldn't share with her the details of his former life. He couldn't tell her he had been an agent for one of the most secret, elite government espionage and enforcement squads. No way did he want to even *remember* his childhood, such as it had been, let alone share those barren memories with someone as sweet and gentle—as giving— as Marybeth.

Erik's thoughts brought him right back to his original resolution. He had no business getting involved with her, no business having anything to do with her. The best thing he could do for both of them was to leave her the hell alone.

He drained the last of his brandy in one gulp, knowing that giving her up was one thing he might not be strong enough to do. For both their sakes, and for Tina's, he had to hope that he was wrong.

Chapter Five

"Well, he has gorgeous brown eyes, but his ears *are* a little strange."

Marybeth bent down and extended her hand to the dog Sandy had brought with her to Marybeth's house. The animal hesitated, trembling slightly. His stump of a tail wagged slowly. After a moment, he sniffed her fingers and his tail wagged faster as she scratched around his pointed ears. One of them stood up straight but the other flopped over, giving the brindle-colored boxer a slightly lopsided and comical appearance.

"See, I told you that Joker's got a great personality," Sandy said while she ran her hand over the short hair on his back. He turned his head to lick her hand with his pink tongue.

Marybeth watched the dog sadly, trying not to think of his fate. "I believe you," she said with regret. "He's a beautiful animal, but I'm full up. I just don't have room for another big dog."

"Only seventy pounds," Sandy said. "More medium-sized, I'd say. He's a year old, housebroken, and obedience trained. We suspect that he's been abused but it only seems to have made him a little timid, not the least bit mean. He'd be great with kids."

"I don't have any kids," Marybeth reminded her.

Sandy's eyes flashed. "I know you can't take him, but don't you know anyone who could? His time's up tomorrow, and he's too much of a sweetheart to put down." She bent and put her arms around Joker's neck. His tail wagged so fast it was almost going in circles and he licked her chin.

Marybeth shook her head. "All my neighbors already have dogs from the shelter. You know I've hit up everyone I can think of to give them homes."

"I know." Sandy frowned, her hand stroking down Joker's dark brown body. When she stopped, he turned and thrust one white forepaw into her hand, whining. "Okay, boy," she said softly. "We'll think of something."

"I wish I could help," Marybeth said.

Sandy straightened, snapping her fingers. "What about Erik?"

"Erik?" Marybeth echoed. "What about him?"

"He has a ranch, you told me, and a little girl. A perfect home for Joker."

Marybeth pushed her hair off her forehead. She had been cleaning house when Sandy arrived and had on her oldest cutoff jeans and a faded T-shirt. "I don't know about that. Maybe he already has a dog. Or maybe he doesn't like them." He hadn't paid much attention to Annabelle and Arthur when he was over.

"Let's find out," Sandy urged. Hearing the excitement in her voice, Joker danced at the end of his leash. "Call him."

"Gee, I kinda hate to hit him with this over the phone," Marybeth stalled.

"Yeah, I agree," Sandy said before she could go on. "The phone's no good. Let's go see him. It will be harder for him to say no with Joker right there in front of him."

Again Marybeth hesitated. Her relationship with Erik hadn't progressed to the point of dropping in on him, even though she'd done that very thing when she delivered the spaghetti. What if he had company, another woman? She didn't know enough about him to be sure he wasn't seeing anyone else. What if he thought she was making excuses to see him?

"Well?" Sandy pressed her. "You do want Joker to find a home, don't you?"

Marybeth looked down at the dog, who was sitting politely at the end of the leash, watching her. Joker returned her stare, brown eyes intent above his square black-and-white muzzle, dark forehead a mass of worried wrinkles. "Of course I want him to find a home." How could she deny him what might be his last chance?

"Then, what's holding us up?"

"Okay," Marybeth sighed, turning toward her house. "Let me put on a clean shirt and lock up."

On the way to Erik's, with Joker sitting behind her on the back seat of Sandy's old hatchback, his nose thrust out the open window, Marybeth tried to follow Sandy's conversation about the other animals at the shelter. It was difficult not to dwell instead on the way Erik had kissed her and then asked to go inside with her the last time she was with him. It wasn't Sandy's fault that Marybeth couldn't keep her resolution not to get more deeply involved with Erik, and it certainly wasn't Joker's.

Maybe Erik would take the dog. She just hoped he wouldn't get the wrong impression of her, since they hadn't discussed getting together again.

"Nice house," Sandy said as they finally pulled up where Marybeth had parked the last time. Erik's truck sat in front of the barn, so he was probably around somewhere.

"I don't know about dropping in like this," Marybeth muttered as Sandy snapped on Joker's leash and let him out of the car. "Erik might be out with the cattle."

"I'll take the blame," Sandy said in a breezy voice. "Just introduce me, and I'll take it from there."

Marybeth wished she had her self-confidence. When it came to animals, Sandy was a crusader. Marybeth glanced at her friend's curvy figure in tight jeans and a cropped knit top, not sure she wanted the other woman to "take it from there." Sandy had a flirtatious personality, even when she wasn't trying. What if Erik found her attractive?

Jealousy sizzled through Marybeth at the thought of Erik being interested in her friend. Then she silently scolded herself. She didn't have the right to feel possessive when she had no intentions of pursuing her own relationship with him.

"Is that Erik?" Sandy hissed, not turning toward her.

Marybeth glanced up as he came out of the barn, wiping his hands on a bandanna. A battered black Stetson covered his silver-blond hair, shading his expression. With his plaid shirt, faded jeans and scuffed western boots, it completed the image of a rough and rugged male at home in the domain he had carved out for himself.

Marybeth swallowed dryly. Beside her, Sandy murmured, "My, oh my." Joker slunk behind her, pulling on his leash until it was taut.

"Okay, boy," Sandy murmured in a distracted tone. She bent to pat his head, and he ducked away. Marybeth ached to see his nervousness and know it had been caused by some cruel, bullying human. At that moment, she decided that Erik had to take him.

"Hi," she called as he moved closer. "I hope we aren't interrupting."

He sauntered over to stop in front of them. Before he glanced at Sandy, his narrowed eyes sent Marybeth a message that she couldn't interpret. "I was just heading out to check on some cattle," he said in his deep voice.

"This is my friend Sandy McPherson," Marybeth explained quickly, sensing his impatience.

She and Erik exchanged greetings.

"Who's this?" he asked, reaching to pat Joker, who again ducked away, almost pulling Sandy around with the tight leash.

"He's a little shy of strange men," she explained, shifting. "His name's Joker."

"We're trying to find him a home," Marybeth interjected.

Erik's piercing gaze returned to her. "Sorry. If you were thinking of me, you'll have to forget it."

"Why?" Marybeth asked, surprised at his blunt refusal. "He'd be great company for Tina."

Erik frowned, then directed his attention to Sandy. "Aren't boxers pretty fierce?"

"Not around children. They're usually very gentle."

He shook his head. "No. I can't take the chance."

"I've seen Joker with children who come to the shelter," Sandy continued. "He's very good with them."

Erik's jaw was set, his expression negative. Marybeth wondered if there was anything she could say to change his mind. Just then a small dynamo burst from the door of the house.

"Daddy! Who's here?" She ran down the steps and slowed as she looked at Sandy and Marybeth, her straight black hair swinging above her red shirt and blue denim overalls.

"Hi, Tina," Marybeth said. "Do you remember me?"

"You brought the spaghetti." Her dark eyes were direct, her expression cautious.

"That's right."

Tina glanced up at Erik. "Daddy said it was better than Mrs. O's."

Marybeth met his rueful expression. "That's nice," she replied, trying not to chuckle.

"This is Marybeth's friend Sandy," Erik told Tina.

"Aren't you a darling?" Sandy cooed. To Marybeth's surprise, Joker rose from his sitting position, one ear pricked to attention, tail starting to wag. He strained at his leash and whined softly.

Tina saw him and came forward, extending one hand. "Nice doggy. Who are you?"

Sensing an ally, Sandy said, "This is Joker. He'd like to meet you and shake hands."

"Really?" Tina's dark eyes sparkled as she looked at Erik. "Can I, Daddy?"

He nodded, but Marybeth could tell that he was ready to leap to Tina's defense if the situation changed. His stance reminded Marybeth of something but she couldn't remember what.

His lean body was coiled tensely as he said, "Move slowly now, Tina. Let him sniff your hand."

The minute she extended it, palm up, Joker nuzzled her fingers while she laughed in delight.

"He tickles."

"Joker, give her five," Sandy encouraged.

Joker offered a white paw for Tina to shake.

"He likes me!" she exclaimed, delighted. Before Erik could stop her, she moved closer and threw her chubby arms around Joker's neck. He licked her cheek. "Now he's kissing me." She dissolved into giggles.

"Did you coach this dog," Erik asked Sandy from the side of his mouth, "or does he do this to everyone he thinks might take him in?"

Sandy looked pleased. "He's acting on his own." Then her voice became more serious as she said quietly, "We're putting him to sleep tomorrow, so maybe he can sense that his time is running out."

For a moment, something grim flashed across Erik's deeply tanned face, then he looked at Marybeth. "This your idea?"

"Actually it was mine," Sandy said quickly. "I'm desperate."

Erik was already shaking his head. "I'm sorry, I can't help you."

Sandy clutched at his arm, and Marybeth felt a possessive charge go through her. "Keep him for a week," Sandy urged. "Then, if I have to take him back, he'll have more time coming before we put him down."

Erik looked doubtful, but Tina pulled at his hand. "Please, Daddy," she urged. "Let him stay, and then I'd have someone to play with."

Marybeth watched an expression of pain cross his face before he quickly covered it up. "You'll get attached to him, and you won't want to give him up," he said.

"No, I won't." Her high voice rose even more. "I promise I won't get 'tached to him. I promise!"

Erik's eyes flashed as he looked at Sandy and then Marybeth. "I bet you were counting on this to happen."

Sandy's grin held not a hint of remorse. "Whatever works."

Marybeth shifted uncomfortably. She could see that Erik hated to be manipulated. He ignored her.

"A week?" he asked Sandy, watching Joker wiggle his compact body as Tina stroked him, crooning in her light voice.

"Only a week," Sandy agreed. "I guarantee it." She glanced around. "Boxers are house dogs. I hope you don't plan on keeping him in the barn or anything like that. He needs to be around people."

Erik took off his hat and raked his hand over his pale hair in a gesture that was becoming familiar to Marybeth. There was the faint suggestion of humor on his face. "Of course. Can I feed him regular dog food or does he need a special diet?"

Marybeth relaxed, not realizing until then how tensely she'd been holding herself. Beside her, Sandy thrust the leash at Erik and turned away.

"I have a bag of dry food in the trunk of my car," she said. "Just a sec."

Erik looked at Marybeth, quirking a brow. "Just don't bring me any cats," he said.

She managed a smile. "I won't. Thanks."

"Thank you, Daddy," Tina echoed, throwing both arms around his legs.

He patted her head and then rubbed Joker's neck. "Remember, it's only for a week."

Marybeth watched him with his daughter. He must be a good father; she seemed happy and relaxed around him.

"I'll remember," Tina promised solemnly.

After ten days on night shift, Marybeth was glad to be going back on days. Tonight had been particularly heavy, with two emergency admissions to her section. All she wanted was to go home and get some sleep. Instead, Sandy was waiting by her car when she walked outside at eight the next morning.

"Hi. Thought I'd catch you here." Sandy was wearing her usual uniform of jeans and T-shirt, its message faded from repeated washings.

"Hi." Marybeth summoned a smile, hoping that Sandy didn't want to go out for breakfast. "How come you aren't at work?"

"I am," Sandy replied. "Right now I'm running an errand."

Marybeth's brows rose as she walked up to her Escort and unlocked the door. "Oh?"

"Joker's week with your buddy is up today," Sandy said. "And I might have found him a home."

Marybeth was fully aware that Erik had kept the dog for the promised length of time. He had called twice, once to ask if it was normal for Joker to refuse his food, which Marybeth assured him wasn't unusual in a strange new environment, another time just to ask her how she was bearing up under her temporary schedule change. Neither time had he suggested they get together.

"I'm glad for Joker," she told Sandy, "but I don't see why I have to go out there with you. You know the way."

Sandy's grin wavered. "I didn't want you to go with me," she said. "I need you to go *for* me. I've got some other things to do that can't wait. But I don't want to lose this opportunity for Joker. The family's looking for a boxer as a birthday present. If they can't see him today, they're going to buy a puppy." She clasped her hands together in a petitioning pose. "Please, please. Do this one little thing for me, and I promise I won't ever ask for another thing."

That was what Sandy always said. Marybeth couldn't keep from whooping in disbelief. "Another thing this week," she added dryly.

Sandy's expression was unrepentant. "Yeah, this week," she agreed.

Marybeth was beginning to wonder if contact with Erik Snow was preordained, but she couldn't make herself pretend she would mind seeing him again as well as finding out how Tina and Joker had gotten along.

"Okay," she said, ignoring her exhaustion. Her sudden capitulation obviously surprised her friend, who no doubt had been prepared to give her a hard sell.

"Can you go right now?" Sandy said. "Bring Joker to the shelter and tell Rachel to call the Brannigans immediately."

Marybeth glanced down at her rumpled uniform and nibbled at lips devoid of artificial color. The least she could do was to put on some gloss and run a brush through her hair.

"I guess. But you owe me. Big time."

Sandy, not one to dally when the battle was won, was already climbing back into her car. "Sure thing."

Somehow, Marybeth doubted she would ever collect.

Erik was loading some gear into the back of his pickup when he saw the familiar little red car coming down the road to the house. Another five minutes and he would have been headed for the far pasture. As he waited for Marybeth to pull up and stop, he wondered why she had come out and tried to convince himself that he wasn't glad to see her.

Tina and Joker, who had been inseparable all week, came running from the barn. After watching Joker stand off a stray dog that wandered onto the property, Erik had pretty much stopped worrying about the animal around Tina. He even slept in her room at night. Erik knew he'd made a big mistake in agreeing to keep him for a week.

"Hello," Marybeth called to him as she got out of the car. Her cheeks were pink and she looked uncomfortable.

"Hi, yourself," Erik said, walking closer. He could see fatigue in her eyes and the lack of her usual energy in her movements. "Been up all night?"

She grinned. "And then some. Sandy corralled me to run an errand for her." She stopped to smile at Tina. "Here's the reason for my trip now."

"Me?" Tina asked incredulously.

"No, sweetie. Sandy found a permanent home for Joker. The people want to see him this morning."

Even though Erik had reminded Tina more than once that week that Joker was only a temporary guest, he wasn't prepared for her reaction to Marybeth's announcement. Tina went pale, and an expression of pure anguish crossed her small face.

Erik looked at Marybeth, who had glanced at him for guidance. Tina threw her arms around Joker's muscular neck and began to cry. None of Erik's extensive training in antiterrorism had prepared him for the heartbroken sobs of a six-year-old who was about to be separated from an animal she loved. He immediately crouched beside her, mumbling something about her knowing that Joker's stay was up today.

Tina only cried harder. Thoroughly lost, Erik tried to peel her hands from their grip in Joker's short fur.

"Nooo," she wailed, clutching the dog tighter. Joker's whines joined the noise Tina was making. Erik wasn't sure if the dog understood enough of the situation to sympathize with his small friend or if her grasping fingers were pulling his hair. After another moment, Erik gave up on trying to loosen her hold.

He straightened, looking at Marybeth. She had tears standing in her eyes. If she started crying, too, he didn't know what he would do.

"I knew this was a bad idea," he growled, throwing his hands up in exasperation. He felt like the worst kind of villain, but it would be better for Tina not to get any more attached to a dog that might wander off or be killed. He'd had a dog when he was little, a cocker spaniel named Buddy, but his father made him leave it behind when they moved.

"I'm sorry." Clearly Marybeth didn't know what to do, either.

Erik tried again. "Tina, Joker has been promised to another family. We have to let him go."

Tina looked up at him, her dark eyes drenched with tears. "Joker's mine," she sobbed. "We're best friends. If you send him away, I'll be lonesome again, with no one to play with."

She buried her wet face in Joker's neck as he twisted around and tried to reach her with his tongue. Erik turned away, cursing under his breath. He hated to see Tina cry. She had been through so much. She had lost her mother and her homeland, had been taken from everything that was familiar, even had to learn a new language. Children were supposed to be adaptable, but how much could one little girl take?

Marybeth cleared her throat. She stared at Erik as if she were trying to tell him something.

"Well?" he snapped, irritated that she had gotten him into this fix in the first place. "What is it?"

She hesitated, while he glowered. Tina's noisy sobs were shredding his patience as well as his heart.

"Actually," Marybeth said slowly, "Joker isn't *promised* to the other family. They're looking for a boxer and said they'd like to see him. Sandy's afraid they'll find something else if we delay."

At Marybeth's words, Tina had let go of her death grip on Joker and was staring intently up at Erik. Again he squatted down so that he and the little girl he'd risked so much to make his daughter were looking into each other's eyes.

"You want to keep him?" he asked gruffly.

The smile that threatened to split Tina's face was all the answer Erik needed. He remembered too well a time when she hadn't smiled, no matter what he did. Now his hand trembled when he touched her cheek. Then he reached out to ruffle Joker's floppy ear. The dog responded with a wet kiss from Erik's jaw to his hairline.

He stood and eyed Marybeth. She still looked as if she were going to burst into tears. "You can't have him," he said, realizing that he was just as pleased as Tina that the dog was staying. "Joker's a part of *our* family now. He stays."

"Oh, I'm so glad!" Marybeth threw her arms around Erik's neck, her soft body crashing into his. Tina's piercing shriek of happiness and Joker's deep barks of excitement barely penetrated the buzzing in Erik's ears as his arms automatically came around Marybeth to hold her close. For a moment he almost forgot where they were as she planted a smacking kiss on his cheek.

Then Tina's shouting drew him back to reality. "Thank you, Daddy," she was saying. "You're the best daddy in the whole world!"

Marybeth leaned back in his embrace. "I agree." She smiled as the tears finally spilled over and ran down her flushed cheeks.

For a moment, Erik wanted to duck away from all the emotion. Instead, he let his arms tighten before he reluctantly let her go. He swooped Tina up and whirled her around, then set her carefully back down. "You'll have to keep feeding Joker," he reminded her with a straight face. "And make sure he always has fresh water."

"I will, I will." Tina was jumping up and down, clapping her small hands. Joker caught her excitement and began to spin in tight circles, barking excitedly.

Erik glanced down at the dog, surprised. "This is the first time he's barked," he explained to Marybeth. "We thought perhaps he couldn't."

She grinned at him happily. "Perhaps this is the first thing he's had to bark about."

"We're going to go play," Tina said, and Erik nodded absently.

"Don't go too far." He returned his attention to Marybeth. "I hope this doesn't cause problems for Sandy." Even if it did, he had no intention of giving the dog up.

"No, I'm sure it won't," Marybeth replied. "The main thing is that Joker has a good home with people who love him." She looked at Erik as if she expected a comment.

"Yeah," he said slowly. "He's got people who love him."

Marybeth's expression was pleased. "Well," she said, "now that we've settled the dog problem, I guess I'd better go. I'll let you get on with whatever you were doing when I showed up. I've disrupted your life enough for one day."

Erik realized that he liked having her close to him, her scent drifting up to fill his nostrils, her gray-green eyes narrowed with warm laughter. "Come with me," he said, linking his fingers with hers. "It's pretty up at the far pasture, and I won't be there too long."

She yawned, covering her mouth quickly with her free hand.

"I'm sorry," he said, feeling stupid. She'd told him that she hadn't slept. She probably wanted to get home. He disengaged his fingers stiffly. "Another time, maybe."

She squared around and set her hands on her hips. "I'm perfectly capable of deciding if I want to accept an invitation or not," she told him. "It so happens that I'm all done with night shift and don't have to be back to the hospital until tomorrow morning."

His brows rose and he felt his chest tighten with renewed anticipation. "So you'll stay?" he asked.

"Yes, I think I will," she drawled. "I can always sleep later."

Erik didn't say anything, but Marybeth saw a light in his eyes she would have liked to examine more closely. He wrapped her hand in his larger one and led her toward the house.

"I'll tell Mrs. O'Reilly to plan on one more for lunch," he said. "She'll be pleased to hear that Joker's staying on, too."

They ended up taking Tina and Joker to the far pasture with them. Tina sat on the bench seat between her father and Marybeth while Joker rode in the pickup bed. Marybeth found it hard to remember that she had thought the little girl to be quiet and withdrawn; Tina talked nonstop all the way. She only quieted when Erik interrupted to point out a red-tailed hawk soaring above them, or a patch of wildflowers spreading across the pasture.

"Sheriff Johnson came by," Marybeth told him when Tina turned to watch Joker through the back cab window.

"Oh?" Erik glancèd at her, brows raised.

"He said that Harcourt changed his plea to guilty, right after he had a visit from an attorney Sheriff Johnson didn't know. He said, too, that Harcourt seemed a little shook up."

Erik's slow smile held no surprise; instead he looked pleased. "Well, that will save the taxpayers some money," was all he said.

Before Marybeth could comment further on Harcourt's about-face, Tina thought she saw a rabbit. Eventually she ran out of things to tell Marybeth and started asking questions, some of them uncomfortably pointed. Marybeth glanced to Erik for help but he kept his gaze straight ahead. Only an occasional twitch of his lips betrayed his amusement at her discomfort.

"Why don't you have any children?" Tina asked her.

"Because I'm not married," Marybeth replied, wondering what was coming next.

"Neither's Daddy, but he has me," Tina exclaimed, twisting in the seat to study Marybeth intently. "You don't have a husband, and Daddy doesn't have a wife."

Beside her, Erik made a choking noise. Marybeth slanted him a dirty look. Just you wait, she thought.

"I have dogs and cats," she said, trying to divert Tina's attention.

"How many?"

Marybeth told her, describing them at length and giving their names.

"Can I meet them sometime?" Tina asked.

"Sure." Marybeth shot another glance at Erik, who was studying the land ahead of them intently. "Have your dad bring you over sometime," she said.

"Okay."

Marybeth relaxed slightly, relieved.

"You could marry Daddy, and then we could get some brothers and sisters for me to play with." While Marybeth tried not to blush, Tina turned back around. "Right, Daddy?"

Cheeks burning, Marybeth wondered how he was going to get out of this one. It served him right, since he'd abandoned her to fend for herself.

"Well, Erik," she teased when he remained silent. "Sounds like Tina has come up with quite a plan."

He pulled the truck to a jerky stop, shifting hard and setting the hand brake. "Uh, we'll have to talk about this some other time. We're here, and I have a couple of cows to check on." He leaped out of the truck, his long legs carrying him toward the clump of cattle that were watching him curiously.

Behind him, Marybeth had a hard time stifling her laughter, even though she probably should have been more embarrassed than amused.

"What's so funny?" Tina demanded as Marybeth went around to drop the tailgate and let Joker out.

"Stay here, boy," she told him as he began to sniff around in the tall grass. Then she put a hand on Tina's shoulder. "There are probably some things you shouldn't ask your father in front of me," she began. Again she remembered the expression of blank astonishment on Erik's face when Tina had come out with her master plan, and it was all Marybeth could do not to chuckle anew.

Several yards away, Erik tended a large black cow as if he had forgotten entirely the existence of the two females he had brought with him.

Chapter Six

"When can we take Joker and go to Marybeth's house? I want to see her animals."

Erik raked a hand over his hair and realized he needed to get it cut. He took another bite of the chicken and dumplings that Mrs. O'Reilly had fixed for their dinner.

"Daddy!" Tina's fork paused midair.

Erik met her anxious expression with a resigned one of his own. She wasn't going to forget, and she sure wasn't going to give up.

"All right," he said, surrendering to her wishes as well as his own. "I'll call her when we're done eating and set something up, okay? Now will you finish the rest of your dinner before it gets cold? Including the peas."

Tina beamed until he mentioned her least favorite vegetable, but even then her smile only dimmed a little.

"Yes, Daddy," she said obediently. Then she concentrated on her dinner.

Erik remembered what meals at home had been like when he was growing up, his silent father sitting across from him, cold eyes watching every move that Erik made. Watching for mistakes.

He had dinner with Tina whenever he could, and he made a point of talking to her while they ate. Minx that she was, Tina used to leave whatever food she didn't like until last, and then complain that it was too cold to eat. Erik had nipped that when he got the microwave. Now she usually ate a little of everything without complaining.

Once she tried to slip a spear of broccoli to Joker, but Erik saw her. His threat to shut the dog out of the dining room during dinner had stopped that practice. Since Joker was never fed from the table, he was content to lie on the rug without begging, happy to be near the little girl he had clearly come to love.

Erik wondered what Marybeth was doing right now. Was she out or at home, perhaps eating a solitary meal and thinking about him? Suddenly eager to hear the sound of her voice, he cleared his plate quickly, then urged Tina to finish so he could make the call.

"Can we take Joker when we go to Marybeth's?" she asked as they carried their dirty dishes to the kitchen, where the housekeeper was cleaning up.

"Everything was great, as usual," Erik told her.

"Except for the peas," Tina added.

Mrs. O'Reilly gave Erik a wink over Tina's head. "Your dad asked for them special," she teased. "Says he wants them every night until you learn to like them."

Tina turned an astonished face to Erik. He couldn't help but laugh at her chagrin.

"Did you say that, Daddy?"

He scooped her up and gave her cheek a smacking kiss. "No, but I might. Then when you get used to the peas, we could start on brussels sprouts."

Tina's giggles delighted him. What would he ever have done without her in his life?

"Silly daddy. I know *you* don't even like brussels sprouts."

"Maybe I'll fix them and you can both develop a taste for them," Mrs. O'Reilly commented when she turned back toward the kitchen counter.

"We'll talk about that later," Erik said. "Right now Tina has to take a bath, and I have a phone call to make." He told the housekeeper good-night and carried Tina down the hall while Joker followed.

"Can't I talk to Marybeth, too?" Tina asked.

"Not this time. Take your bath, and then we'll read a book before bedtime," Erik promised, thinking quickly. As soon as he had started the water and adjusted the taps, he went down the hall to use the phone in his bedroom. He left the door open so he could hear Tina if she needed him and picked up the receiver. Then he took a deep breath.

Marybeth was cleaning the oven. Her hands were covered with bright yellow rubber gloves and she had spread newspaper on the floor in front of the stove to catch the drips.

"When I buy kitchen appliances of my own, you can bet I'm getting a self-cleaning oven," she announced to no one in particular. Then she rinsed out the sponge she had been using and reached into the oven to clean its back wall. She had barely started to wipe away the vile-smelling spray cleaner when the phone rang.

"Damn," she muttered, straightening and tossing the sponge into the sink. "This had better be good." The phone rang again as she stripped off the rubber gloves, then a third time as she hurried over to pick up the receiver.

"Hello." Her greeting was brusque.

There was a pause at the other end of the line. "Marybeth? Is that you?"

She recognized Erik's voice, and a warm glow began somewhere in her midsection. "Hi. How are you?"

"Did I catch you at a bad time?" He sounded fully prepared to hang up, but that was the last thing she wanted him to do.

"Oh, no. I was cleaning the oven, and it's not my favorite chore."

"I could call back later."

She gripped the receiver harder. "No, it's okay. I'd rather talk to you than breathe noxious fumes while I get a crick in my back."

Again there was a pause. "Thanks, I think," he drawled after a moment.

"I didn't mean that the way it sounded," she told him while she rolled her eyes. What was wrong with her tongue? Her mind?

"I called to see if I could bring Tina over sometime soon, like we talked about. She's been bugging me about meeting your menagerie."

Marybeth's pleasure at his call took a sudden nosedive. "Oh, sure. When do you want to come over?" She wondered if the only reason he'd called was that Tina had been nagging him.

"I thought we could make it an afternoon when you weren't working," he suggested hesitantly. "Maybe have another picnic?"

Marybeth thought fast. "I'm off the day after tomorrow, if that's good for you. Why don't we dig for clams? We can steam them and have a salad and rolls, too."

"Good idea." Was it her imagination or had his voice warmed slightly? "We'll bring dessert. See you around three?"

"Sure. That'll be fine." She hesitated, reluctant to let him go.

"Oh, I almost forgot. Okay if we bring Joker?"

"No problem. He'd probably enjoy a romp with my dogs."

After another pause that made Marybeth wonder if he, too, was reluctant to end their conversation, Erik said goodbye. When she donned her rubber gloves and turned to tackle the oven again, her mood was much improved. She was looking forward to seeing Erik and Tina. She was even looking forward to seeing the dog.

Tina watched Erik and Marybeth dig a few clams, but she was more interested in looking for shells and pretty rocks. Anticipating her inclination, Erik had brought along a blue plastic bucket with its own red shovel. Tina walked along the water's edge and studied the sand intently as she searched for treasure. All three dogs followed her, tongues lolling and tails wagging.

"I think we've got enough clams," Marybeth said finally. She rocked back onto her heels while she tried to brush the wet sand from her hands.

Kneeling across from her, Erik dropped the clam he had just captured into the pail. "I guess you're right." He allowed his gaze to rest on her face. In the background he could hear Tina's voice as she showed the dogs her latest find.

In the sunlight, Marybeth's hair shimmered with reddish highlights. When she pushed the curls off her forehead, the gesture left a sandy streak on her velvety skin.

Erik got to his feet. He brushed off his hands and held one out to her. When she rose in front of him, he glanced in Tina's direction, saw that she was squatted over a pool of water with her back to them, and leaned forward to give Marybeth a kiss. Tempted to linger, he forced himself to pull away.

"Thanks for inviting us. Tina's having a wonderful time."

Marybeth glanced at the child, who was totally engrossed in whatever she had found. "I'm glad. The two of you seem to have a really close relationship."

"I guess it's normal when there's only one parent." He knew Marybeth was curious about Tina, but she had never asked. Perhaps now was the time to tell her—not everything, but a little.

He put his arm lightly across her shoulders. They were bare except for the red polka-dotted halter top she wore with ragged cutoff jeans. Her skin was warm. All afternoon he'd been sneaking looks at the length of her legs below the shorts and the lightly tanned expanse of her shoulders and throat above the curving, clinging top.

Perhaps it was a good thing they had a pint-size chaperon with them. His thoughts had definitely not been G-rated. He didn't know how Marybeth would feel about that, but he did know that she wasn't the kind of woman to take a physical relationship lightly. As much as it complicated things, he realized that he wouldn't want her any other way.

Erik turned away from where Tina still played. He knew that the sound of the waves would drown out any possibility of her overhearing him if he kept his voice down.

"Since she was two years old, I'm the only parent Tina has known," he said to Marybeth. "Her mother was killed in Argentina, so I brought her back with me and adopted her."

Marybeth's eyes were warm and approving. "That was a wonderful thing for you to do."

Erik shook his head. "I think her father's dead, too, but I'm not sure."

Marybeth tilted her head to one side, obviously puzzled, but instead of bombarding him with questions, she waited patiently for him to continue. Erik appreciated her thoughtfulness. It was difficult for him to talk about such personal things.

"Were you working in Argentina?" she asked finally, urging him to continue.

He was used to thinking on his feet and coming to fast decisions. He wasn't sure just how much he wanted to reveal about his past, but certainly not enough to put her off. He knew he didn't want that!

"I used to do some work for the government," he said slowly, testing the waters.

Marybeth's expression changed only slightly, her brows quirked in curiosity. "What kind of work?"

He grinned without humor. Now came the tricky part. "A little espionage, a little undercover work."

For the first time, she looked shaken. "You were a spy?"

He nodded, wondering if he had gone too far.

"Now I'm beginning to understand why you acted the way you did at the bank robbery," she murmured, half to herself. "I wondered at the time."

Erik glanced past her to see that Tina was still playing in the rocks. Joker sat beside her patiently while the other two dogs splashed in and out of the water.

"I was on assignment in Argentina," he continued. "An important American drug supplier was holed up there, waiting for the heat to die down here in the States. I'd infiltrated his band of merry men, but there was some kind of a leak and everything blew up. That's when Tina's mother was shot.'' Erik suspected that the leak had something to do with his efforts to get her and Tina out of there before things did go sour.

Marybeth's face had paled, her mouth drawn into a tight line. ''That's awful. You and Tina might have been killed, too.''

Erik remembered how Marybeth's husband had died in the line of duty. ''I'm not in that kind of work anymore,'' he reminded her. ''I raise cattle now.'' He stared down at her intently. ''Tina's mother was the drug lord's mistress.''

''And he was Tina's father?'' Marybeth guessed, eyes darkening.

''Yeah. He was shot, too, but before we could check him out, he disappeared in all the confusion.'' Erik wasn't about to tell Marybeth that it was a wild shot from his own gun that had killed Tina's mother. He couldn't risk seeing a look of revulsion on her face. Not yet. Maybe not ever.

''What about family?'' Marybeth asked. ''If her father was an American, Tina probably has other relatives, people who might not be criminals.''

Erik spun away. He didn't want to hear what she was saying. ''Don't you think I've already considered that?'' he demanded, forcing himself to calm down. Tina looked over her shoulder and he managed a smile for her, then lowered his voice. ''Bernadetti was scum, the worst kind of parasite. Do you want Tina exposed to people like that?''

Marybeth nibbled at her bottom lip. ''Of course not. I'm sorry, I'm sure you've already done everything you could. Anyone could see how happy Tina is with you. *Does* she have anyone else?"

Her innocent question irritated him, and he had to clamp his mouth shut to keep from snapping at her. The truth was, he hadn't checked. He'd been too busy hiding out with Tina, hoping that no relatives would ever find out about her. He wouldn't give her up. His former agency wasn't even sure if the drug supplier himself was alive or dead. Bernadetti had completely disappeared after the botched attempt to bring him down.

Erik shrugged. "I didn't find anyone." That was the truth as far as it went. He was more than ready to talk about something else.

Marybeth didn't ask any more questions. Instead, she touched his bare arm lightly. "It must have been difficult for you at first," she commented. "A man alone taking care of a toddler. Is that why you quit the agency?"

His eyes searched hers. He saw no condemnation there, no horror at his former occupation, only sympathy and the desire to understand. "Part of the reason. It was hard at first," he admitted. "Tina spoke only Spanish. I was the only one who could understand her. She didn't like the food. We had to find a place to live."

He didn't add that the agency had helped him with the adoption, keeping it very quiet, or that they had provided him with a new name and identity to protect him from any enemies who might still be trying to find him. Especially Bernadetti's men. Or even Bernadetti himself, who could be searching for his daughter.

"What made you decide to live on Whidbey Island?" Marybeth asked. "It's a long way from St. Louis."

"A friend at the agency told me about it. We came here and liked it, so we decided to stay." He didn't tell her that the friend at the agency was a woman specializing in relocating agents with pasts too hot to live down.

"Well," Marybeth said with a smile, "I'm certainly glad the two of you chose Whidbey." She was too trusting to look for holes in his story.

Erik shoved down the niggling guilt that he hadn't been completely honest with her. Instead, he glanced at his watch. "Let's go back and eat," he suggested. "I'm getting hungry."

Her eyes lit up. "Me, too. I can't wait to sample that chocolate cake you brought. Did Mrs. O'Reilly bake it?"

"No, actually Tina and I did," Erik admitted as he went over to pick up the pail of clams and the short-handled shovel they'd been using to dig. "I'm surprised she didn't tell you that the minute we got here."

"She was too interested in my zoo," Marybeth said as she collected the soda cans they'd emptied while they'd been digging. Then she followed him back to where his daughter was examining the treasure she had collected in her bucket. "Remember how she said she never met anyone with *three* cats before?"

Erik nodded. He called to Tina. "Time to go."

She skipped over to them, carrying her bucket and shovel. Marybeth called the dogs. All the way back to her house, Tina chattered about the rocks and shells she'd found.

The three of them pitched in to fix dinner. Erik cleaned the clams while Tina buttered the French bread and helped Marybeth with the salad. By the time they'd eaten, the little girl was doing her best to stifle yawns behind her tiny hand, and her eyelids were drooping.

"Let's have some of that cake you made. Then you can have a rest on my bed," Marybeth said.

Worn out from their afternoon at the beach, Tina didn't even argue. "I'm going to show my shells to Mrs. O," she told Erik as he cleared the dirty dishes, and Marybeth cut the cake.

He was a handy man to have in the kitchen, she thought, watching his spare, efficient movements. He turned and the light from the overhead fixture gleamed against his pale hair and the hard planes of his profile. His normally stern mouth had softened into a smile for Tina.

Swallowing, Marybeth turned her attention back to their dessert. She refused to speculate about what might happen after their little chaperon went to sleep.

"Mmm," she said when she had taken her first bite of the round layer cake. "You and your dad are sure good cooks. Chocolate is one of my favorite foods."

"I frosted it," Tina said importantly. "And Daddy let me put the 'gredients in the mixing bowl. All but the eggs. I can't do eggs yet."

"Sometimes the shells go in, too," Erik explained, patting Tina's head. "But we're working on it."

When they were done, Marybeth gave her a hug and poured more coffee while Erik settled her in the strange bedroom. Joker, who had just been outside, went with them.

"Is she okay?" Marybeth asked him when he came back. She handed him a steaming mug.

"She'll be fine. Joker's made himself at home on the rug next to the bed."

Marybeth led the way to the living room. She stepped over the prone bodies of her own dogs and sat at one end of the couch. Erik sank next to her and took a sip of his coffee.

"Joker seems to have made a place for himself in your family," she observed, watching his expression.

His grin was reluctant. "Yeah," he finally admitted. "I'll have to hand it to your friend. Getting a dog was a good idea. I just hope that nothing happens to him. Tina would be heartbroken."

Marybeth wondered about his excessive worrying, but she didn't say anything. Maybe he had lost a pet as a child. There was still so much she didn't know about him.

"Did you have a dog growing up?" she asked after a moment.

Erik's expression closed, and he took a long swallow of coffee. "One," he said evasively as he rose from the couch. "Come on, I'll help you do the dishes."

Before Marybeth could reply, he had gone back to the kitchen. So much for personal questions, she thought grimly as she finished her coffee and followed him.

"Wash or dry?" he asked from where he was standing at the sink.

"What?" He looked so out of character holding the flowered apron she kept on a hook that she forgot to be annoyed.

One side of his mouth quirked upward. "Do you prefer to wash or dry the dishes?" he asked patiently, as if he were talking to Tina.

For a moment, Marybeth thought that what she'd prefer would be to take away the apron and step into the circle of his arms. Really, she had to stop thinking such lustful thoughts before something in her eyes gave her away and embarrassed both of them.

"I'll wash," she said, "though I would have loved to see you in the apron."

Returning her grin with a slow smile of his own, Erik stepped aside while she ran water into the sink. His response was enough to make her wonder if she had imagined his shortness when she asked him about his childhood.

After a few moments of companionable silence, she handed Erik the last pan to dry, and let the water out of the sink. When she wiped off the table and turned to ask if he wanted to watch television or listen to music, she almost bumped into him. He had moved quietly up behind her.

Now, while she returned his stare, he leaned forward and rested his hands on the table on either side of her, penning her in. Unsure of his intentions, she leaned back away from him.

Amusement twinkled in his blue eyes before they darkened, and his expression sobered. He lifted one hand to run a finger down the side of her cheek.

Marybeth failed to hide the reaction that shivered through her. Without thinking, she leaned her cheek into his hand. As lightly as the brush of a butterfly wing, he caressed her jawline and then stroked his thumb across her mouth.

Her lips parted as she watched him. The warmth from his body ignited hers. For a moment, his fingers cupped her chin.

"Want to watch TV?" she asked in a rush.

"No," he muttered hoarsely. "I don't want to watch television. Do you?"

"I don't think so." Her voice sounded thin to her ears, as if all the breath had been squeezed out of her.

He tipped up her chin while his gaze slid to her mouth. Then he shifted, widening his stance and crowding closer. As he put his arms around her and pulled her to him, her hands slipped up his chest to clasp behind his neck. She was aware of his muscular thighs pressed against her. Then his mouth came down to cover hers, and she noticed nothing except the way he made her feel.

Her fingers tightened in the short strands of his hair. His hands slid down her hips to imprison her against him and his arousal nudged her insistently.

The fire in her own body began to burn out of control. Erik tore his mouth from hers, pressing kisses across her cheek until he reached her ear. Carefully he touched the sensitive lobe with his tongue. When she moaned softly, he traced the delicate outer rim, his shallow breath tickling her.

She arched her neck to give him more access while her lower body rubbed against him. His swift intake of breath was ragged; then his open mouth returned to hers, and his tongue thrust deep. His big hands tightened their hold on her hips as his body surged once against her, then stilled as if he had temporarily lost control.

"You bring out feelings in me that I had forgotten even existed," he groaned against her mouth. His hands slid up to rub slowly across her breasts, making the nipples bead, before they continued on up, stroking her throat and then grasping her jaw to hold her face immobile. For a moment, his eyes burned into hers. His widened pupils almost blotted out the lighter irises. Then he branded her mouth with a series of scorching kisses, breaking away each time before she could quite get enough.

Marybeth's own breathing was labored. When he stopped the sensual assault and bent to scoop her into his arms, it clogged in her throat. To her surprise, he turned and set her on the edge of the kitchen counter. Spreading her knees gently with his hands, he stood in the V he had created. Then he reached for the back clasp of her halter top, giving her time to object before he released it. She didn't, and he slipped the narrow straps down her arms. When the top fell to the floor, he took her hands in his and raised her arms slowly. He never took his gaze from her breasts. His attention riveted on them made the tips bud even tighter. Marybeth would have given anything for him to touch them and ease their tingling pressure.

"My Lord, you're lovely," Erik murmured, voice gruff.

She couldn't speak, could barely think, as the waves of longing washed over her. He placed her hands on his wide shoulders. With a will of their own, they went to the buttons of his shirts.

"Do it," he urged.

Trembling, her fingers released them all, baring his chest. It was tanned and firm, dusted with blond hair a shade darker than his head. She spread the edges of the shirt as his hands moved across her shoulders. Urging her forward until her breasts were cushioned against his bare skin, Erik leaned his head back and drew in a hissing breath between clenched teeth.

Marybeth buried her face in his shoulder while the rush of sensation poured through her. With rough urgency, Erik grasped her hips and ground himself against her. Marybeth hooked her legs around his, straining to get closer still. His hand skimmed up her thigh to the ragged edge of her cutoffs; his fingers teased the sensitive skin of her inner thigh. Marybeth gasped and clutched at his shoulders. Finding the leg opening of her shorts too snug for what he had in mind, he rubbed his fingers over the zipper to fumble with the snap.

For a moment, Marybeth pressed against him, drowning in the sensations he was coaxing into a fiery inferno of need. Then, suddenly, as the snap of her shorts gave with a sharp click, reality hit her like a wave of icy water.

She stopped the progress of his hand with her own, her eyes flying open as she remembered that they were in her kitchen, with his little girl asleep only a couple of dozen feet away.

What had she been thinking?

Nothing, obviously. She had been enslaved by the feelings he had raised in her so effortlessly. Feelings he might not return. He was a man; lust was probably enough for him.

Abruptly she straightened away from him, hands over her breasts.

"What?" he asked. His eyes looked sleepy but in their depths burned the fires of passion.

"Tina," she whispered. "We can't do this—she might wake up."

For a moment, Erik froze, listening. Then he groaned and straightened. "I forgot," he admitted, voice raw. "You could make me forget my own name." His gaze slid to where she shielded herself from him. "Damn," he said. "She's in your bed." A flash of regret crossed his face, and then he bent to pick up Marybeth's halter top.

"Would you let me put it back on?" he asked.

Surprised, she searched his face for some clue as to what he was feeling, but he gave away nothing. She nodded, disappointed and shaken.

With gentle strokes, he smoothed the fabric over her breasts. They still tingled from their contact with his chest. Then he reached behind her to hook the halter, leaving the straps dangling across her arms. He bent forward and pressed a kiss to her shoulder before he slid the first strap into place. Then he did the same with the other.

While Marybeth watched him silently, he rebuttoned his shirt. "Bad timing," he said finally.

She wasn't sure how to respond. She hadn't meant to let things go so far. Physical intimacy didn't come casually to her; she had been a virgin when she had married Mike.

"Yes," she agreed finally, while she wondered if their reasons for considering the timing bad remotely matched.

She wasn't sure she was ready to take such a big step while so much of Erik was still unknown to her, but she wasn't sure how to voice her doubts.

He glanced at the wall clock above the sink. "I'd better take Tina and go," he said, "before I decide the couch would make a dandy temporary bed."

"With Arthur and Annabelle looking on?" she managed to ask, trying to lighten the pulsating tension between them.

He chuckled and lifted her down from the counter before she could slide off herself. Before he let her go, he dropped a surprisingly tender kiss onto her mouth. His eyes were narrowed, screening their secrets. Marybeth supposed he wanted to leave before they were tempted again to ignore the present circumstances. There didn't seem to be any easy way to tell him that she wouldn't have continued, anyway. At least she didn't think she would have. Surely her sense of self-preservation would have kicked in before it was too late!

Watching him in the glow from the overhead light, she wasn't so sure. He was an almost overwhelming temptation.

"Keep the rest of the cake." His offer brought her abruptly back to reality. "Mrs. O'Reilly makes too many desserts as it is."

Marybeth watched his hand go to his flat abdomen and pat it meaningfully. Her gaze drifted lower and she swallowed dryly, remembering how he had felt when he rubbed against her. Maybe she wouldn't have stopped him. The thought was a sobering one.

"Well," she said briskly, "if you don't mind, I'll take it to work and share it with the staff. Now, let me help you with Tina. You carry her, and I'll bring her bucket and shovel. Did you have anything else?"

Erik's hands came up to grasp her upper arms, and he pinned her with his stare. "Don't forget where we left off," he said urgently. "I know I won't."

Marybeth was frozen by the intensity of his gaze. She wanted to say something but wasn't sure what. Her common sense had certainly deserted her when she needed it most tonight.

Erik apparently took her silence for assent. His arms fell away and he turned toward the bedroom. Marybeth followed along behind him, feeling light-headed and about as communicative as one of her dogs.

He brought a very sleepy Tina out of the bedroom, cradling her against his chest. "'Night," she murmured to Marybeth, rubbing her eyes with her fists. "Thank you."

Marybeth smiled at her. "Thank you for coming, sweetie. I'll see you later."

Erik settled Tina onto the seat of the truck, directed Joker into the back and took the shovel and pail that Marybeth handed him. He glanced at Tina, who had sat up and was watching them. Then he gave Marybeth a frustrated frown. His male annoyance almost made her smile.

"Thanks," he said, touching her cheek with his finger. She wished him good-night, and he slid into the cab of the truck. After he had turned it around, he lifted his hand in a brief farewell.

When the truck disappeared into the darkness, Marybeth realized he hadn't said a word about seeing her again. Well, good, she told herself as she let her dogs out one last time before bed. Things were getting too complicated anyway. Maybe it was best if they *didn't* see each other again.

Three nights later, she was tossing and turning in bed, unable to sleep. She hadn't heard from Erik and had been doing her best to convince herself that he was probably out of her life for good. He had undoubtedly come to the same conclusion as she had, that things had been moving too fast. They were both better off this way.

She turned over and thumped her pillow until it was the shape she wanted. Outside her open door, Annabelle whined softly.

"Go to sleep," Marybeth said. On the bed next to her, one of the cats shifted and stretched, then settled back down. Anyway, she thought half hysterically, there was no room in her life for a man like Erik, not literally and not figuratively.

After a few more minutes of sleeplessness, she muttered a curse under her breath and slid from beneath the covers, doing her best not to disturb the cat that slept on top. The other two usually curled up together on the couch. Glancing down at the short, clingy nightshirt she wore, she decided it wasn't cool enough for her robe. She certainly needed some warm milk or an aspirin to help her sleep or she'd be awake for hours—again. She stepped over the dogs and told them both to stay put, then turned on the kitchen light. Before she could cross to the refrigerator, a knock sounded against the front door. She hadn't heard a car. Both dogs immediately rose to their feet, barking loudly.

Marybeth glanced at the clock, surprised to see that it was only midnight. It felt as though she had been tossing and turning for hours. She shushed the dogs and crossed to the front door as the knock sounded again.

"Who is it?" she asked through the wooden barrier.

"It's Erik. I know you're up, I saw the light. We have to talk."

For a moment, she stared at the closed door, too shocked to move. What was he doing here at this time of night? Who was with Tina? Perhaps something had happened to her!

Giving no thought to her own appearance, Marybeth whipped open the door, intent on asking him. Before she could say a word, he glanced at the dogs, who both stopped barking, and then crossed the threshold to yank Marybeth roughly into his arms.

"Thank God," he groaned into her tangled hair. "I don't think I could have held out for another minute."

Chapter Seven

Marybeth stepped back, out of the way of Erik's embrace. "What are you doing here?" she asked, eyeing him warily.

He frowned and dropped his arms. "May I come in?"

She wasn't sure who she distrusted the most, him or herself. "It's late."

His expression of frustration intensified. "I know. I had to wait for Mrs. O to come back and watch Tina."

"Is Tina all right?" Marybeth asked. She recalled her thought that something might have happened to the child.

If anything, Erik grew even more tense. "Tina's fine." A muscle along his jaw quivered.

She glanced beyond his wide shoulder to the empty driveway. "Where's your truck?"

"I left it parked down the road."

Her brows rose, but he offered no further explanation. They weren't getting anywhere.

"Well," she said after a moment that ticked between them like a time bomb, "I was going to fix myself some cocoa. Would you like a cup?"

He grimaced. "No, thanks." Then he looked her up and down, his leisurely perusal reminding her of the thin nightshirt she wore. "Couldn't you sleep, either?" His tone was wry.

"Either?" Now that she looked closer, he did appear to be tired, his face drawn.

"Come on." He glared at her with a thunderous frown. "Give me some help here. If you think I make a habit of lurking outside women's bedrooms at night, waiting for a light to go on, you're crazy. This is a first for me."

"I don't know what you're talking about," she protested. "*I* didn't ask you to lurk around outside. And there's no need to snarl."

Erik turned away and threw up his hands. "Why me?" he intoned to no one in particular. Then he faced her again. "I haven't been sleeping too well since the last time I saw you. When I do manage to sleep, you haunt my dreams. I thought, just maybe, you might be having similar trouble. That *was* you in the kitchen with me, wasn't it? All hot and responsive? I wasn't the only one caught up in what we were doing, in what we almost finished right there, was I?"

His blue eyes were narrowed, his mouth a grim line. Seeing his belligerent expression, no one would make the mistake of thinking he was happy about the situation.

"I don't know what to say," Marybeth stammered. She was unused to such an outpouring of emotion, especially from Erik.

"Then let's not waste time talking," he urged as he pulled her into his arms. "You know why I'm here." He pressed a kiss to the side of her throat, his mouth open and hot. "I've been full of your scent for days," he muttered against her skin.

Marybeth began to melt in the heat of his desire. She could readily admit, if only to herself, that she had longed for him, had wanted to be with him. Like this.

She turned her head, seeking his lips. With a rough groan, he obliged. His mouth devoured hers, his tongue thrusting deep. One of his hands skimmed up her side to lightly cup her breast. Considering the wildness of their kiss, his fingers were surprisingly gentle as they reshaped her nipple.

Pleasure splintered through her and turned her limp in his embrace.

"I've been going crazy with wanting you," Erik muttered. "I need you—your warmth, your kisses." His mouth covered hers again, as if to give proof to his words.

Want. Need. The words echoed through her muddled brain as his lips and hands began to transport her once again to a state of mindless passion.

But what of feelings? Her arms, in the process of pulling him closer, hesitated. Her mouth, returning his kiss, faltered. Her desire, driving her ruthlessly, dimmed.

Erik must have sensed her sudden doubts. He stopped and drew slightly away.

"What?" His face was flushed, his eyes dark. His mouth looked less intractable after kissing hers.

She lifted her fingers to his cheek. It was hot to the touch. He grabbed her hand impatiently and pressed a kiss to its sensitive skin.

"Come on," he said, urging her toward the bedroom.

"No."

He stopped in his tracks. His head swiveled in disbelief. "What?" he repeated.

"How do you feel about me?" she asked, crossing her arms over her tingling breasts.

A long moment passed. Marybeth could have counted her heartbeats.

Erik's expression chilled. "I told you." He made a visible effort to regain control. "I want you." The muscles of his face were taut. "Come closer, and I'll show you how much."

Instead, she stepped away. "You want me." Her voice was flat. "But how do you *feel?*"

He was clearly puzzled—groping for words. Finally he gestured with his hands, a movement of confusion, indecision. "What do you want me to say?"

"Excuse me a minute." Marybeth darted around him to grab her robe from its hook on the back of the bedroom door. While he watched, she shrugged it on and tied the belt.

As if she had thrown down a gauntlet, Erik turned toward the living room. "What do you want from me?" he asked again. While she watched, he paced like a tiger in a trap.

"I asked how you feel." She followed him and dropped onto the couch.

"I thought I told you." Clearly he wasn't in the mood for words. He came to stand over her. His gaze searched her face. Then he whirled away again. "I don't know what you want to hear."

Marybeth bolted to her feet, almost bumping into him. "It isn't what I want to hear, it's what you need to feel!" Realizing that her voice had risen, she made an effort to calm herself. Maybe she was expecting too much, but he was expecting a lot from her, too.

"*I* need more," she said, finger tapping her chest. "More than an itch that needs scratching."

He threw his hands out, palms up. "Of course I have feelings for you," he shouted. "I—" He stopped, looking away.

She waited, hopeful. "Yes?"

He swore through gritted teeth. "It's not just some damned itch. I thought you could tell that." He flung himself into a chair, then immediately stood again. His narrowed eyes searched the room as if for some object that might help him out. "Do you want me to tell you that I love you?" he demanded, pinning her with his stare.

"No! Of course not." How could she say, only if it's true? "I think you'd better leave," she said instead and went to the front door.

Long strides brought him across the room, until he was in front of her again. "Maybe I made a mistake, coming here tonight," he said. "I just thought…" His hand raked over his hair. "Never mind what I thought. I was obviously wrong." His voice had softened, a deadly softness.

Before Marybeth could respond, he jerked open the door. She thought he was going to leave without another word, but instead he grabbed her by the shoulders and hauled her to him. He kissed her hard, as if he were staking a claim. Then he set her back from him.

"I wasn't completely wrong about you," he ground out. Then he moved swiftly down the steps to the road.

Speechless, part of her relieved and part of her wanting desperately to call out to him, Marybeth watched his broad back and long legs until he disappeared into the darkness.

"But *why* can't we go see her?" Tina demanded.

Erik bit down hard on the impatient response he'd been about to make. It wasn't Tina's fault that he'd been moping around like a bear with a bee-stung nose since he'd shown up at Marybeth's in the middle of the night. He'd expected her to jump into the sack with him. Dammit, how could one grown man be so stupid?

"I told you, honey," he said, pulling Tina onto his lap, "Marybeth and I had a misunderstanding. It wouldn't be a good idea to visit her right now."

"But she and I aren't misunderstanding," Tina argued. "Why can't I go see her?"

Erik's patience was beginning to wear thin. How was he expected to forget about a certain sexy, stubborn nurse if his daughter kept bringing up her name every five minutes?

"Last I heard, you still depended on me for transportation," he said. "And I think she'd probably sic her dogs on me the second I pulled onto her property."

Tina giggled. "But Annabelle and Arthur like you."

Erik sighed. "Let's just say that, for now, anyway, I don't want to test their friendship."

Tina frowned. "Sometimes you're hard to figure out."

"I know." Erik planted a smacking kiss on her cheek and then lifted her down. "Why don't you and Joker go watch television for a half hour until time for your bath, okay?"

For a moment, he thought she was going to argue further. Then she gave him a sunny smile. "Okay, Daddy."

Erik kept a matching smile plastered to his face until she left the den. Then he rubbed his aching forehead with his hand. If he didn't do something soon, he was going to go mad from thinking about Marybeth and remembering the way she had made him feel, wrapping her soft arms around his neck and returning his kisses as though she couldn't get enough of him.

Damn. Forgetting wasn't going to be easy.

Frustrated, Marybeth added up the column of outstanding checks for the third time and got yet a third tally.

Maybe if she paid attention to what she was doing instead of letting her mind wander, focusing on mental images of a certain rugged blonde with eyes the color of the sky on its best day, she would make some progress. She pushed her hair back off her forehead and tried again.

A fourth tally. Marybeth tossed down her pen in a gesture of defeat. Maybe now she would remember to pick up a battery for her calculator the next time she went to town. Meanwhile, this was a waste of time. Rising, she stepped outside, shutting the front door behind her, and whistled for the dogs. Perhaps a walk on the beach would clear her head of cobwebs and unwanted images of the man she had decided to prune from her life.

Not that it seemed to matter what *she* had decided; it was obvious he had given up on her. It had been two weeks since his surprising nocturnal visit. Two weeks since he'd turned away from her in disgust.

Did she really have the somewhat outdated notion of having to be *in* love before she made love? Marybeth jammed her hands into the pockets of her baggy shorts and set off down the beach, the dogs running ahead. Just because she had been a virgin when she married Mike, just because she had chosen not to sleep with anyone since his death, didn't mean she had antiquated ideas, did it? Erik obviously liked her well enough to spend time with her. She found him appealing, and he certainly managed to turn her on. What more did she need?

She frowned and stopped to pick up a flat rock. When she tried to skip it across the water, it bounced once and sank.

She missed Erik, and she missed Tina. Her life, which had been fulfilling enough before the bank robbery, now stretched in front of her with all the excitement of lukewarm vanilla yogurt. Bland. Dull. Harmless.

What she needed was some danger, some risk, a little spice. What she needed was Erik, as much of him as he would share for as long as he was willing. It didn't have to be forever. It only had to be long enough to cool her obsession—if she was careful—without breaking her heart.

Over the next few days, Marybeth tried to come up with a plan. She hated the idea of appearing at Erik's ranch with what he must surely see as yet another flimsy excuse. What she needed was an accidental meeting, but where? Erik wasn't in a bowling league, he didn't attend any of the local churches that she knew of, and he didn't hang out at one of the nearby watering holes.

While Marybeth was trying to scare up a few possibilities, fate stepped in and took charge. She was ascending the steps to the bookstore, talking to a resident from the hospital, Peter Atkins, who had parked next to her in the small lot. Some of the nurses thought that Peter looked like Kevin Costner, but Marybeth had discovered during her one and only date with him months before that Peter, though nice enough, was rather boring.

He stopped suddenly in front of the open bookstore doorway. "How about lunch?" he asked Marybeth. "Are you free today?"

She turned to reply and ran right into Erik as he came out the door. His hands lifted automatically to steady her while she apologized profusely.

"You okay?" he asked her, eyes narrowed against the bright sunlight.

More shaken up than she was willing to admit, Marybeth stammered a positive reply and glanced around him, looking for Peter. Erik's hand clamped down on her shoulder.

"Come on," he said. "We're in the way here."

Behind him, Peter gave her a helpless smile and then disappeared into the bookstore. His hasty retreat annoyed Marybeth a lot more than it should have.

"You with him?" Erik asked when they reached the sidewalk. His hand still held fast to her shoulder. His expression was grim. For a moment, Marybeth was tempted to lie. Pride, however, kept her from claiming anything more than a passing acquaintance with a man as easily discouraged as Peter.

"No," she admitted to Erik. "He works at the hospital, and I just happened to run into him."

Erik's sudden grin gave her courage. "I'm glad to see you, though."

He looked surprised. "Me, too. You need anything in there that can't wait?" He gestured at the bookstore with his thumb.

She was having trouble not staring. In his work clothes and black Stetson, Erik looked even better than she remembered. Her gaze followed his to the shop behind him.

"No, I guess not." Even John Saul's latest thriller couldn't compete with Erik Snow in the flesh.

"Good." His hand released her shoulder. "Got time for a little ride?"

As he waited for her answer, she studied his weathered face. Some instinct all women seemed to have, that only came out when they needed it the very most, was telling her that she was answering a much more complicated question than the one Erik had spoken aloud. She took a deep breath.

"Yes," she said, voice firm. "I have as much time as we need."

Erik's eyes darkened with approval. His arm snaked around her waist and, for a moment, he pulled her close. Then he let go and took her hand. His steps, as he led the way to his pickup, barely contained his impatience. Sending up a silent prayer that she was doing the right thing, Marybeth hurried to keep up with him.

"This is the highest point of my land," Erik said, after he had driven through a gate he locked carefully behind them and parked the truck at the end of a dirt road. "Come on." He climbed down and held out a hand to her.

When Marybeth slid over to follow him, he clasped her waist and lifted her down, so close that she could feel the warmth from his body, smell the faint scent of after-shave. When her feet were on the ground, he didn't release her right away. Instead, he stood looking down at her.

"I'd like to show you what I think's one of the prettiest spots on the island," he said. "I come here sometimes just to sit and look at the view."

"Okay." Her voice came out a little high, but Erik didn't seem to notice. Instead, he led the way down a faint path through the tall grass.

After a couple of minutes, they walked past a stand of alder trees, branches sighing in the breeze. Erik stopped at the top of a steep hill. At their feet, Marybeth could see a rolling pasture dotted with black cattle and, even further, his white house and barns. It was not the view of his ranch spread out before them that brought the soft gasp to her lips, though. It was the sight shimmering beyond the fields and roads of Whidbey Island, of the silver-blue waters of Admiralty Inlet that stretched to the horizon. A few boats skimmed the surface, as tiny as water bugs. Above it all glowed the sapphire blue of the cloudless sky.

"This is glorious," she said as they stood side by side and studied the beauty before them.

"I thought you'd like it." Gently Erik turned her toward him. His knuckles skimmed her cheek. "No one comes here but me," he said softly. "It's quiet and private." She saw him swallow as his expression revealed a shadow of anxiety. She remembered the shadows she'd first noticed in his eyes back at the hospital. She had thought then that he must be the loneliest man she had ever seen. Now she had learned a fraction of his secrets, and wanted to know more.

She glanced around, breaking the hold of his steady gaze. The ground beneath them was covered with thick grass, the place where they stood sheltered from prying eyes.

"There's a sense of peace here," she said.

Erik's hand came up to tilt back her chin. "Maybe I can't give you all the right words," he said, voice deep. "But, ever since we met, I've wanted to bring you here. You're the only person I've ever wanted to share this place with." His fingers tightened on her chin and his gaze dropped to her mouth. "Every time I come here, you're with me. I've missed you a hell of a lot."

"I've missed you, too," Marybeth admitted. "And maybe words aren't as important as I thought."

Her gaze clung to Erik as he studied her face. "You sure?" he asked finally.

When she nodded, he didn't wait for her to speak. Instead he urged her down onto the soft green carpet. Kneeling beside her, he held out his arms. When Marybeth went into them, he stretched out and pulled her alongside him. Her head was pillowed on his shoulder, her hand over his heart. Beneath her palm, its beat was strong and steady. All around them was the silence of the land, birds calling, the wind sighing.

Erik shifted so that she was lying on the soft grass, the sun behind him as he leaned over her, so she couldn't see his expression. For once, she wasn't worried about what he was thinking or how he felt about the two of them. She was too happy being here with him.

He pushed back her hair with his hand. Then his fingers traced a meandering path down her cheek and across her lower lip. Marybeth smiled, pulling his head down toward hers.

She sighed with repletion and pleasant exhaustion, turning her face into Erik's bare, sun-warmed shoulder and inhaling his special scent. She hadn't really understood before that loving could be like this, its own special form of communication.

"You okay?" he asked, voice laced with tenderness.

She nodded, too full of emotion to speak.

He put his arm around her shoulders and cradled her close as he dropped a kiss onto her hair. "Me, too."

His voice sounded more relaxed than she had ever heard it. She ran her hand over his arm, trying to convey some of the wonder and contentment she was feeling.

A bird flew overhead, its cry loud in the silence. Erik shifted, nuzzling her neck. "I suppose we'd better get dressed." His hand skimmed her back, leaving a trail of reaction on her sensitized skin.

For a loner, a man unused to sharing himself, he was a generous lover. He had transported Marybeth to new heights of sensuality, controlling his responses until she cried out his name and begged him to end her torment. Then he had done so, filling her with the raw power of his hunger and hurling the two of them into a fire storm of sensation.

Afterward, he had held her close while they both recovered from the beautiful intensity of what they had shared.

Erik was sitting up to pull on his jeans when Marybeth turned over onto her back, completely shameless in her nudity. The sun felt good on her skin. No one could still be self-conscious after listening to Erik's halting praise as he had slowly uncovered her like a precious gift.

"I could stay here forever," she said now, wondering if she could tempt him to linger.

Immediately he bent over her. "And I could stay with you, at least until the temperature turned cooler." His grin was cheeky, relaxed.

Marybeth shifted from beneath him and slid away. "A fair-weather lover?" she teased.

Erik reached for her, but she eluded his grasp and reached for her clothes. Perhaps she had better not be greedy. It had been a long time for her, and her body was pleasantly tender in spots.

She sorted through the jumbled garments until she found what she was looking for. After she had slipped on her bra, Erik reached around to hook it for her.

"I like having you for a lover," he whispered. His breath tickled her neck and bare shoulder.

She clung to him. "I like it, too." It was then she realized what a dangerous position she had gotten herself into. If the time came, leaving Erik might very well be the most difficult thing she had ever done. But would he share enough of himself to allow her to stay in his life? Was what they had just experienced together the beginning of a new openness or merely an afternoon's illusion? And did she have the courage to stick around and find out?

"Are you sure?" Erik demanded, pressing the phone closer to his ear. "This is important to me."

"I'm sure," the raspy voice answered. "Saw the body myself. There's no question."

Erik felt himself slump in reaction to the news. Tina's father was dead, his men either captured or scattered, his entire organization smashed.

For Erik, the years of looking over his shoulder were over. He thanked the agent for passing on the news and was about to hang up.

"Wait. There's more," Moody said. He was one of the very few who knew most of Erik's situation.

Erik's grip on the receiver tightened. "Oh?"

"Grandparents," the agent continued. "They've been looking for Tina."

Erik felt his stomach sink like a cable-cut elevator. "They've got nothing to do with us. Not anymore." He could hear the defensiveness in his voice. He ignored it.

"They seem like good people," Moody said, in measured tones. "Loved their son but didn't understand him. Not connected with his business, as near as we can tell. Bernadetti was their only child, his daughter—"

"I said, that's got nothing to do with us." Erik's voice rose. Deliberately he calmed himself. It would do no good to wake Tina now.

"All I'm saying is keep it in mind," the man on the phone said. "I've got their name and address if you need it."

"I won't."

There was a pause while Moody undoubtedly considered Erik's refusal. "I heard that Harcourt pleaded guilty," he said, breaking the silence.

"Yeah." Erik was surprised at the abrupt change of subject. "The local sheriff said the man got a visit from some out-of-town lawyer who made him nervous."

"Lawyer?" Moody chuckled. "I'll have to tell Taggart he's in the wrong line of work."

"That was Taggart?" Erik remembered him. An agent who could think on his feet.

"Yeah. He outlined Harcourt's options for him, suggested he not waste the taxpayers' time and money."

"Tell Taggart I appreciate it," Erik said.

After a few more moments, Moody wished him well and broke the connection. Erik drifted back to the leather recliner where he had been reading when the call interrupted him. It was late; the house was still. Joker, who had come out of Tina's room when the phone rang, placed a forepaw on Erik's knee and whined softly. His brown eyes were intent.

"Okay, boy," Erik said. "Let's go outside one more time before bed." As he watched Joker sniff around for the right spot, Erik replayed Moody's news about Bernadetti and his parents.

It changed things.

The confirmation of Bernadetti's death could eliminate the necessity of ever having to tell Tina the whole truth about her real father. Or, it could complicate things further by giving her grandparents. Family.

Erik couldn't bear the idea of losing her—the one person who accepted him without reserve, who loved him without question. Once the grandparents knew about her, and him, his shaky legal standing might well collapse. How could he risk it? And how could he build anything meaningful with Marybeth when he and his daughter might have to pack and run at any moment? Did he dare tell her any of this?

Would she condemn him for keeping a child to whom he had no right? Or would she understand? Would she reject him for the things he had done in the past, things he'd had no choice in doing? For killing Tina's mother, although it was an accident? Marybeth had already lost one man to violence; would she accept another who had made it a big part of his life?

Thoughts racing, Erik swore softly. Joker came back from his nocturnal exploring and followed him inside. When the dog went down the hall to Tina's bedroom, Erik peeked in at her. She slept peacefully. As he watched her, possession and love washed over him with all the force of a tidal wave. Joker curled up on the floor beside her bed, expelling a long breath, and Erik shut her door quietly.

How could he tell Tina about her grandparents? How could he not? It was a dilemma that kept Erik up long into the night and plagued his thoughts all the next day as he and his hired hand worked the cattle.

Part of him wished he dared confide in Marybeth, taking advantage of her good sense and her affection for Tina. But, deep down, he knew what she would say.

Erik wanted what was best for Tina, a child who had already lost so much. She was happy with him; she loved him. For four years, he had been her sole protector. Now he had no intention of gambling Tina's future on a couple who had failed so completely with their own son. If he had to deny her the opportunity of knowing her only living relatives in order to keep her with him, he would. He was not willing to lose her, even if it meant looking over his shoulder for the rest of his life.

Chapter Eight

"You aren't listening to a word I said." Sandy shook her head, exasperated, and prodded her spinach salad with her fork.

"Sorry," Marybeth told her while she shoved her wayward thoughts aside. "I guess I'm just tired."

"Horsefeathers, as one of my ancestors would no doubt have said. You're lovesick," Sandy pronounced, with the air of one who knew the illness well. "Tell me all about it." She took a drink of her diet soda, watching Marybeth expectantly.

Marybeth picked up half of her turkey sandwich, eyed it with disinterest, and dropped it back onto the plate. Around them, the sounds of the busy hospital cafeteria rose and fell. Sandy had come over to have lunch and tell her about the animal shelter's new, more aggressive stand on spaying and neutering. Marybeth had tried to listen, but her mind kept wandering to Erik and why he hadn't called her since that magical afternoon she had spent in his arms.

Was he the kind of man to disappear after he got what he wanted? She doubted that, but it had been two days now, and she was beginning to worry.

"There isn't much to tell," she said to her friend. "I thought that my relationship with Erik was progressing at a satisfactory pace, but now I'm not so sure."

"Why?" Sandy asked around a mouthful of salad.

Marybeth shrugged, nibbling on a potato chip. "Every time I think we're getting closer, he backs off."

Sandy leaned forward and lowered her voice. "Have you slept with him yet?"

"What?" Marybeth was surprised by the blunt question. And a little embarrassed.

Sandy grinned. "You heard me. I mean, the man's gorgeous. No one with eyes in her head would blame you."

"He's driving me crazy with his secrecy," Marybeth said, skirting Sandy's question. "I wish he'd open up about himself. What does he think I'm going to do, sell an article to some supermarket scandal sheet?" Maybe making love with Erik had been a bad idea. She had thought it would bring them closer; instead it seemed to have driven him away.

"Maybe there's something in his past that he's ashamed of," Sandy said. "Something about Tina's mother, perhaps."

Marybeth shook her head. She couldn't tell her friend about Erik's activities as a spy or anything else he had confided in her. "No, I don't think that's it," she hedged. "It's like he's not used to talking about himself. He won't even tell me about his childhood."

"Maybe he doesn't want to remember it," Sandy said dryly. "Not all of us grew up like you did, in a nice house with Ward and June Cleaver for parents."

Marybeth remembered what Sandy had told her about her own childhood. Her father drank and her mother tried to support them with menial jobs, leaving little time for Sandy or her two younger brothers. As a result, it had fallen on Sandy to take care of the house and practically raise the boys. Now they were scattered, and no one kept in touch. Sandy vowed never to get married and land in that rut again.

"I just wish Erik would trust me," Marybeth mumbled as she glanced at her watch. "Oh, I have to get back. Thanks for coming over."

"Give him time," Sandy said. "Want to go to a show in Everett tomorrow night? A Steve Martin comedy's playing."

Marybeth feigned surprise. "You don't have a date?"

Sandy made a face. "No, I don't." Her tone was slightly defensive. "If you've already got plans, don't worry about it, all right?"

It didn't look as though Marybeth was going to be busy this weekend, judging from the silence of her telephone. "I'll let you know tomorrow," she said. "Okay?"

Sandy grinned knowingly. "Sure. I don't mind coming in second, after Erik." Her grin faded slightly. "I hope he calls."

"Thanks. So do I." Marybeth wanted to say more, but she really had to get back to her station. "I'll talk to you tomorrow." She dumped her tray and hurried off, turning once to wave. Despite their differences, with Sandy being outgoing and dating a lot while she was more content with her own company—or had been, until Erik came along—

Marybeth valued their friendship. They could say almost anything to each other and know the other would listen.

So why hadn't she told Sandy about what had happened with him? She knew her friend wouldn't judge her. Sandy had had a couple of steady boyfriends since they'd known each other. She always broke it off if the man became too serious, though, and said the only long-term relationships she was interested in were ones with animals.

Back at the nurses' station, Marybeth prepared to administer afternoon medications. She was too busy for the next half hour to think about anything else. When her patients were finally quiet, most of them napping or watching television, she sat down to catch her breath.

She was sure that something troubled Erik deeply. If only he would confide in her. She frowned and admitted to herself that she had thought he would surely open up after they had made love. Apparently she'd been wrong about that.

Erik's lovemaking had made changes in her. By sharing himself with her the way he had, he'd let Marybeth see that he was capable of reaching out—in a way that moved her deeply. What she and Erik gave each other was entirely different from what she had shared with Mike during their marriage. She couldn't accept that Erik hadn't felt the same wonder, the same all-encompassing emotional experience she had. They had been so good together, so honest in their needs and responses.

Marybeth was relatively inexperienced. Maybe what they had shared hadn't been unique; perhaps that level of satisfaction was common among more experienced lovers—but she doubted it. Erik's tender behavior afterward certainly hadn't led her to think he considered it just another ordinary exchange of sexual favors. He, too, had been moved—she knew it.

So why was he pulling back now, if that was truly what he was doing? Why was he acting as if it didn't matter, when she knew from what she had seen in his eyes and heard in his voice that it had been important to him?

She cared about him; she wanted him happy. So why wouldn't he let her in, to comfort him with her love and soothe him with understanding and acceptance? Why couldn't he trust her just a little?

Marybeth started violently when a patient's call button yanked her back to the present. It wasn't one of hers; another nurse hurried to answer the summons. Marybeth stared down at her hands, shaken with what she had just realized.

She loved him.

Erik might have secrets and a painful past, but he was also a good father, a hard worker. From what she'd heard about him after the bank robbery, he was an honest and respected businessman. She had seen firsthand his courage, his gentleness. And there was something about his emotional aloofness—an unconscious armor she was sure hid a fear of being hurt—that had reached out and captured Marybeth's heart.

She doubted he even believed in romantic love, let alone felt that way about *her.*

"Well, my girl," she muttered softly to herself, "you've gone and done it now." She picked up the phone to tell Sandy she couldn't go to the movie after all. She wanted time alone, to sort things out. To deal with her new feelings. Could she handle loving *another* man who refused to share himself—all of himself—with the woman who loved him?

As he drove from Dr. Hamilton's office to the hospital parking lot, Erik flexed his shoulder experimentally. He'd been examined with annoying thoroughness, even though the aftereffects from the gunshot wound were almost completely gone.

Erik had thought about calling Marybeth at work to see if she would go to an early dinner with him, but then he decided to ask her in person instead. He needed to see her. Since her shift was almost over, he had just enough time to find her car and park the truck nearby. In only a few more moments he would be with her.

Perhaps, before the evening was over, she would be in his arms again, uttering those sweet little noises that drove him wild. It would be so easy to let her make him feel as if he had someone of his own, that he belonged, that he mattered to somebody besides Tina.

Two nurses came through the double hospital doors, and Erik straightened from where he had been leaning against Marybeth's red Escort. Then he relaxed again when she saw that neither of them had her particular bright caramel shade of hair.

When the two women walked by, one of them gave him a provocative smile. Her gaze drifted down his long body and then back to his face, her eyes bright with speculation. Uncomfortable with her blatant interest, Erik nodded briefly before looking away. Then he saw Marybeth coming across the parking lot and a bolt of reaction shot through him, making him forget all about the other nurse. He forgot everything but the woman who was approaching him with a welcoming expression on her beautiful face.

As she hurried toward him, Marybeth decided not to mention any of her concern about his silence over the past two days. There was no quicker way to make a man feel hog-tied than to start demanding an accounting of his time. Erik had probably been busy with work and not thought about how vulnerable she might feel. What mattered was that he was here now—and he was obviously waiting for her.

When that notorious man-eater in a nurse's uniform, Marcy Ketchum, had given him the eye, Erik had barely even noticed. For that alone, he deserved a kiss.

Marcy looked around one more time as she bent to unlock the door of her white Corvette. Marybeth was tempted to throw her arms around Erik and stake an unequivocal claim while the other woman watched. Instead, she redirected her attention to his handsome face and greeted him quietly.

"Hi. This is a nice surprise."

Erik returned her grin with a rather wary one of his own. "Sure? I'm sorry I haven't called."

Marybeth made a dismissive gesture with her hand, vaguely aware of the muted roar of Marcy's Corvette as she left the lot in a cloud of dust. "No problem. I figured you must be busy."

He looked almost disappointed by her amiability. "Yeah," he said slowly. "I guess I was. Something came up that it took me a while to work through."

"Not trouble, I hope?" she asked as she stopped in front of him. For once, she wished that he'd quit talking and kiss her.

Erik hesitated. "Nothing I can't handle," he said finally. "Are you hungry? I thought you might want to grab an early dinner somewhere."

Marybeth studied Erik's face, doing her best to ignore her concern over whatever was bothering him. If he wanted her to know, he would tell her. "I'd like that," she said.

He looked tired, as if he hadn't been sleeping well. She would have liked to think it was because he'd been missing her. He raked a hand through his hair and then shot her a grateful look. "Good," he mumbled while he hugged her close. She thought he touched his lips to the top of her head, but couldn't be sure.

"How about Mexican food?" he asked. "Mrs. O'Reilly told me about a new place down toward Langley. She said it was pretty good."

Marybeth agreed quickly. She realized how hungry she was, as if Erik's appearance had rejuvenated the appetite that had been sadly lacking since she'd last seen him.

For a moment he hugged her even closer as she savored his warmth and the scent that was uniquely his. Then he helped her into the cab of his truck. As he climbed in after her, buckling her seat belt before he did up his own, she wondered again what was on his mind. When he asked how work had gone, she directed her attention to him and the evening ahead of them.

After a spicy, enjoyable meal spent filling each other in on news about Tina, Joker and the most interesting of Marybeth's patients, she and Erik enjoyed a comfortably silent ride back to Coupeville.

"How about a walk along the beach?" he asked as they neared the turnoff to the hospital. "Or we can go back to my place and watch a movie on the VCR."

"A walk on the beach sounds nice." She slipped her hand over his as it rested on his thigh.

He glanced down at her before returning his attention to the road ahead. "I want to be alone with you," he muttered, raising her hand to his mouth. He kissed the back and then turned it over. His tongue stroked the sensitive palm. As her fingers curled protectively, he replaced their joined hands on his hard-muscled thigh. Warmth seeped through the heavy denim of his jeans, reminding her of the heated passion they had shared. It was all she could do to keep from squirming restlessly on the bench seat.

"What about my car?" she asked faintly.

"We'll get it later."

For a moment, she rested her head against his shoulder. "Being alone with you sounds good to me," she murmured in his ear. She was pleased when he glanced at her again, his eyes dark with barely restrained desire.

"The walk might have to wait," he said, voice husky. He pulled up in front of her house and shut off the truck.

Marybeth's dogs came running up, barking effusively. Erik spoke to them through his open window and they quieted. Then they ran up the steps to sit expectantly on the front porch. One of the cats was curled up on the porch railing.

As soon as Erik and Marybeth were both free of their seat belts, he reached for her. His hands were greedy, his mouth open and hot against hers. Marybeth returned his ardor with a passion that made her tremble in his arms. She wondered if he realized how easily he could hurt her. Then he held her tighter while his marauding mouth trailed a line of fiery kisses down her jaw and into the sensitive hollow of her throat above the open collar of her uniform smock.

She arched her neck to allow him better access. Her hands clenched in his short, silky hair as he nipped her with his teeth. Then he soothed the tingling spot with rough strokes of his tongue.

"Sweetheart, you don't know how much I've missed you," he groaned, flicking open the top button of her smock with fingers that shook.

Marybeth stilled his hand, suddenly aware of their lack of privacy. She needed a moment to catch her breath before he dominated her will completely. Besides, some small perversity demanded that he be made to wait before he took so effortlessly what they both wanted.

"Uh, someone might come along," she stammered when he shifted impatiently, holding her away from him while he studied her face.

His brows rose in disbelief. "You expecting company?"

"No." She glanced away. "But you never know. Let's go for that walk."

Erik's eyes took on a sudden predatory gleam as he continued to study her. "Sure thing." He was grinning when he slid out of the truck and dragged her after him. Bending close, he nuzzled her neck. Then, before she could protest, he stepped back, hands raised innocently.

"I know," he said, his good humor apparently restored. "You want to walk." He tucked her arm through his.

Arthur and Annabelle galloped back down the steps to join them. "Walk" was a word they both recognized, along with biscuit, dinner and sometimes, when it suited them, no. The dogs ran ahead, plumy tails wagging. Every few steps, one or the other would look back, checking to see if the humans were still following.

While they made their way down the beach, Marybeth probed gently. She was trying to discover what troubled Erik. After more than one evasive answer, she fell silent, but she was frustrated with his continuing unwillingness to open up.

A moment later, Erik guided her to a fallen log and pulled her down beside him.

"Look," he said when she sat stiffly next to him, refusing to glance in his direction. "I know you seem to be convinced that some deep, dark secret is eating away at me, but I swear I'm fine."

She said nothing, only raised her chin a notch as she steadfastly watched the water. Finally he made a sound of exasperation in his throat.

"Have it your own way, then," he said, picking up a handful of pebbles and tossing them into the water one by one.

"I wasn't trying to pry," Marybeth found herself saying defensively. "People who care about each other are usually willing to talk, really talk, about what's bothering them."

"I told you, nothing's bothering me." Erik's voice held the first threads of annoyance.

"I don't believe you." She held her breath, waiting for his burst of anger. It never came.

Instead, he put a muscular arm around her and squeezed. "I'm not one of your patients, remember?" he teased.

She shifted away and he let her go. "You used to be, and a very annoying one, I might add."

"I don't need a nurse anymore," he said, voice low. "I need a woman." One callused finger came up to trace a line down her cheek.

Marybeth pushed it away. "Any woman?" she burst out.

Chuckling softly, Erik captured her chin in his fingers and gently turned her head. "You know better than that."

For a moment, Marybeth almost let herself yield to his tempting persuasion. Then she stiffened. "If you really cared about me, you'd trust me enough to be honest," she insisted. She could scarcely believe that the unguarded words had come out of her mouth. Braced once again for his anger, she waited silently.

Erik released her chin. "You mean cared about you as in love you?" he asked.

She couldn't meet his eyes. "Not necessarily," she told him in what she hoped was a breezy tone. Where was that staunch feminine courage when she needed it?

"What makes you so sure that love even exists?" he asked, surprising her.

"Well, I..." she stammered, biting off the obvious explanation that she *loved* him. "Aren't you?"

He tossed another pebble at the water. "I haven't had much proof of it," he finally admitted.

She was surprised by his frankness. "Your parents must have loved you," she probed, while she recalled Sandy's words. "Didn't they?" Her own daring shocked her, after she had crumbled so quickly in light of his last challenging look. After all, he had made it abundantly clear he didn't like discussing his childhood.

"I suppose my mom loved me," he said slowly. "She died when I was real young, so I don't remember a lot." He sighed, staring toward the water. "I don't think my dad knew how to love anyone. At least, he sure didn't act like it around me."

Marybeth put a hand on his arm, silently encouraging him to continue.

"Dad was always waiting for me to do something wrong," Erik added after a moment. "Sooner or later, I would. Then he'd punish me. He never yelled, never lost his temper. He was cold, through and through." Erik turned to look at Marybeth, his face expressionless. "Dad didn't smile, never laughed. Didn't talk much. But he knew I'd screw up again, and of course I always did."

Marybeth's heart ached for the little boy who must have longed for his father's approval, and had never gotten it. "Was it just the two of you?" she asked.

He nodded. "Can't imagine him doing what it takes to make more children," he drawled. "I learned early to count on myself, and I left home as soon as I graduated from high school."

"Do you keep in touch?" she asked, appalled at the idea that they might not, no matter how barren their relationship.

Erik shook his head, reaching for another handful of pebbles. "I called him once, after boot camp. I was shipping out and feeling sentimental, I guess."

"What happened?" she prompted when he fell silent.

He threw several more pebbles before he resumed talking. "I told him what I was up to. He said good riddance and hung up."

She sat, speechless with shock at the cruelty of it. Rubbing his arm with her hand, trying to give some small measure of comfort, she shook her head. "I'm so sorry," she managed, after swallowing the tears that threatened to clog her throat. No wonder he found it hard to trust.

Erik shrugged. "Don't worry. It all happened a long time ago, and I've gotten over it." He sighed, long and deep. "Ugly story, isn't it? Are you glad now that you got me to talk about it?" His voice was bitter.

"I never wanted you to talk about it to make you feel bad," she said. "I only wanted to share a little of your pain."

"Why?" he shot out. "You can't share my pain."

She searched for an explanation he would accept. "To help," she said finally, "just to try to ease the loneliness."

He turned to look at her, his expression defensive. "Who said anything about being lonely?"

It was her turn to shrug. "You didn't."

His head jerked. "Damned right."

"You said you're not sure you believe in love," she said after a moment, changing tactics. "But you love Tina. It's clear she loves you."

"What's your point?" He dropped the rest of the pebbles and got to his feet, wiping his hand on his jeans.

She rose beside him and felt her way cautiously. "Isn't that proof that love exists?" she asked. "Your father didn't show you any warmth, but you've given Tina a home, and love. Surely you can't deny its existence after all that."

She watched Erik closely as he looked away, down the beach. He seemed to be thinking over what she had said. Then he turned back to her, his face troubled.

"I've got to go," he said abruptly.

She understood that she had gotten too close, making him uncomfortable. She resisted the urge to question him, to plead with him to stay and share with her again the powerful lovemaking that had brought them so close. She needed the reassurance they could find that closeness again. Still, she refused to speak the words that might persuade him to stay. Perhaps that very closeness she craved was more than he could handle right now. Instead she reached up to hug him briefly. If he needed so urgently to be alone, perhaps it was to think about what she had said, to consider that love did exist, maybe even to realize that it could exist between the two of them if he would only let it.

He didn't return her embrace, but the corner of his mouth lifted into a lopsided smile as they stood looking at each other. "You aren't upset?" he asked.

She shook her head. "No." She wanted to add something more but wasn't sure what.

He touched her cheek with one finger, then his hand dropped back to his side. "I'll call you, okay?"

"Sure." She wondered if he meant it, or if it was just a kiss-off phrase, like guys said when they had no intentions of really doing it.

Watching him walk back down the beach, his broad shoulders straight, she remembered that her car was still at the hospital. She thought about calling him back, then decided not to. She could always get Mr. Isaacson to run her in to pick it up.

By getting Erik to talk, had she made things better or loused them up completely? It might be days before she knew for sure.

When she was almost back to her house, the phone started to ring. Muttering under her breath, she hurried to catch it before the caller hung up.

All the way home, Erik thought about what Marybeth had said. He loved Tina. Tina loved him. Therefore, love existed. Therefore, he and Marybeth could live happily ever after? He thumped the steering wheel with his fist, knowing from firsthand, painful experience that life just wasn't that simple.

Thinking about Tina and how far they had come together, he began to realize that Marybeth had been right about one thing. He *had* changed since the little girl first entered his life. Without his realizing it, her love had nurtured a side of him he wouldn't have admitted before even existed. He'd only known from the beginning that he wasn't going to raise her with the coldness his father had shown him. Instead, he had made every effort to give her acceptance, patience, and encouragement, to arm her with confidence and security. In trying to give her the best, he had brought out the best in himself. Rather, she had brought it out in him, too. With her love.

The realization made him pause. In giving to Tina, he had gained even more. Giving love had brought him love back, tenfold. It was a revelation he hadn't thought about before. One he needed more time to examine. Maybe trusting in love wasn't quite as foolhardy an idea as he had decided it was, so many years ago.

Erik pulled into his usual parking area by the house, surprised when Mrs. O'Reilly came rushing outside, followed closely by Trevor, his ranch hand.

"Oh, Mr. Snow, I'm so glad you're here," the housekeeper exclaimed as he got out of the truck. Her hands were twisted into the front of her apron. "I tried to call you at Mrs. MacNamara's, but you'd already left."

Erik glanced from her agitated face to Trevor's, which was equally upset. "It's Tina, isn't it?" he exclaimed as his gut twisted anxiously. He'd been tempting fate, thinking about love. "Where is she? What's happened?"

When neither the housekeeper nor the ranch hand answered immediately, Erik grabbed the front of Trevor's shirt. "Tell me!" he demanded, hauling the slighter man close. "What the hell is going on? Where's my little girl?"

The concern on Trevor's face made Erik drop his hands. His heart lurched painfully, as if it were going to quit beating altogether.

"That's just it, man," Trevor said, spreading his hands helplessly. "We don't know where Tina is. She and the dog are gone."

Chapter Nine

"Tina's missing?" Erik echoed. Cold, raw fear knotted his stomach. "How long has she been gone? Where have you looked?" He whirled, muscles bunching, his hands doubled into fists. He wanted to strike out at something. If anything happened to her, he didn't think he could survive it.

Mrs. O'Reilly touched his arm. "Tina and the dog were right in the house," she said. "The next thing I knew, they had disappeared. It's only been a few minutes, really, and I'm sure that she's okay as long as Joker's with her. That dog wouldn't let any harm come to her."

Erik took a deep breath. He forced down his helpless rage. Getting upset wouldn't help Tina. "Where have you looked?" he repeated, fighting for the icy control that had always gotten him through the most dangerous of situations. This time, control didn't come easily.

The housekeeper glanced at Trevor, who was holding his beat-up straw hat and worrying the brim with both hands.

"Well, Mrs. O'Reilly thought they had followed me outside, and I thought they were still playing in the house," he said in his measured drawl. "When I went in to get some iced tea a few minutes ago, she asked me what they were up to."

Erik's accusing gaze shifted back to the older woman, who couldn't keep an expression of concern from her plump face. "We were just about to split up. I called around for her in the house, but she isn't there. Trevor was going to search the barn when we saw your truck coming, so we waited."

"She's got to be close by," Erik said, growing impatient. "Maybe she's hurt, lying somewhere unconscious." He swallowed painfully. "She knows not to wander off."

"Yes, and she's just a little girl," the housekeeper reminded him. "Sometimes children forget the rules. Or they fall asleep. She might have been so caught up in her playing that she just forgot."

"Not Tina," he disagreed with confidence. She wouldn't do that kind of thing. She knew he'd worry; she'd always seemed to have a sixth sense about that. As if she understood the dangers. Even when she had been a toddler, and they'd fled her father's mansion, she hadn't made a sound to betray Erik. For a moment the fleeting horror that perhaps she had been *taken* wrenched through him, but he did his best to ignore it. Bernadetti's men were no longer a threat. Moody had told him so. Besides, Joker would have sounded the alarm if a stranger had set foot on the property. It was too soon for Erik to be worrying about those kinds of possibilities.

Perhaps, though, she *was* hurt and unable to hear them. But where? Erik's brain, usually as organized as a computer, seemed to be spinning helplessly.

"Something has been bothering the child, I think," Mrs. O'Reilly said when he would have turned away. "Ever since she came back from that birthday party yesterday, she's been abnormally quiet."

Erik berated himself for not noticing, but he'd been too wrapped up in his own concerns. Even now, he longed for Marybeth's gentle presence to hold on to in the face of the blind panic that was trying so hard to engulf him. Would she come, after the abrupt way he had left her? She knew that Tina was missing; Mrs. O'Reilly must have told her so.

It wasn't as if he needed someone to hold his hand, after all, he assured himself. He didn't *need* anyone, except perhaps Tina. Erik rubbed at a headache that was working its way up the back of his neck.

"Well, we aren't going to find her by standing around," he said. "Trevor, you go ahead and look in the barn. Mrs. O, would you mind checking the smaller buildings?"

"Of course not," she said. Beside her, Trevor hesitated.

"What is it?" Erik asked.

"You don't think she would have gone to the creek, do you?" The younger man's face was rigid with worried strain.

An icy hand squeezed Erik's heart. The creek was low this time of year, but a child could drown in very little water. "That's pretty far for her to walk," he managed to say in a fairly normal voice. "I'll take the truck up there, though, just to be sure." He felt powerless against the emotions churning through him.

"Maybe we should call the sheriff," Trevor suggested.

Tina would be terrified. "No, not until we've looked around first." Erik hurried to the truck. The creek was defined by a line of trees that bisected the nearest pasture. It was still quite a walk for a small child. He hoped like hell it was too much of a walk. Tina had been specifically told never to go there without an adult. She had to be somewhere else. If only the dog had enough sense to keep her from getting into real trouble.

As Erik drove the pickup toward the creek, bouncing over the uneven ground, his hopes that she wouldn't have gone that far grew. She wasn't comfortable with the cows when they were loose, and there were quite a few of them grazing in his pasture. As Erik steered through their midst, they lumbered toward the truck to see if he had brought them extra feed. It took all his patience to maneuver around them.

"Go on, git!" he yelled out the window, one hand on the horn.

When he got to the creek, he found himself muttering a litany of half-forgotten prayers as he slid from the pickup. Normally stoic, he was almost afraid of what he might find along the sandy bank. Then he got a grip on himself and glanced around. Seeing nothing unusual, he began to look for signs as he listened for a shout that would mean she'd been found in one of the outbuildings.

Instead he heard a horn honk. Marybeth's car was coming down the road. The rush of feeling that raced through him was a shock, and he realized then how worried he'd been that she might not come.

Marybeth brought the Escort to a stop and leaped out, looking around for a glimpse of Erik's blond head. She hoped that Tina had already been found, the emergency aborted. Instead, Erik's housekeeper hurried over. Her face was lined with concern.

"Haven't you found her?" Marybeth asked.

Mrs. O'Reilly shook her head. "Not yet. Erik's up at the creek, but we don't really think she would have gone that far."

Marybeth glanced in the direction the older woman pointed. She could see the truck and Erik's lean figure but couldn't tell if he was looking her way. The poor man must be going through hell.

"How's he doing?" she asked the housekeeper.

Mrs. O'Reilly shook her head. "He tries to hide it but I know he's distraught. That little girl means the world to him."

"I know," Marybeth said, aching for the man who had come to mean so much to her. "What can I do to help?" Any self-consciousness she had felt at coming over after Erik had made it so clear he wanted to be alone had vanished when she got to his ranch. No matter if the news about Tina was good or bad, she wanted—no, needed—to be with him.

"You can help me look. Come on," the housekeeper said. "I think that something upset Tina yesterday while she was at a friend's house." Marybeth followed her to a large garden. "When I asked her about it, she said no." Mrs. O'Reilly stopped beside several rows of tall berry bushes. "Other children can be cruel, though."

"Did you tell Erik about it?" Marybeth asked as they began to look around.

"I tried, but he didn't really pay much attention. Now's not the time, I guess."

As they looked among the rows of berry bushes and corn stalks, calling out, Marybeth wished with all her heart that Tina would be found soon, and unharmed. Not just for

Erik's sake, but for hers, too. She had become extremely fond of the little girl, not to mention her floppy-eared canine companion.

Despite his careful search, Erik could find nothing to indicate that Tina or Joker had been to the creek. The only tracks in the mud along the bank were cloven ones. He stared into the shallow water for a moment and then turned away. He was desperately relieved that he hadn't found her beneath its surface.

Now the question was, where to look next? He could see Marybeth and Mrs. O'Reilly searching through the raspberry and blueberry bushes at the far end of the vegetable garden. He supposed it was possible for a little girl to fall asleep there in the shadows from the sun, but from where he stood he could see no telltale flash of color that might be her clothing.

When he got back to the yard, Trevor met him at the truck.

"Any sign?" the ranch hand asked. There was sweat beaded on his forehead and a bloody scratch down one gaunt cheek.

"No," Erik admitted. "How about you?"

"Nothing." Trevor pulled out a bandanna and blotted his face.

Erik couldn't keep ignoring the nagging fear that someone had slipped in and spirited Tina away against her will. She would be so frightened of strangers! What if Moody's information had been wrong? What if Bernadetti's men were still a threat? Maybe they wanted Tina for some twisted sense of revenge and had stumbled on her whereabouts. They would have killed Joker without a second thought.

Erik raked a hand through his hair as he swallowed and tried not to think of the possibilities. If anyone had hurt her, he would kill them with his bare hands.

"How are you holding up?"

Marybeth's welcome voice distracted him from the lurid details his well-trained imagination conjured up. Grateful, Erik pulled her into his arms and buried his face in her cloud of silky hair as a shudder of tension racked him.

"Thanks for coming," he murmured. "I'm doing okay, I guess." He let her go, drowning in her wide hazel eyes.

"I'm glad you're not upset that I came," she told him. "I thought perhaps I could help. Especially..." She hesitated, and then plunged on. "Especially if she's hurt, since I'm a nurse."

Erik linked her fingers with his. "Let's keep looking," he said to the others. "We have to find her." Suddenly he remembered something. "What about that old shed on the other side of the house? Has anyone checked there yet? Mrs. O?"

Marybeth could just see one corner of a small, white building past the sprawling ranch house.

"I never gave it a thought," the housekeeper admitted. "It's so hot and dusty in there, and full of junk."

"But I'd talked to Tina about turning it into a playhouse," Erik reminded her. "We were poking around in there a couple of weeks ago, making plans.

"Come on," he said, hope rising as he glanced at his watch. "If she's not there, I guess I'll have to call the police before we lose the light."

Following his rapid footsteps, Marybeth sent up a silent prayer that Erik would be spared the pain of seeing volunteers dragging the creek and fanning out with search dogs, knowing all the while that he had to be prepared for the worst. How she wished she could protect him from it.

"I'm running out of ideas," Erik said as he hurried her along. When they got to the shed, he pushed open the door and called Tina's name. Marybeth's heart cramped at the suffering she could hear in his voice. There was no response.

The small room was full of abandoned furniture, stacks of boxes, and a jumble of other items. Marybeth's ears strained for any revealing sounds but all she heard was the blast of a horn from the highway. Behind her, Trevor and Mrs. O'Reilly waited, expressions anxious.

"Come on, Tina," Erik muttered under his breath as he began to shove things aside. "I'm running out of ideas."

Marybeth thought she heard a faint cry. "Wait." She grabbed his arm, straining to catch the noise again. Beneath her fingers, his muscles bunched.

In the pasture, a calf bawled.

Erik hefted an abandoned door and leaned it against a wall. "Tina! Are you in here?" he demanded.

"Joker," Marybeth shouted on an impulse. "Where are you, boy?"

This time, the dog's plaintive whining was easy to hear, followed by a childish whisper trying to quiet him.

Marybeth's body went limp with relief as she murmured a fervent prayer of thanks.

"Tina, come on out," Erik called, and there was underlying steel in his voice. "If you're okay, you'd better get out here right now."

Marybeth held her breath, hoping he wouldn't be too hard on the child. For a moment all was still; then something rustled in the back of the small room and became a blur of brown fur as Joker galloped out to meet them, tail wagging. Tina came behind him at a much more hesitant pace. Her cheeks were flushed and her light blue shorts and white T-shirt were streaked with dirt. Her mouth was drawn into a petulant pout.

It was clear that, physically at least, she was okay. Marybeth's heart went out to the small, dejected figure.

Erik stood watching his daughter's progress, hands on hips. He looked ready to pounce. Marybeth hoped he would hold his temper in check even though he had good reason to be out of his mind with worry.

He didn't yell. For a long moment Tina seemed to shrink even smaller as she returned his stare, big eyes sparkling with tears. Then he crouched down to her level and cupped her thin shoulders in his big hands.

Beside him, Marybeth fought tears of her own.

"You gave us quite a scare," he told his daughter in a surprisingly gentle voice. "Are you okay?"

She bobbed her head, looking down at her dusty shoes. "Yes, Daddy."

Erik muttered something that Marybeth didn't hear, and pulled Tina into his embrace. For a long moment, he held her tight, and then he released her with great reluctance.

"Then would you please share with us what's going on?" he asked.

Tina looked at the housekeeper and the hired man, as if she were searching for allies. Her pleading gaze lingered on Marybeth, who tried to give her an encouraging smile. Then Tina peered back at Erik and her tears spilled over.

"Joker and me were hiding," she gulped.

"I think we've figured that out." Erik's voice was dry. Marybeth could almost feel his determination to hang on to his control. "Why were you hiding, sweetheart?"

Tina hung her head. "I don't know."

He tipped back her chin with his hand. Marybeth remembered how tender those hands could be, and how commanding. She licked lips gone suddenly dry.

"Who were you hiding from?" Erik prodded patiently. "Tell me."

Tina hesitated for so long that Marybeth thought she wasn't going to answer. "A girl at Sara's party said parents don't love adopted kids as much as they do kids who are really theirs."

Marybeth had to blink fast at the woeful tone of Tina's voice. Beside her, Erik stiffened.

"She doesn't know what she's talking about!" he thundered. Then he seemed to get a mental grip on himself. He hauled Tina back into the circle of his arms, resting his cheek against her straight black hair. "Haven't we talked about that?" he questioned, his tone slightly hoarse with suppressed emotion. "You *are* my real daughter in every way that counts to me."

The dark head bobbed in agreement.

"And what did we decide when we talked?" He rocked back onto his heels, watching her face. Marybeth was almost overcome with emotion at the patience he was showing, when many parents would be livid.

Tina grabbed at a strand of her silky hair and chewed on the ends while she again returned Erik's relentless stare.

"We decided that you love me more because you chose me special," she said, as if she were repeating a familiar litany.

"That's right. Our relationship is *very* special. Was this little girl at Sara's party adopted?"

Tina frowned in concentration. "I don't think so. She has a big nose, just like her mom's."

A smile tugged at the corners of Erik's mouth, but he didn't give in to it. "Then how could that little girl know?

Maybe she was just trying to sound important. She probably didn't realize that you *are* adopted.''

Tina pulled the strand of hair from her mouth, letting it slide through two fingers. ''Maybe.'' She didn't sound totally convinced.

''Did you tell her that you are?'' Erik asked.

Tina shook her head.

''What else is bothering you?'' he persisted.

Marybeth marveled at his perception. She wanted to lean forward and touch him, just to feel his warmth, but didn't.

''I've got chores to do,'' Trevor said quietly, turning away.

''Me, too.'' Mrs. O'Reilly's eyes were suspiciously moist.

''Thanks for your help,'' Erik told them both.

After they left, he and Marybeth both looked back at Tina.

''It bothers me that I don't have a mother,'' she admitted finally.

The softness of her reply made Marybeth wonder if she should leave, too. This conversation was getting awfully personal.

Before she could decide what to do, Erik glanced up at her and mouthed the word ''stay.'' It was all the encouragement she needed. Perhaps he was finally learning to share what he was feeling with her.

''You had a mommy who loved you very much,'' he told Tina. ''But she died. Otherwise, she would never have left you.''

The little girl was quiet for a moment, digesting what he said. ''Was she pretty?''

''She was very beautiful, and you're going to look just like her.''

Tina looked at him for what seemed like a long time. "I need a new mother," she announced suddenly.

Marybeth saw Erik brace himself and then spread his hands in a gesture of helplessness. "That's not something I can get at a toy store, like another dolly," he said, a new thread of exasperation in his voice. This subject must have come up before.

Tina's slightly rounded chin thrust out, her expression turning stubborn. "You *always* say that," she complained. "So this time Joker and I decided to go on strike."

Caught by surprise, it was all Marybeth could do to choke back a laugh. "Strike?" she echoed.

Tina glanced up. "Yes. Like the teachers do."

Erik's expression was rueful. "I told her the beginning of school might be delayed by a strike," he explained. "We had quite a talk about it." His voice carried a certain wryness.

"So, why are you on strike?" he asked his daughter.

"I want you to get me a mother," she said. "Joker and I are on strike until you do."

Marybeth was speechless, torn between admiration for Tina's bravado, and helpless laughter at the expression on Erik's face. Apparently he wasn't sure what to say, either. He rose to his full height and looked down at Tina, who stared up at him defiantly. Her hands were on her hips in a miniature imitation of his own stance.

"We'll talk about this later," he said and for the first time, Marybeth heard the beginnings of real annoyance in his voice. "Meanwhile, you'd better get into the house. I think an early bedtime is in order."

For a moment longer, Tina continued to look up at him. Her chin started to wobble. Erik swooped down and picked her up. "I love you," he said softly. "That will *never* change. The other thing is going to take a lot of time.'' He hesitated. ''Meanwhile, I don't know that a strike is the answer.'' He set her back down.

''It's what people have to do sometimes to get what they want,'' Tina said, obviously quoting him.

Erik rubbed his hand over his face. Marybeth thought she saw another flicker of a smile on his hard mouth. ''I said for you to go inside,'' he repeated. ''I'll think about what you've told me, and we'll talk some more tomorrow.''

Tina looked at Marybeth, who tried to appear encouraging.

''Good night, honey. I'm glad you're okay.'' She bent forward to give Tina a hug. The soft arms came around her neck, and the little-girl scent roused all of Marybeth's maternal instincts. Again she had to blink rapidly.

''Good night,'' Tina echoed, running to the house with Joker at her heels.

Erik found himself watching Marybeth. ''Whew,'' he muttered. ''Talk about a mine field. Perhaps I should be glad I don't always know what she's thinking.'' He slid an arm around Marybeth's waist, drawing her closer as she turned into his embrace. Surrounding them were shadows, the day's brightness fading to twilight.

''Come inside with me,'' Erik implored when she remained silent. The words surprised him. He hadn't meant to beg. ''I don't know about you, but I could use a drink.'' He hesitated, clearing his throat of the words that wanted to stick there. ''I'm sorry about the way I left you before.''

After the crippling worry over finding Tina, he felt hollow, as if he had been drained. Maybe he did need the woman at his side. At least for now. The need bothered him, but the wanting that came with it was sharp, fierce.

When Marybeth still didn't say anything, he looked into her eyes. They were dark with concern for him. "Please stay," he urged again.

For a moment the expression on her face softened, and she raised a hand to touch his cheek. "You must have been frantic, with Tina gone and no idea what had happened to her."

"I was." Erik didn't want to be reminded of the helpless feeling. He was used to being in charge, being in control. It would be too easy to confide these new fears to the woman at his side, to reveal his weaknesses. "I kept thinking of the creek," he burst out, unable to bite back the words. "I tried to tell myself she couldn't have walked that far, but I wasn't sure." He closed his burning eyes for a moment. "Thank God she's okay."

Marybeth's head rested briefly against his heart. "Yes, thank God," she echoed. "I guess I can stay for a little while."

Erik was glad that she seemed to accept what he told her without asking for more than he wanted to reveal. They climbed the steps together, and he opened the door for her.

Mrs. O'Reilly was coming down the hallway. "Tina's in bed," she said in a low voice, "and I think she fell asleep before her head was on the pillow. Poor little mite, with so much on her mind."

"Thanks for sticking around," Erik said. "You can be sure that she and I will have a long talk in the morning. We'll deal with her concerns."

"Don't forget that she's supposed to go to Katy's house for the day," the housekeeper reminded him. "I was going to drive her on my way to the market, if it's still all right that she go."

Erik thought a moment. "I guess she can. Why don't you still do that? Don't worry about breakfast. Just get here in time to take her to Katy's."

"Okay, I will." The housekeeper looked at Marybeth. "He's so good with her," she confided as if Erik weren't there. "Mr. Snow might think he doesn't need anyone for himself, but I'm glad you're here now. He needs someone to be good to him sometimes, too."

She glanced at her employer somewhat defiantly. "Even if you won't ever admit it."

He wanted to argue with her, but more than that, he wanted her to leave him alone with Marybeth. Mrs. O'Reilly meant well, but sometimes she thought she saw more than was there.

"Don't let us keep you," he said pointedly. "Thanks again for staying late."

With a last goodbye to them both, the housekeeper left, easing the door shut behind her.

"She's nice," Marybeth said as Erik pulled out a kitchen chair for her.

He went to the counter. "Coffee?" he asked, not sure what to say now that they were alone. All he wanted to do was drag her down the hall and make love to her, reaffirming life until the dark corners of worry and reaction receded completely. Given the raw pain he still felt, that could take all night.

Marybeth glanced at the pot he held up. "No, thanks. Why don't you check on Tina yourself? You know you want to. I can wait in the living room."

"Promise?" He managed to keep his voice light, but urgent hungers were beginning to claw at him, twisting his insides. Making sure that Tina was safely in her own bed, asleep, would ease one of his needs. Other, more pressing desires clamored for fulfillment, too.

How had he been able to walk away from Marybeth earlier? He must have been crazy.

"I promise I'll wait," she told him, her expression slightly maternal.

Erik frowned. That was the last emotion he wanted to evoke in the woman who aroused him as no one had in such a long time. For once, he wanted to entrust himself to someone else's care for a little while, someone who wouldn't betray him. He wanted Marybeth to take him into her body and shelter him, not as a mother but as a lover with hungers of her own. Hungers that only he could satisfy.

Thoughts churning, Erik hurried down the hall to Tina's room. She lay in a boneless heap, obviously exhausted by the day's stress. Poor kid. Erik padded silently to the side of her bed and looked down at her sprawled form. Her lashes rested on her cheeks like black feathers, her hair falling across her face. Beneath the covers, her thin chest rose and fell with reassuring regularity.

On the carpet beside the bed, Joker stirred and looked at Erik in the gloom. Then he rested his head back on his paws with a noisy sigh.

"Good boy," Erik murmured. He resisted the urge to brush the hair off Tina's cheek, afraid he might disturb her even though he knew she slept like a rock. She probably wouldn't stir until morning. Permitting himself one butterfly kiss on her forehead, he left the room.

Tomorrow he would have to find some words of wisdom and reassurances to vanquish her ghosts, but tonight Marybeth awaited him. His blood began to heat as he hurried to the living room and then paused in the doorway to study her unobserved.

She was curled on the couch, shoes off and feet tucked beneath her, leafing through a farm management magazine with all the concentration she might give a medical journal. Some instinct must have alerted her to his presence because she raised her head and gave him a sweet smile.

"Everything okay?"

"Yeah." His voice was rusty. Closing the space between them, he took her hands and urged her to her feet. Without shoes on, she was shorter, bringing out his protective instincts. Those feelings warred briefly with his hunger. Then he dispelled them and slid his hands up her throat to cup her jaw with new possessiveness. In the past hours, he'd been reminded how quickly someone he cared about could vanish from his life. Now he felt as if he could drown in the depth of Marybeth's eyes.

He stroked the hollows below her cheekbones. "Will you stay with me tonight?" he asked, chest knotted with tension.

Her smile, when it came, was rather shy. It filled him with exultation and something more that he had tried to shield himself against—an aching tenderness. For the first time in his life, he felt an almost overwhelming urge to explore these new feelings.

"I'd like to stay," she said quietly.

Erik bent to scoop her into his arms. She laced her fingers together behind his neck and he found that he liked her proprietary gesture. Her expression was as guileless as Tina's. It filled him with a humble kind of pride that she would entrust herself to him so completely.

With a heartfelt sigh, he buried his face in the silky radiance of her hair. The scent of flowers swirled around him, making him dizzy with wanting. His arms tightened as he held her close to his thundering heart. The tension that had racked him earlier began to seep away, replaced with a different kind of awareness that hummed along his nerves with a life of its own.

"I'm glad you're here," he found himself admitting. "I need you so desperately." The confession didn't bother him nearly as much as he had thought it would only a short while before. Perhaps it was all right to need, in certain circumstances.

When he looked down at Marybeth, he could see that her eyes were brimming. Her smile was tremulous as she blinked away the moisture. "I want you to need me," she said softly.

"I do." An echo of the alarm that always sounded at any sign of vulnerability shivered through him, but he shrugged it away. Tonight was for the two of them, without the armor he used to shield himself from the rest of the world. Old fears would have to wait.

In his room, Erik set Marybeth down carefully next to the wide bed. He felt the gentleness in him begin to melt away in a blaze of heat that threatened to consume his shaky control. His hand shook as he stroked her cheek.

"You're so lovely," he whispered hoarsely.

She lowered her gaze while her flawless skin turned pink in the low light from the bed lamp. Forcing himself to move slowly, he raised his hands to the neck of her plaid shirt. While his trembling fingers fumbled with the buttons, he leaned forward to cover her mouth with his.

He had meant to make the magic last as long as possible, but when he touched his tongue to her lips they parted eagerly. Fire raced through him. One hand bunched the fabric of her blouse immediately, threatening to tear it; the other slid around her slim body as his tongue plunged deep, staking a purely masculine claim. Intent on possession, he bent her backward over his arm as if he could absorb her into himself.

Marybeth's clever fingers pulled his shirt free of his jeans, then tunneled beneath its hem to dance across his heated skin, leaving small but intense fires wherever they touched. Her lips fueled his growing desire as her tongue lured and then seduced his.

Wholly caught up in the passion that roared between them, Erik dealt with her clothing. He was vaguely aware that she was doing the same to his. With barely contained reluctance, they broke apart to finish undressing as quickly as possible. Then he gathered her up and laid her gently on the big bed. When he followed her down, she smiled at him. His body covered hers, burning skin to bare, burning skin. He remembered all the tortured nights he'd dreamed of her here with him.

A hiss of wild pleasure escaped his lips as fresh needs tore through him. Marybeth moaned softly. He tried to give voice to what he was feeling, but words, even thoughts, were too elusive to form. Frantically his mouth raced over her scented skin. His head spun with dizzying sensation. His eager hands renewed their claim while she twisted beneath him, trying to capture his mouth with her own.

Eluding her kiss, he bent to her breasts. He pleasured first one and then the other with his tongue while she sighed. When he drew a beaded tip into his mouth, she arched beneath him, her fingers tightening in his hair. Her sigh became a gasp.

"You taste so sweet," he muttered hoarsely, releasing one nipple to pull at the other until it, too, hardened in response. Her fingers, buried in his hair, tightened. His hands explored the rest of her, making her whimper with need. His mouth traced a path back to hers as she clutched at his shoulders. He held her tight against him and turned so they lay side by side.

Erik searched for new ways to tantalize her, watching the way her eyes darkened as her lids fluttered closed and then flared open again. He had never been a selfish lover, but he found that giving enjoyment to Marybeth brought him sharp, aching pleasure of his own.

Her hands traced sensual patterns on his skin. They lingered to investigate his reactions with maddening thoroughness while the raw passion building inside him intensified. When she reached down to cup him tenderly, tracing his hot length and murmuring her approval, Erik was sure he would explode. His control in ribbons, he eased himself onto his back. Before he could urge her over him, she crawled up his body herself, rubbing against him like a starving man's heated dream.

They lay together as she pressed a burning kiss to his mouth. Her tongue glided between his lips to tease him before swiftly escaping again to caress his ear with feline strokes. Rising to her knees astride him, she bent to nibble at a puckered male nipple before trailing kisses down the line of golden hair that bisected his abdomen. Before she could shift and move even lower, he gripped her head with hands that shook.

"What's wrong?" she whispered.

"Wrong?" His hoarse laugh balanced on the narrow edge of control. "Not wrong," he gasped, "too right." He was afraid she would strip him of whatever shreds of discipline remained.

"I'd meant to go slow with you," he added on a shaky breath. "To make it last."

Her smile was as knowing as Eve's. "Next time," she murmured in a throaty drawl rich with promise.

Erik's temperature soared.

With a ragged groan, he pulled her back up his feverish body. Before he could prepare himself for the sensual assault, she shifted, impaling herself. Erik's hands clenched on her hips and he bit back a groan as she rode him hard, driving the two of them to new heights of soul-shattering ecstasy. Then, when it was over, they curled into each other and embraced the oblivion of sleep.

Marybeth opened her eyes to darkness. She wasn't sure how much time had passed or what had dragged her back awake. Turning slowly as not to disturb Erik, she glanced at the clock. Soon it would be dawn. After that first greedy explosion of passion, they had made love a second time. Their leisurely exploration of each other had been in direct contrast to the first frantic coupling. Its ending, though, had been the same intense race to completion, culminating in such raw, aching sweetness that Marybeth had almost feared she might soar off into space and never come down.

Now as she lay remembering, a smile on her lips, Erik threw out an arm and groaned. His head thrashed wildly on the pillow as if he were in torment.

"No," he muttered. "No! Not like this." The words melted into indistinguishable sounds of distress as his hands curled into fists. While Marybeth was trying to decide whether to wake him, he sat up in bed. The sheet fell to pool in his lap. His eyes stared at unseen terrors. His voice, when he spoke again, was filled with dread.

"No! Oh, God, no!"

Chapter Ten

The stifling Argentina heat had barely lessened with the setting of the sun or in the dark hours since. Erik slipped quietly into the garden. He concealed himself by a screen of bushes. While he watched the lights in the main house wink out, one by one, he waited impatiently, craving a smoke. The minutes crawled by. The heavy perfume of numerous tropical blooms clogged his nostrils, nauseating him. He dragged in another breath as he strained to catch a glimpse of Bernadetti's mistress in the shadows.

The longer Maria delayed, the better their chances of being caught by her lover's men. Erik knew they still didn't trust him completely, despite his elaborate cover story. If he was to get Maria and her daughter out of the compound before the rest of his team arrived, he had to do it now. Erik knew that if Bernadetti even suspected Maria's betrayal, he would certainly kill her.

Erik glanced at the luminous dial of his watch and swore softly as sweat trickled between his shoulder blades. So where the hell was she?

He was about to break cover and look for her when he heard a hoarse shout, followed by several gunshots. Adrenaline raced through him. He drew his weapon as the floodlights surrounding the main house flashed on, turning night into day.

Erik swore again. Before he could move, Maria came running toward him. Her two-year-old daughter was clutched in her arms.

Maria had pulled back the luxurious black hair from her face. She was dressed in the dark red that Bernadetti favored, but her full skirt and flimsy sandals made Erik frown. They had miles to cover on foot before they would be relatively safe.

Maria saw him, and he motioned for her to hurry. Another shot rang out. She looked back and tripped over a vine in the path. Falling heavily, she rolled and twisted her body to keep from dropping her precious burden. Erik crouched low and hurried to where she lay sobbing.

He took the frightened child from her as she struggled to rise. Trying to help, he grabbed her elbow but she fell back down, face twisted with pain.

"Come on," he urged. "We have to go!"

Maria tried again. Again she sank to the ground, moaning.

"I've hurt my ankle," she cried in Spanish. "I can't walk."

Erik could see that the joint was already swelling. "We can't stay here," he told her, glancing around. In his arms, the child trembled but didn't speak.

Maria reached up to pat her daughter's dark head. "Save Tina," she pleaded. When Erik hesitated, her voice rose urgently. "Go! I beg of you. I'll follow, I promise."

An Uzi began spitting bullets near the house. Tina trembled again and buried her small face in his shoulder. The assault team must be inside the walls, but Erik knew that didn't guarantee their safety.

"You'll have to catch up to us, or Bernadetti will kill you," Erik said harshly. He could see no one in the shadows of the numerous trees and ornamental shrubs, but he could hear the fighting all around them. The spacious compound echoed with shouts and gunfire. A man screamed as a bullet undoubtedly found its target.

Shifting the toddler to his other arm, Erik tried again to help Maria to her feet. "Come on," he urged. "You can make it if you lean on me."

Her body crumpled when she put weight on the injured ankle. "Take Tina and go," she implored him tearfully. "I'll follow you. I will."

Erik hesitated, sweat running into his eyes. If he left her, she might not make it. If he delayed, they might all three die. "Are you sure?" he demanded, wondering what had gone wrong with his plan. Perhaps Maria had confided in one of the servants, even though he had warned her to trust no one.

"Yes, I'm sure. Now, go!" she repeated. The tears that had been swimming in her dark eyes streamed down her face. "Take my baby to safety."

Regret and admiration filled Erik. "I will," he promised, shoving his spare pistol into Maria's hand. He half dragged her to a stand of tall shrubs. There was nothing else he could do for her now.

More gunfire exploded around them. Maria shrank into the darkness as a voice that was too near called out in

Spanish. Tina whimpered, and Erik shushed her. He had no choice but to try to get to the wall. He had hidden supplies there earlier.

Cautiously, hugging the shadows, he began to make his way toward the perimeter. At one point, he saw a guard and doubled back. Tina clung to him as he muttered reassurances under his breath. The frailty of her small body dismayed him.

Abruptly, another escape route was cut off. *We're not going to get out of here,* Erik thought for a fleeting moment. His arms tightened around Tina, and his resolve hardened. They had to make it.

He zigzagged through the elaborate pattern of plantings, but the guards surrounded him. Where were his fellow agents?

Erik heard Bernadetti's voice and caught a glimpse of the man he had been stalking for months, an American drug dealer waiting for the heat back home to die down. Bernadetti's hair was black, his dressing gown the same dark red as Maria's blouse. The color of blood.

As Erik hid, praying that Tina would remain quiet, the drug lord disappeared behind a large clump of bushes with razor-sharp leaves. Erik swung around to see another guard with a gun headed his way. The man hadn't spotted Erik yet. Pistol ready, he turned back toward where he had last seen Bernadetti.

A hunched figure left the shadows, outlined against the glare of the floodlights. Erik saw a flash of red and a gun pointed at his own heart.

Instinct took over as he fired at the dark silhouette. As his finger squeezed the trigger, the figure shifted, face catching the light.

Shock twisted Erik's gut. He uttered a low cry. His arm tightened on Tina, pressing her tiny face into his shirt. She struggled in protest.

As he watched in agony, it was Maria who staggered before him, Maria whose frightened expression turned to puzzlement and then Maria whose body fell heavily to the ground, eyes still wide and staring.

"No!" Erik cried, horrified. His gun hand dropped to his side.

Frightened, Tina began to cry.

Bernadetti appeared in the path and looked down at Maria's still form. He bellowed in rage and leveled his gun at Erik.

"I'm going to kill you, pig!" he shouted.

Frozen, Erik stared into Bernadetti's hate-filled eyes.

"No!" he shouted again, trying to shield the child in his arms, as the sound of one more gunshot filled his mind.

The burst of pain didn't come. Instead, a hand touched Erik's arm. Through the whirling blackness, a welcome voice called his name. He tossed his head, still lost in the coils of the familiar nightmare. His heart was racing; his breathing forced.

"It's okay, everything's okay," the gentle voice chanted. Gradually Erik became aware of the scent of perfume he had come to know so well. He struggled to consciousness, as he realized that he no longer held little Tina in his arms. Instead, it was Marybeth who cradled him in hers, shushing him softly as she stroked his cheek.

"Don't be afraid," she murmured. "You're here with me."

"Tina," he croaked.

"She's safe, too, in her own bed."

Erik blinked and shuddered, fighting for control. He rubbed his eyes with the heels of his hands. Gradually his pulse rate slowed as he peered up at Marybeth in the darkness.

"How did you get here?" he asked.

"We're in your room. It was only a nightmare," she soothed. "A bad dream."

Still upset, Erik rose from the bed and went to the window. He saw his own barn, his own pasture beyond the glass.

After a moment, he heard the sheets rustle behind him. Marybeth came to the window, slipping an arm around his naked waist.

"Have you had the dream before?" she asked.

"It was no dream," he muttered, voice raw. He had thought the nightmarish memory finally vanquished. Perhaps Tina's earlier disappearance had triggered its recurrence.

Marybeth turned to him, stroking his chest with her free hand. "Want to talk about it?"

Erik looked down at her as a primal hunger filled him. "Maybe later," he growled, jerking her into his arms. Her warmth pulsated through him. "Right now I need to banish the face of death, and I need you to help me forget."

Marybeth wanted Erik to need her, but she wasn't sure that the frantic, almost obsessive way he had gripped her as they made love, thrusting into her as if that final, sweet explosion would exorcize his nightmares, was exactly what she'd had in mind. Afterward while she held him and they both came down from the euphoric heights he always took her to, he lost himself in sleep. Unwilling to disturb him, Marybeth was left with a dozen unanswered questions.

When she woke later, he was gone. The pillow that still bore his imprint had grown cold.

She showered and dressed quickly, then went to find both Erik and a much-needed cup of coffee. Hearing voices from the kitchen, she headed in that direction.

"Hi," she said, feeling slightly self-conscious in front of his daughter.

"Hi!" Tina responded. "Daddy said you slept over."

Marybeth glanced at Erik for guidance. As he handed her a steaming mug, his expression revealed nothing of what he might be thinking or feeling.

"Yes, I did," she stammered. "It was late when we got done talking."

"Too late to let her drive home alone," Erik said blandly, sipping his coffee.

"What did you wear to sleep in?" Tina asked, face alive with curiosity.

Marybeth's wits scattered like dry leaves in the wind.

"I lent her one of my T-shirts," Erik drawled.

"Daddy's T-shirts make good nightgowns," Tina agreed, apparently satisfied with his answer.

"Yes," Marybeth agreed, face burning.

"Sit down. I'll cook you some breakfast," Erik said. He turned toward the stove while she wondered what he was thinking.

"Oh, no thanks. Cereal and coffee would be just fine." She wanted to question him about the nightmare but couldn't very well do that in front of Tina.

"Where's Mrs. O'Reilly?" the little girl asked as Erik let Joker in the back door.

"She'll be here pretty soon. I told her not to come so early, since she stayed late last night." He tried to look stern. "She's taking you to Katy's to swim today, remember. I should probably make you stay home after that stunt you pulled, but I won't this time."

Tina beamed. "Thank you, Daddy," she said, rushing over to hug him.

"Finish your breakfast." He handed Marybeth a box of cereal and a bowl. The milk and spoons were on the table.

"Are your mommy and daddy still alive?" Tina asked her abruptly as she sat back down.

The question surprised Marybeth, who was glad Tina had apparently abandoned her interest in the night before. "Yes," she replied. "They live in Seattle, in the house where I grew up. Why do you ask?"

Tina studied her intently. "So if Daddy married you," she mused, "I'd get grandparents, too."

Marybeth tried not to choke on her coffee as her gaze met Erik's over his daughter's head. To her dismay, he was frowning darkly.

"What made you think of that?" he demanded.

"Sara's grandparents were at her birthday party," Tina explained. "She has four of them, two grandmas and two grampas. And I don't have any grandparents at all. I thought, while you're getting me a mother, you could—"

Erik straightened from his casual slouch against the counter. His cheeks were dusky red beneath their tan. "That damned party again!" he snapped, surprising both Marybeth and Tina with his vehemence. Then he made a noticeable effort to regain control.

"You'd better get your swimsuit and a towel," he reminded Tina in a calmer tone. "Mrs. O'Reilly will be here soon to take you to Katy's house."

And the reason for Marybeth's presence would be more than obvious.

Clearly forgetting all about stocking her family tree with Marybeth's relatives, Tina rushed from the room. "Okay, Daddy," she shouted as she ran down the hall.

Erik came over to where Marybeth sat drinking her coffee and dropped a kiss on her forehead. "How are you?" he asked tenderly, the frown from moments before completely gone.

"I'm fine," she managed warily, "but how are *you?* Any more bad dreams last night?"

His expression closed and his lips compressed as he shook his head. He was clearly unwilling to discuss the incident. Before Marybeth could say anything else, a knock sounded on the back door. At Erik's hasty invitation, Mrs. O'Reilly bustled in, including both of them in her cheery greeting, which helped reduce Marybeth's feelings of awkwardness.

"How's Tina this morning?" she asked.

"No worse for her adventure," Erik told her. "I wish grown-ups rebounded as quickly as kids seem to do."

"Isn't that the truth?" the housekeeper agreed. "We're left stewing while they go on to the next adventure."

"Not right away, I hope." Erik's voice was dry. "I don't know if I'm up to it."

Chuckling at Erik's comment, Mrs. O'Reilly excused herself to get his daughter. After a few minutes, the two of them left. Was it her imagination, Marybeth wondered, or had Erik hugged the little girl with unusual fervor before he let her go?

As the sound of the departing car faded, he poured more coffee for Marybeth and then himself. "When do you have to work today?" he asked, joining her at the kitchen table. "I can't seem to keep track of your schedule."

"I don't have to be there till three. I'm filling in for vacations again." She had offered to work second shift for a week while another nurse went on her honeymoon, but she didn't tell Erik that. Instead, she debated how to bring up the subject of the nightmare.

Across from her, he fidgeted restlessly and glanced at the wall clock. Marybeth's cheeks grew warm at his obvious hints, but then the stubborn side of her nature grabbed hold. She was reasonably sure that Erik's rudeness stemmed only from his mulish reluctance to discuss anything more personal than his taste in movies or food. Well, for once she wasn't going to be sidetracked by her attraction to him and oblige.

"We have to talk," she said baldly, ignoring his sneaky glances at his watch. "I think now, while Tina and Mrs. O'Reilly are away, would be a good time for you to tell me what really happened last night."

Erik managed to look incredulous. "Don't you ever have dreams?" he demanded. "They're so vivid at the time that you think they're real and then, by morning, you can hardly remember them."

His evasive maneuvers didn't surprise Marybeth, but she was disappointed all the same. Despite the closeness they shared in bed, he was still unwilling to trust her enough to be honest about himself. To talk about whatever it was that put the shadows in his eyes.

"Are you telling me that you *don't* remember the dream?" she asked.

Erik's gaze dropped away. Perhaps he drew the line at telling her a deliberate lie. Feint and parry seemed to be more his style.

Her annoyance and determination rose in equal shares. After a moment's hesitation, she took a sip of her rapidly cooling coffee and let the silence stretch between them. Erik rubbed a hand down the side of his cheek and rose from the table. He jammed his hands into the back pockets of his jeans and studied the scene from the window over the sink. After a few minutes, she began to wonder if he'd forgotten her presence.

"I remember all of the dreams," he said finally, voice resigned. He turned away from the counter. The pain in his face made Marybeth want to cry.

"I lived the dream, and I've been reliving it for four years. Lately I thought it had finally stopped." He made a vague gesture with his hand. "I guess I was wrong."

Marybeth settled into her chair, but inside she was trembling. "Something happened when you were in Argentina," she guessed. "Before you brought Tina back with you."

He neither confirmed nor denied her comment.

"I'm a good listener," she offered, breaking the strained silence. "And I'm pretty unshockable."

Erik straddled the chair across from her, knuckles white against its back as he studied her with his vivid blue eyes. Apparently he came to a decision. "What do you want to know?"

At the last second, Marybeth's courage failed her. "Whatever you want to tell me," she said. Perhaps she was unconsciously afraid of the secrets she suspected he was keeping from her. What if he had done something so terrible she couldn't accept it? Something illegal or morally wrong? He certainly acted like a man whose conscience sometimes tore him apart, even though she couldn't believe him capable of doing anything really awful.

"I've already told you part of it," Erik began as she struggled with herself. "Tina's mother was the mistress of the guy I was there to get out, an American in hiding. A real sweetheart. He was one of the biggest drug dealers on the East Coast, responsible for the destruction of a hell of a lot of lives. And I'd seen him abuse Maria and Tina, too."

"Tina must have been only a baby," Marybeth exclaimed, shocked.

"She was two. A little angel. I knew that I should stay away from both of them. I couldn't break my cover. Bernadetti seemed to trust me, or maybe it was just his twisted sense of humor that made him assign me to watch Maria when she took Tina for walks." Erik drew in a deep breath. "Once Maria had a black eye. She often had bruises. So did Tina. I wanted to kill him."

"I can understand that," Marybeth said. A man like Erik would abhor violence against anyone who was weaker or smaller.

"I'd been feeding information to my agency," Erik continued. "They got tired of waiting for Bernadetti to come back to the States, so they decided to help him along a little." His glance was wry. "The agency doesn't always follow the rules too close, either." When Marybeth remained silent, he shrugged. "I wanted to get Tina and her mother out of there before the shooting started."

Marybeth nodded her agreement. She could understand how he must have felt, wanting to help and needing to preserve his cover. Torn between what he wanted to do and what he had to do.

"Something went wrong. Maria was late meeting me that night." Erik stopped talking and, for a moment, his attention seemed to wander. His mouth became a grim line, his face haunted.

"By the time she came out with Tina, my men were all over the place. So were Bernadetti's guards." He swallowed, his expression shadowed with pain. "Maria was killed," he said in an emotionless voice. "Shot to death in the fighting."

Marybeth gasped, her hand flying to her mouth. "How awful."

"Yeah." His gaze held hers. "I didn't know for a long time about Tina's father. He'd been shot, too, but I got her out of there without knowing if he'd been killed. Afterward they couldn't find his body. I only heard recently that he didn't die then.''

"Is he looking for you? For Tina?" Marybeth asked, afraid for him.

Erik shook his head. "He was killed in a recent drug bust. I just heard the other day."

"How did you ever get Tina back here?" she puzzled. "It must have been difficult. Did you have papers?" Had the agency he worked for arranged it? What of Tina's other family?

Erik's smile was humorless. "I got her out of Argentina with the worst false papers I've ever seen," he admitted. "And a lot of bribes. You don't want to know how I got her into the States. Once I was here and the agency realized I wasn't about to hand her over to some government pawn, they arranged the adoption. I owe them for that."

He stopped and took a long drink from his coffee mug. "Maybe they thought I'd go back to work for them."

"And did you?"

His brow quirked. "Not yet."

That gave her something to think about. She had assumed he was out of that life for good. A little of what she was thinking must have shown on her face.

"No," he said with a crooked grin. "I'm not going back. I blew my cover too well for that."

"I'm glad," she said defiantly.

His grin widened, then faded completely. "The rest you know."

Marybeth couldn't help but wonder if he was holding something back. Otherwise, why would his act of heroism in saving Tina return to haunt him so? Why was he so secretive if the adoption was really legal as he claimed it was?

How much weight did this mysterious agency have, anyway? There was a lot she would have liked to ask.

"Didn't Maria have any relatives in Argentina who would have taken Tina?" she asked finally, when it was clear no more information was forthcoming. At least not voluntarily.

Erik shook his head. "They all knew what Bernadetti was, and they hated him. Maria had shamed her family by going to him, but she was dazzled by his charm and the gifts he lavished on her. Once she'd had Tina, he only had to threaten to keep the child if Maria left. She was a virtual prisoner when I arrived."

Marybeth shook her head in horror. Again she wondered what preyed on Erik in the form of the disrupting nightmares. What wasn't he telling her?

"Is there more?" she asked.

He hesitated. "Nothing worth mentioning."

Marybeth closed her eyes. In her mind, she could hear her husband's voice speaking the same words, over and over. Anything he hadn't wanted to tell her was "nothing worth mentioning." It was not too farfetched, she supposed, that Erik would choose the same unremarkable phrase. Still, the coincidence made her shiver, as if with a sudden, icy chill.

While she was thinking, he rose from the table. "I've got work to do," he said. "Want to come with me and see how a real ranch is run?" Grinning, he held out his hand.

Marybeth, who had expected him to excuse himself, promptly banished her unhappy thoughts for another time and linked her fingers with his.

"There's one thing I didn't tell you," Erik said abruptly. He had been watching her stroke one of the calves while it tried to lick her face with its long pink tongue. Seeing her take such pleasure in the ranch and its animals gave him a feeling of contentment. Now he was probably going to destroy the fragile peace that had been growing between the two of them, but he found himself eager for her understanding and approval.

"What's that?" As soon as she glanced away from the calf, it lowered its black head and butted her, sending her sprawling in the long grass. Marybeth shrieked, and Erik shoved the animal roughly aside, momentarily panicked by her cry of surprise.

"Are you okay?" His voice was brusque, throat knotted.

With his help, she got up and brushed herself off. "I'm fine. That'll teach me to be so trusting."

Her words shook him.

He tried to dust off her rounded derriere but she laughed and pushed his hand away. Then she hooked her arm through his as they began walking back to the truck. The calf followed for a few steps and then, distracted, started to pull on a tuft of grass.

"What didn't you tell me?" Marybeth prompted when he remained silent.

Erik braced one booted foot on the front bumper and studied the face that had grown so precious to him in the weeks since the bank robbery. He wondered if he was doing the right thing. Then, with a sigh, he decided to risk it. What could she do besides disagree?

Would she go to the authorities and report him? She'd never do that to Tina, no matter how she felt about what he was doing. He liked to think she wouldn't want to hurt *him*, either. Surely she would understand that he could take the risk of exposing Tina to possible danger.

"Tina has grandparents here in the States." He studied the toe of his scuffed boot intently, waiting for Marybeth's reaction to his bald announcement.

"You mean Bernadetti's parents?" she asked after a moment.

"Yeah. One of the guys at the agency, the same one who told me about Bernadetti's untimely demise, said that his parents have heard rumors of a child. They've been making inquiries."

"You mean the agency knows who they are? Where to find them?" she asked, frowning.

He searched her face. "*I* know. So what?"

"Why haven't you gotten in touch with them?" she demanded, eyes flashing more green than hazel. "They must have been going through hell all this time, wondering."

He shrugged, reaching down to pluck a long stalk of grass and stick it between his lips. He'd rather be kissing her sweet, soft mouth than talking. "Their son was a gangster. Doesn't that bother you?"

She shook her head as if to clear it. "Oh," she said. "I didn't think. Are they in the drug business, too?"

For a moment he was tempted. A little white lie would extricate him from the situation he'd managed to get himself into. Why had he thought she would ever understand the motives behind his secrecy? Defensive now, he plunged ahead.

"No, they don't seem to have any connection to Bernadetti's seamier side. Moody says they appear to be decent folks."

"Moody?" Her brows rose.

Erik flushed darkly. He was really getting sloppy around her. "Forget you heard that name," he cautioned her.

She nodded. "Okay. So, what are you going to do now? Are you going to tell Tina?"

He nibbled on the blade of grass. "No."

Marybeth turned away, the furrows in her brow deepening. "You're waiting until she's older? That might not be the best way." Then her expression cleared. "Oh, of course. You probably want to meet them yourself first. To make sure it will all work out before you raise her expectations. So she won't be disappointed." Marybeth's expression was hopeful, as if she were willing him to agree.

"No." Erik hated to disappoint her. All of a sudden, he realized what else she could do, besides turning him in, if she didn't agree with his decision. She could stop seeing him. If she didn't like what he was doing, she could just remove herself from the situation. From his life. A shiver of something close to fear sliced through him. What a hell of a time to realize that he didn't want to lose her.

Damn!

"You aren't going to contact them at all?" she asked.

He shook his head, blanking his expression. Doing his best to blank the feelings clamoring inside him—with little success.

"You aren't going to tell Tina about them, either?"

He sighed, shaking his head again. "No."

"But you can't play God like that," she said after a moment of obvious pondering. "If she has *family,* you have to check them out. You can't just pretend they don't exist because it suits you."

He turned, watching her out of the corner of his eye. "That's where you're wrong. When it comes to Tina, I can do whatever I damn well please. Whatever I think is best for her. That's what I've always done." Since he'd watched her mother die and known he was responsible. "I earned the right. Believe me," he muttered. "I earned it."

Marybeth's frown bristled with disapproval.

"I have to do what's best," he added stubbornly.

"To do what's best!" she echoed. "That's what Mike always used to say to end an argument. That he knew *best*. It's—it's arrogant! How could either of you be so sure of that?" She waved her arms in a gesture of frustration. "Don't you think you have an obligation to check out those people? To not cut them off from Tina but to unite them with her? They might be the only family she has."

"You're dead wrong," he said, tossing down the grass stalk he'd been absently chewing. "*I'm* the only family Tina needs. My duty is to protect her from anything, anyone that might hurt her." He wrapped one hand around Marybeth's upper arm and hauled her closer. "She's never going to hear about Bernadetti's parents," he said grimly, frustrated that he couldn't make her see his side of it. "Not from me, and not from you. I want your word."

Marybeth looked from where he gripped her arm to his harsh face. "You've got it," she said finally when he didn't budge. "But you are undoubtedly the most selfish, insecure man I've ever met. And you are wrong!"

Chapter Eleven

Disgusted by his weakness, Erik ground out the cigarette he'd been smoking with little pleasure and rose from the kitchen table to toss the rest of the pack into the garbage. The pressure of coming to the right decision in a matter that could truly affect the rest of his and Tina's lives still wasn't reason enough to renew a bad habit he'd finally kicked several years before.

He opened a window to air out the kitchen and returned to the straight-backed chair, staring without interest at the half-empty cup of cold coffee at his elbow. There was no help for it. He'd been over the situation more times than he cared to remember in the last several hours since Tina had gone to bed, and he always arrived at the same conclusion.

He couldn't step into the future until he settled the past. Despite the gut-wrenching guilt that welled within him, he

knew the issue was both that simple, and that complicated.

The questions that had haunted him since he'd first
learned of the existence of Tina's grandparents rose in his
mind again. Would they try to obtain custody if they knew
about her? If they did, what were the chances of them
succeeding? The senior Bernadettis were, after all, her only
blood relatives besides a family in Argentina who had
turned their backs on her mother years before. Erik had no
claims other than those of his heart and a definitely shaky
adoption decree, whose validity he held in serious doubt.

He reached absently into his shirt pocket for another
cigarette, cursed at the speedy return of a craving he'd
thought he had licked, and rocked the protesting chair
onto its two back legs. If Mrs. O'Reilly had been there she
would have *tsk-tsked* under her breath. She probably
would have given him her opinion of the wisdom of contacting Tina's grandparents, too, if he'd been inclined to
solicit it. He wasn't.

After Marybeth's opinion, he definitely wasn't into
garnering others. If he had it to do again, he might not be
so quick to seek hers, either. Must be his roiling hormones that had temporarily affected his judgment. Her
reaction had only served to muddy a decision he'd thought
was final.

In his den, the grandfather clock he'd assembled himself the winter before chimed once. Erik rose to dump the
ashtray and his cup. He put them into the dishwasher,
turned out the kitchen light, and moved quietly down the
hall. Beyond her partially open door, Tina slept soundly.
Joker raised his head when Erik looked in.

"Good boy." Like it always did at the sound of a
friendly voice, the stub of a tail wagged several times.

Erik hesitated in the doorway of the master bedroom. Ever since Marybeth had shared it with him, the room— and the bed—seemed unbearably empty without her. He shut the door behind him and stripped off his clothes, missing her with a physical ache. He knew he wouldn't sleep in his present condition and headed for the adjoining shower.

The cold water did little to banish her image from his tired brain. After he dried off, he flipped aside the covers and settled onto the bed. He turned automatically toward the other side before he could remind himself that, as usual, he was alone.

He thought about calling but then remembered that Marybeth was back on day shift and was undoubtedly asleep now. Resigned to his own company, he stretched out on the cool sheets with his hands behind his head and began to make plans.

"I thought you said you weren't going back." Marybeth cradled the phone against her shoulder and glanced around warily. There was no one else near the nurses' station. She felt like an actress in a suspense movie, talking about agencies, contacts and secret missions.

"I owe them." Erik's voice sounded tired, as if he hadn't slept. "I should only be gone a few days, but I just wanted you to know, in case you might have worried."

"I would have. Thanks for letting me know." She wanted to ask him if this sudden trip had anything to do with Tina's grandparents, but she already knew his decision on that. Better not to bring it up again and chance an argument before he left.

"Well, I guess I'd better let you go back to work."

She could sense his impatience, his eagerness to get on with his new assignment. Was that what he missed, the adrenaline rush a secret mission gave him?

"Is it going to be dangerous?" she burst out, unable to keep the concern from her voice. Would he ever trust her completely?

"Dangerous?" His echo conveyed surprise at her question. Then his voice softened, became almost tender. "No, not in the way you mean."

Her arms ached to hold him again before he left. Impossible.

If his reply was meant to placate her, it only did the opposite. "Then in *what* way?" she asked.

He sighed, voice flat. "I can't tell you."

"You haven't told me anything, only that you're going somewhere you can't reveal for an uncertain length of time to do something you can't divulge." She didn't try to hide her frustration. Maybe it was time to admit defeat. First Mike, and now Erik. What was wrong with her?

His soft chuckle affected her like a trail of damp kisses, banishing thoughts of Mike and making her senses leap. "I'm sorry that you're frustrated," he told her. Then his voice deepened to a masculine growl. "Well, actually that's not true. I'd love to leave you so frustrated that you'd be waiting for me with open arms when I got back."

"I might be waiting in your bed if I knew when you were getting back," she murmured without thinking, senses alerted by the unleashed desire she could hear in his voice.

His groan pleased her immensely. "I knew that calling you was a mistake. Now I'll have to take another cold shower before I leave."

"Serves you right." She tried to match his lighter tone. "When's your flight?"

"Not till the middle of the afternoon, but with the drive to Sea-Tac and the early check-in, I'd better get moving."

"Yeah," she agreed, hating to let him go. Not even knowing if he was leaving the States made her miss him even more.

"Trust me," he coaxed, as if he could read her thoughts. "It'll be okay."

"Why can't *you* trust *me?*" she demanded.

"I do." For a moment his voice was achingly sincere. "More than you know. More than I've trusted anyone in longer than I can remember."

There was a pause Marybeth didn't even try to fill. "When I get home, we'll talk," he added, fueling her curiosity.

She didn't know what to say, didn't know what she was going to do if he went back to the agency. It represented the kind of secrecy she could no longer accept. Didn't he know how he was tearing her apart?

"Yes," she agreed, almost regretfully. "We'll talk."

"I wish I could kiss you goodbye," he confessed, the longing in his voice weakening her knees. His voice was husky with promise.

"Then kiss me hello instead," she suggested, blinking away the sudden stinging moisture.

"I will, sweetheart. I'll call you as soon as I get in."

After he hung up, she clung to the receiver, warmed by his term of endearment. She hated to break that last tentative link, but then someone signaled her, and she had no choice. She wondered if he'd meant he was going to call when his plane landed at Sea-Tac or when he got back to Coupeville, a drive of at least ninety minutes from the airport—longer by the time he collected his bags and walked to the parking garage. Either way, she had no choice but to wait.

And she would hate every minute.

From his table in the corner of the New Orleans coffee shop, Erik watched the elderly couple as they came in. The man, tall and spare, had an unsettling resemblance to his drug-dealing son. While Erik watched, he bent his gray head to speak quietly to the short, plump woman at his side. She took his hand, and Erik could tell that she gripped it tightly.

He watched as they looked around the coffee shop, knowing they couldn't recognize him. The way he had set up the meeting, he would find them. For the length of an indrawn breath, he toyed with the idea of getting up and leaving, as anonymously as he had come.

He wondered what they were thinking as they waited for a voice from the telephone to identify himself. He had told them only that he had information about a possible grandchild and wanted a meeting.

Now Erik rose. The man glanced up, his expression painfully eager. Again, Erik was tempted to walk on by. Instead, he forced himself to stop before the couple. Close up, there was a frailness about them he hadn't noticed before.

The woman put a trembling hand to her mouth. The man waited, tension in every line of his face. For the first time, Erik wondered at their feelings for their son. Had they hated him? Loved him? Forgiven him in the end?

He broke the silence. "Mr. and Mrs. Bernadetti?"

The man seemed to slump. The woman gasped.

"Yes, that's us," he said quickly. "And you're...?"

Erik wanted to give them no clues if his instincts warned him off. "You can call me Rick." His hand went out automatically.

Bernadetti gave him a look before taking it. There was pride in that glance, and pain. Erik wondered if they thought he had been an associate of their son's.

"Let's sit down," he suggested, then turned to lead them back to his table. The three of them remained silent until the waitress brought more coffee.

"Please tell us what you know," the woman pleaded. "We've searched for so long."

"You have to understand that we've been waiting for news, and hoping, without much to go on but rumors," the husband said firmly. "It's been—difficult. Especially for Betty. Robert was our only child." His gaze flickered away, then back as he raised his chin. "We've asked ourselves many times what we could have done differently, what we didn't do that we should have." He shook his head, and for a moment his shoulders drooped before he straightened them resolutely. "I'm sure you don't really want to hear this."

"Yes, I do." Erik wanted to understand all he could about what kind of people they were before he entrusted them with the knowledge of Tina's existence. "Please."

"Robert was always a handful," Betty volunteered, glancing at her husband. "Maybe I was too easy on him when he was little, but we both adored him."

"Go on," Erik urged, searching for some explanation. How could people as ordinary as these two seemed, raise a monster like Bernadetti? He needed answers.

The old man cleared his throat and then took a sip of his coffee. "He began getting into scrapes when he was a teenager. We begged, we threatened. Nothing seemed to reach him." He took another swallow of coffee.

"He was the only child we could have," his wife added softly.

Erik imagined this was terribly painful, admitting their failures to a stranger. "When did he get involved with drugs?"

The old people exchanged another glance, communicating silently.

"Robert got involved with drugs in jail." The man's voice wavered. He swallowed, steadying it. "He served some time for robbing a convenience store. After he got out, we didn't see him much."

"It's not that we didn't try," Betty interjected. "We wanted him to feel welcome, but he just never came around. Then, about ten years ago, he disappeared completely. We knew, long before, that he was in pretty deep."

"The money, the people he kept around him," the old man continued, shrugging. "You didn't need a guidebook to see. Still, we tried to stay in touch, to let him know that if he ever wanted to—" He paused briefly. Again, the silent exchange of glances. "Wanted to change, we'd stand behind him."

"When did you hear about, uh, his death?" Erik asked, feeling awkward. These people had loved the man he'd known as an international drug lord, the man he'd hunted and tried to bring down. He knew that with certainty. Just as he knew they probably had no more hand in their son's descent into crime than any other loving, overindulgent parents who couldn't say no.

Erik wondered briefly what it would have been like to grow up with an abundance of parental love.

The man spoke again. "We got a call. The man said Robert had wanted us to be told if anything happened to him. He didn't leave his name." Tears misted his faded eyes. He took a moment to blink them away. "The man also intimated that Robert left a child. When we tried to find out, no one could tell us anything for sure."

Erik's own eyes narrowed as he looked for signs, something to guide him. Were these people sincere or too good to be true? He had expected to find them cold, ruthless individuals like their son. Now he wasn't sure.

"Please," the woman said. "Tell us what you know about our grandchild."

Acting on the instincts that had usually served him well in numerous life-or-death situations, Erik came to a quick decision. He'd already called Moody to make sure that Tina's adoption, despite its shaky origins, was ironclad legal before he contacted her grandparents. Now he took out his wallet, extracting the pictures he'd brought, just in case. Sliding them across the table, he said, "Her name is Tina, and she's six years old."

"Those are mussels, and that's a hermit crab. He has his house on his back." Tina looked up from the tide pool she and Marybeth were squatted over. "What's that little fish called?"

"I'm not sure. Maybe we can find him in the book I have back at the house." Marybeth had brought Tina home with her for the afternoon. After a lunch of hot dogs barbecued on the hibachi, fresh fruit and cookies, they'd come to the beach to look for shells. The two of them had chatted about whatever popped into Tina's lively mind. The more Marybeth got to know the little girl, the more she liked her. If things didn't work out with Erik, there would be two good-sized dents in Marybeth's heart.

"I wish my daddy would come home," Tina said, straightening. "I miss him."

Marybeth drew her into a hug. "Me, too, pumpkin. He's only been gone since the day before yesterday, though. It's probably too soon to expect him back yet."

She had hoped that he might call, but he hadn't. She refused to ask Tina if he'd called *her*.

It was hell, not even knowing where he was or if he was safe. He'd said this trip wasn't dangerous, "not in the way she meant," but that had only made her worry more.

"What do you want to do now?" Marybeth asked.

"Go back to your house and have an ice-cream cone."

Marybeth chuckled and held out her hand. "Sounds like an excellent idea." She whistled for the dogs.

The phone started to ring as they were coming up the front steps. "I'd better get that," she said. "It might be the hospital."

Tina followed her into the house as she picked up the receiver. "Hello?"

"I understand that my two favorite ladies are spending the afternoon together."

"Erik!" How close he sounded. "Where are you?"

"Is Daddy home?" Tina asked.

"I'm still at the airport. My flight just landed, and I couldn't wait to call." His voice was deep, filled with something Marybeth wasn't quite willing to analyze.

She nodded to Tina, who was waiting expectantly. "How soon will you be home?" Marybeth asked.

"As fast as I can get there," Erik replied. "Why don't you call Mrs. O'Reilly and tell her you're keeping Tina with you? When I get there, we can go eat and then take her home together."

Marybeth was too busy dealing with the emotions pouring through her to answer immediately. Happiness and relief warred with desire, curiosity and a reluctance to let her concerns go completely.

"Well, do you have to work?" he asked impatiently.

"No. We can't wait to see you." She would deal with her reservations when she had to.

* * *

"Daddy, Daddy!" At the sound of Erik's truck in the driveway, Tina ran out the front door.

Marybeth followed at an only slightly more sedate pace. Her heart was beating fast, and her mouth had gone dry. She felt as if a great hollow place inside her was about to be filled, but she wasn't sure how warm a greeting Erik would expect in front of his daughter.

Her question was answered when he got out of the truck, scooped Tina up with one arm and wrapped the other around Marybeth, pulling her close. She snuggled into his body heat, inhaling his scent.

"God, I missed you two!" His voice was fervent, eyes dark with emotion. First he gave Tina a smacking kiss, then buried his face in her neck, making loud snorting noises until she giggled and pushed him away.

"Silly Daddy," she scolded, kissing his cheek.

Erik's eyes met Marybeth's over Tina's head. "Come here." His arm drew her closer. His gaze flashed to her mouth as his head dipped.

The kiss he gave her was neither as short as she expected nor as long as she needed. When his mouth left hers, he mouthed the word "later" and gave her a smile that sent a shaft of pure longing spearing through her. His arm tightened briefly and then she was free.

His big hands gripped Tina's waist as he lifted her high and then set her down gently. "Have you been good?" he asked.

Tina's happy laugh rang out like bells. "Of course I have! Marybeth and I had fun." She took a quick breath. "We saw all kinds of creatures in the tide pools, and we had hot dogs for lunch, and I played with the dogs."

Erik looked at Marybeth. "Sounds like a full day. I bet she sleeps well tonight," he drawled.

At his blatant inference, she felt the color race up her cheeks. "You must be tired, too, after your trip," she said sweetly. "Was it a long flight?"

He grinned. "Not bad."

"Going to have an early night?" she persisted.

"Lord, I hope so." His tone was so sincere that her blush deepened. "You're still coming home with us, aren't you?"

Wanting to assert herself a little after he'd been so mysterious, she hesitated.

Immediately his hand snaked around her wrist. "I missed you," he rasped, pulling her hard against his length. "I can't wait to show you how much."

Marybeth's gaze darted to Tina, who was watching them, wide-eyed. "I missed you, too," she said quickly. "Everything else will have to wait."

His blue eyes searched hers. "But not for long. I need you with me tonight."

Marybeth was reasonably sure he'd forgotten all about his daughter, who continued to stare with open fascination.

"Are you sleeping over again?" she asked, before Marybeth could form a reminder to him.

Startled, Erik dropped Marybeth's wrist. She turned toward the house. "How about something cold to drink?" she asked, unable to face either of them. Without waiting for replies, she hurried up the steps and pushed open the screen.

Let Erik deal with his daughter's awkward questions.

"Wait here," she heard him say, seconds before he followed her inside.

She turned, intending to admit that nothing could prevent her from going home with him. Before she could utter a word, he yanked her into his arms. His possessive gaze burned into hers.

"You'd better be sleeping over," he growled. "It's the only thing to prevent my going completely crazy." Without giving her time to answer, he swooped, taking her mouth in a punishing, completely captivating kiss.

Even when one of the dogs began barking he didn't let her go. Instead, his lips raced over hers, drawing a response that made him groan deep in his throat. When her lips parted, his tongue plunged inside, reclaiming the territory he'd made his before, melting Marybeth against him like sealing wax on a love letter. Her hands, braced against his chest, went limp. She slid them around his neck to bury her fingers in his short blond hair. Her body, ablaze with longing, pressed closer to his, and she savored the unmistakable proof of his passion.

Again he groaned, raising his mouth to change angles, moving his hands down her body in long, possessive strokes. Marybeth's fingers slipped inside his collar, touching the tight muscles of his neck and shoulders. She freed another button on his shirt as the next wave of response crashed over her, spinning her senses.

Erik cupped her buttocks, lifting her against the throbbing ache that clamored for her soft, moist warmth. Desire drove him relentlessly as he did his best to restrain his overriding passion.

"Daddy! How long do I have to wait out here?" Tina's voice brought him sharply back to the present, to parental responsibility and adult control. Freezing, he sucked in a tortured breath, as Marybeth stepped hastily back and smoothed her blouse.

Erik released a string of frustrated curses. "Sorry," he muttered finally, hardly believing that he had lost control so thoroughly that he had all but forgotten his daughter's presence.

Marybeth glanced away, cheeks fiery red. "It's okay."

"Could I have that cold drink now?" he asked, unable to assess her mood.

When she looked back at him, her eyes brimmed with laughter. "Do you want it in a glass or over your head?"

He laughed, too, relieved at her reaction. "Whichever will cool me down the quickest." His body still signaled its frustration by ignoring his attempts at control.

As Marybeth went to the kitchen, still chuckling, Erik headed for the door to get Tina. Maybe the promise of a special dessert after dinner would distract her.

By the time Mrs. O'Reilly left, and Tina had been settled into bed with two stories, Erik needed Marybeth with an impatience that bordered on the unbearable. The way she looked at him when he came back into the living room, he guessed she must feel the same way. His desire for her became even stronger.

She held up the television guide. "There's a good movie on," she said, "or a program about Eskimo artifacts that I'd hate to miss."

Erik never slowed his steps, reaching for her when he got close enough and tossing her over his shoulder like a bale of hay.

"I'm sorry to be the one to tell you this," he muttered over her muffled shriek, "but your chances of seeing either show are about zero." With one arm across her legs and the other hand planted firmly on her derriere, he crossed the room, intent only on gaining his bedroom before he threw her down and ravaged her.

"We could tape one of them on the VCR," she suggested as her nimble fingers hiked up the back of his shirt and began to explore the curve of his spine.

Erik nudged open the door to his room with one elbow, stepped inside and booted it gently shut. Not until he was next to the bed did he release her, and even then it was only to let her down from his shoulder before he turned and fell to the bed on his back. He still held her tight against him.

"One problem," he gasped as he felt her softness pressing into him. "How're you going to get out there to program it?" Rolling to his side, he began freeing the buttons down the front of her blouse.

"You won't let me go?" she asked.

His voice rang with promise. "Never."

Neither one of them spoke again except to murmur softly of desire or pleasure until much later, when they lay locked in each other's arms beneath the top sheet.

"So," Marybeth found herself asking, as she tried her best to distract him by trailing her hands over his bare chest. "Tell me about your trip."

The minute she felt him stiffen beneath her touch, she wished she could recall the words. At least then she might have kept pretending that he meant to enlighten her.

"Nothing to tell," he said, bending his head to press his lips against her forehead. He moved them down her cheek but, when he reached her mouth, she turned away. All she could hear was the echo of Mike's words, back again to taunt her. Regret burned through her like acid as she sat up in the bed.

"What's wrong?" Erik asked as he pulled himself up beside her.

She could feel his eyes on her, boring into her, demanding she look at him. Instead, she reached for her clothes where they'd been dropped beside the bed.

"You know what's wrong." She choked, turning away to dress. Disappointment filled her with a bitter ache.

Erik's hands pressed into her shoulders as he urged her back against him. She resisted and he finally released her.

"I told you I couldn't say anything about the trip." His tone was annoyed.

She turned to confront him, keeping her voice low as she remembered the child asleep in the other room. "Not even where you went? What the weather was like? If your mission was a success?" She heard the angry tone of her own voice and realized she had come too far to turn back.

He hesitated, and she knew he was stalling while he searched for some insignificant, *safe* detail he could throw her as a sop to her temper.

"Don't bother," she blazed through gritted teeth. "Wouldn't want to endanger national security, would we?"

His face flushed in the dim light. "It's not like that," he insisted. "If you'd just give me a little more time—"

"Time!" she echoed, incredulous. "I've given you time, and patience and trust. And what have you given me? Half-truths, evasions, awkward silence when I ask too many questions." Now that she'd started, her bitterness spilled over.

"I made that mistake once," she said. "I gave my husband so much time, he managed to get himself killed in a dangerous situation I wasn't even aware existed. Can you imagine how I felt? Waiting for him, blissful in my ignorance while he was out there risking his *life!*" She stopped long enough to take in a breath, to zip and snap her jeans and then smooth down her hair. "If you want a secret life, that's just *fine* with me," she continued. "Just don't expect me to be *in* it! I won't do that to myself again. I ca-an't!"

She spoiled the effect she'd been striving for, that of icy control, when her voice cracked on the last word. Furious with herself and with him, she jammed her feet into her shoes and fled.

Erik, at a definite disadvantage since he was completely naked beneath the sheet, grabbed his jeans and rushed after her, one eye on Tina's door. It remained partially closed. At least they hadn't awakened her. He paused to pull on one leg of his jeans, cursing when he almost fell. Then he heard the kitchen door open. He swore under his breath, still too close to his daughter's room to risk raising his voice. As he stepped into the other leg and pulled his jeans up, the door shut with a firm click. Fumbling with the zipper, not even bothering with the snap, he hurried after Marybeth.

He yanked open the door in time to see her climb into her car and cursed his earlier agreement that she drive it over. When he was halfway across the gravel parking area, hopping from one bare foot to the other and cursing steadily, she left him in, literally, a cloud of dust.

"Dammit!" he shouted after her, digging his keys out of a tight pocket. He limped over to his truck and was about to climb in when he stopped, chest heaving. He couldn't leave Tina alone.

Besides, what was the use? Maybe Marybeth would be more rational after she cooled off. Meanwhile, he had other things to take care of. Perhaps when she found out what it was that he had planned to do, she would forgive him his secrecy.

Chapter Twelve

"Would you please just be here at seven?" Erik asked again into the receiver. He was probably lucky that Mary-beth had even consented to speak with him on the phone, after the way they'd parted.

"Why should I trust you?" Her voice was belligerent, but he hoped it was just to cover up the hurt. After tonight, maybe they could get their relationship back on track. God, how badly he wanted that!

"Trust me because you care about me," he told her, gambling that what he said was still true. "And because I care about you. I promise that after tonight a lot of things will be made clear. Please say that you'll come."

"All right," she said grudgingly, "but, so help me, if this is just a trick, I'm outta there."

"That's your right," he responded, pleased. "But I don't think you'll want to leave, once you've gotten a look at my surprise."

"We'll see about that," she muttered. If she was curious, she kept it to herself. "For now, I have to get back to work."

After repeating the time once more, Erik said goodbye and let her go. He still had a lot to do.

He wished he could have shared his news with her. He was immensely relieved that the Bernadettis didn't want to fight him for custody of Tina. They had reassured him that they felt they were too old to raise a child. He believed them. They only wanted to meet their granddaughter, to share her life in some small way, and to know that she was happy. They still thought that Erik had adopted her through the usual channels. All he had been able to tell them about seeing her before he left New Orleans was that he would think about it and let them know what he decided.

And he had.

He'd made the painful decision alone, after a lot of thought. He had wanted to spare Marybeth any part of the responsibility, which rested, as it should, squarely upon his own shoulders. It was better to keep her out of it until the past was resolved. Then perhaps he could come to her free from the problems that had kept him their prisoner. If everything worked out the way he wanted, that might be very soon.

Erik glanced at his watch and went off to find Mrs. O'Reilly. It was almost time for him to leave.

"I think Daddy's planning a surprise," Tina confided in Marybeth as they waited together in the living room. A Disney movie played on the VCR. "It isn't my birthday. Is it yours?"

"No, not for several months." Marybeth, who'd been surprised to see that Erik's truck was gone when she arrived at the ranch promptly at seven, regarded his little girl absently. Where was he? And what on earth was going on?

"I guess we won't know what he's up to until he gets home and tells us," she murmured. "When did Mrs. O'Reilly say he left?"

"Around three-thirty." The housekeeper poked her head in from the kitchen, where she'd been busy since Marybeth got there. "And, no, he didn't tell me where he was going or when he'd be back. Just asked me to make up the guest room and stay with Tina. And to please make sure you didn't leave." When Marybeth didn't say anything, she went back to the kitchen.

After their argument, Marybeth was a little surprised that Erik had even called. Of course, just hearing his voice on the phone had been enough to sabotage all her resolutions to stay away from him, but she was still determined to break things off if he didn't open up, as devastated as that would leave her. All that remained was to find the willpower to carry through with what she was certain would be the best thing for both of them in the long run. Even if it did leave her heart in ruins.

From where he lay quietly at Tina's feet, Joker pricked up his ears. Then he rushed to the kitchen and started to bark.

"He's back," the housekeeper announced.

Pushing away her bleak thoughts, Marybeth followed Joker and glanced out the window. She saw Erik's truck coming down the long gravel driveway. He wasn't alone.

"Daddy's here!" Tina cried as she ran outside to wait. Joker went after her and, after hesitating for a moment, so did Marybeth. Even Mrs. O'Reilly came outside to stand on the back porch and watch him pull up.

A premonition shivered over Marybeth with the touch of icy fingers as Erik got out, waved, and then helped an older couple climb down from the cab. She might have thought they were his parents, but he had told her his mother had died years before. Without being quite sure why, she gave Tina's shoulder a reassuring pat. Then the little girl broke away and ran to Erik. He scooped her up, said something to the people with him and came toward the house.

"Hi," he greeted Marybeth with a dazzling smile. "I'm glad you're here." He kissed her cheek and his familiar scent reassured her. It swamped for a moment the impending sense of disaster she felt closing in like the heavy air before a storm. Erik spoke to his housekeeper and then turned back to the elderly couple. "Let's all go inside, shall we?"

They seated themselves around the living room, with Tina and Marybeth perched on the couch and Erik's guests on the love seat. Marybeth studied them curiously while Mrs. O'Reilly took up a position in the kitchen doorway. After a moment, Erik motioned for Tina to stand beside him. He cleared his throat.

Marybeth was surprised and more than a little alarmed to see that, beneath his cheerful facade, Erik was nervous. She had seen him in many moods, but he had always been self-assured. Her inexplicable sense of doom increased.

"Well," he said, smoothing his hands down the sides of his dark blue dress slacks as if to wipe away the tension that seemed to grip him, "I'd like you all to meet Tina's grandparents, Mr. and Mrs. Bernadetti—Salvatore and Betty—from New Orleans."

His announcement was met with total silence. After a sidelong glance at Marybeth, Erik bent to look at his daughter. She stood frozen beside him, white-faced with shock.

"Who?" she asked, pulling away when Erik would have taken her hand.

Marybeth was tempted to echo Tina's question. Had she heard him right?

He squatted down so that he was on a level with Tina's anxious face, while the people he'd just introduced with such a dramatic flare smiled somewhat hesitantly. Marybeth noticed that the old man was gripping the woman's hand tightly.

"These are your grandparents, sweetheart," Erik repeated. "They're the mother and father of your real daddy, and they came all the way from Louisiana to meet you. I just went and picked them up at the airport. Now, how about giving them both a kiss?"

To his obvious consternation and Marybeth's sudden ache of sympathy, Tina snatched her hands behind her back and retreated even farther. Her dark eyes were wide with shock.

"No!" she shouted, bursting into tears. "It's not true! They're not my grandparents! They're not!" With that startling announcement still ringing through the room, she whirled and ran down the hall. The slamming of her bedroom door was like a shot in the silence of the living room. After he gave Erik a look of reproach that was startlingly human, Joker rose and followed her.

"Erik, how could you?" Marybeth burst out, stunned by his total lack of sensitivity. "Didn't you tell her what you were planning? Didn't you prepare her for this at all?"

Erik's face was almost comic in its consternation. He clearly had no clue as to what he'd done wrong. When he didn't reply, Marybeth threw up her hands, exasperated, and went to see if she could somehow comfort Tina.

"Oh, my Lord," she heard the elderly woman exclaim. Her face had paled at Tina's rejection of her and the man beside her. "How could you land us on that poor mite without any warning? No wonder the precious child's upset!"

Without waiting to hear more, Marybeth knocked on Tina's closed door. The only sound from inside was a muffled sob. Joker whined and cocked his head, brown eyes intent.

"She's okay," Marybeth told him.

Back in the living room, Erik was trying to salvage a situation that had slipped totally from his control. "I thought a surprise would be nice," he explained defensively to the couple who was staring with unsmiling faces. "I didn't want her to worry about anything before you got here."

Sal Bernadetti shook his head sadly. "I'm sure you meant well," he said, "but the sudden appearance of grandparents she never knew existed is too much of a shock to be sprung like this. Who knows what's going through her head?"

Beside him, his wife nodded her agreement. "No wonder she bolted. Her reaction shouldn't come as any surprise, under the circumstances." Her expression was mildly accusing.

"Are you trying to tell me that you know Tina better than I do?" Erik demanded hotly. He was still smarting from the way his great surprise had turned to a big disaster. Even Marybeth had seemed less than pleased.

When she came back into the living room, Erik raked a hand through his hair. She almost felt sorry for him. "Tina doesn't want to come out," she announced. "Under the circumstances, I didn't want to push her."

"No, dear, of course not," said Mrs. Bernadetti, getting to her feet. "Let her be for now."

Across the room, Erik searched Marybeth's face as if he were looking for an ally. "I can't believe this," he thundered, when her expression remained serious. "*You* told me how wrong I was to keep them from her. *You,*" he addressed the two of them, "told me how much you wanted to meet her, to get to know your only grandchild. And when I do what you all wanted me to do, everyone—not to mention my unpredictable daughter, who said she wanted grandparents—jumps all over me! How am I supposed to know what I did wrong?"

Erik's expression was such a confused mixture of justified annoyance and wounded good intentions that, had the subject been a less serious one, Marybeth would have giggled. Under the circumstances, though, she'd never felt less like laughing. This proved her darkest doubts.

"If you don't know, I probably can't explain it," she said quietly. "It wasn't what you've done, it's how you went about it. You didn't discuss your change of heart with me, you didn't see fit to tell me what you decided. You made the decision alone and you carried it out—alone—without telling anyone, springing it as a totally done deal." She dragged in a breath. "Did it ever occur to you to let me in on your plans? To even ask my opinion? No! Not Mr. I-can-do-it-myself-and-I-don't-need-anyone-Snow."

When Marybeth finished, there was another awkward silence. With what she hoped was a dignified air, she crossed to where the Bernadettis were standing, holding hands tightly as the indignation on their faces was replaced with bewilderment. No doubt they were wondering why she was raving like a wild woman.

"Nice to meet you," she said to them both, conscious of the glaring inadequacy of the trite phrase as she extended her hand. "I wish it could have been under different circumstances, and I hope your visit doesn't turn out to be a total disappointment."

They returned her handshake, their expressions still confused.

"Tina's a wonderful child," she felt compelled to add. "And Erik, despite what you've witnessed today, is really a terrific father." She allowed her gaze to fall on him with chilly disapproval. It was the only way she could possibly disguise the heartbreak that was threatening to make a total fool out of her.

"I'm leaving," she told him bluntly. "For Tina's sake, I hope you can straighten this mess out. And I hope you learn something from it, even though I sincerely doubt it." She wanted to say more but couldn't force the words past the lump forming in her throat. She hadn't wanted it to end like this!

Some volatile emotion blazed in Erik's blue eyes, but before he could speak, she whirled and left, afraid to linger lest the tears threatening to overfill her eyes and run down her cheeks humiliated her entirely.

At least he had no idea how much she'd come to care about him. That would have been the final humiliation in the face of his total lack of sensitivity.

"Goodbye, dear," Mrs. Bernadetti called after her.

"Wait a damned minute," Erik hollered, following his demand with a curse that must have shocked the Bernadettis.

Marybeth kept going, determined to reach the safety of her car and then the solitude of her own home before the extent of the evening's events hit her. She was sure making a habit of these hasty escapes.

As she started the car and backed it around, a sense of déjà vu came over her. In her rearview mirror, Erik was standing on the porch, hands shoved into his pockets while he watched her with a furious expression on his face. At least he wasn't hopping across the gravel in his bare feet.

Apparently her loss wasn't worth the effort that running after her would take.

Still shell-shocked by the staggering events of the past few minutes, Erik watched her go, then stomped back inside. He let the door slam behind him as he did his best to ignore the pain beneath his anger. During the fireworks, he noticed, Mrs. O'Reilly must have retreated to the kitchen. If the Bernadettis had had anywhere to go, they probably would have deserted him as well. Instead they remained where he'd left them.

"If you want to go after your friend," Betty said, "we'll be okay."

Her words surprised him. "Uh, no. That's okay," he mumbled. "She probably needs some time to cool off."

"Probably wise," Sal agreed, giving him a sympathetic look. Maybe he understood a little of what Erik felt. After all, he'd made mistakes, too. His son was proof of that.

"Well, we've got two days to undo the harm you've done with Tina," Betty said crisply.

Erik's brows rose. What had happened to the meek, grandmotherly old woman he'd thought so sweet and gentle?

"Now, Mother," said her husband, patting her arm, "I'm sure that when our granddaughter has a chance to properly digest the information, she'll be happy about us."

"I'm sure she will," Erik agreed. Actually he was no longer sure of anything. Maybe it was just females, of all ages, that he didn't understand.

Mrs. Bernadetti surprised him further by rising and coming to give his hand a reassuring squeeze. "We know you meant well, dear, but you went about it as wrong as anyone I've ever seen. Lord knows, you've no reason to trust us after knowing our son, but don't you even trust that poor woman who so obviously loves you?''

Erik's mouth opened and closed, but his mind went blank. If Marybeth had ever felt any love for him, she probably didn't anymore. Was that why she was so furious with him? Because she thought he didn't trust her? He had only meant to spare her. How would she have felt if he'd brought the Bernadettis out here on her recommendation and then lost Tina to them?

A small, insistent voice told him he could still lose Tina if the Bernadettis thought he wasn't doing a good job raising their granddaughter.

He regarded them warily.

As if he could read Erik's thoughts, Sal Bernadetti smiled encouragingly. "Don't be discouraged. If it was meant to be, it will all work out for the best."

Grimly Erik sat down, not at all sure he wanted to leave his future happiness to fate. Meanwhile, he needed to at least try to explain why he had done what he had.

Before he could begin, Mrs. O'Reilly came sailing into the room carrying a large tray. "I figured you'd need some refreshments," she said in a hearty tone. "I've got coffee, tea, and blackberry pie. Tina and I picked the berries and froze them last fall."

"Thanks for coming," Marybeth told Sandy over hospital cafeteria sweet rolls and barely passable coffee.

"You know I only come here for the food." Sandy's smile curved briefly before she took a drink of orange juice. "Besides, I happen to think Erik Snow's a hunk, and when you told me on the phone that you thought the two of you were through—"

"I don't think it, I know it," Marybeth interjected. She swallowed some coffee and grimaced. "There's a lot more to Erik than his looks," she added defensively. "You remember the problems I had with Mike? I couldn't live with that kind of relationship again."

"Ah, yes," Sandy murmured, not without sympathy. "Mike kept a whole chunk of his life apart from you. Wouldn't talk about it. You feel guilty because you let him get away with that, and you think if you'd known what he was involved in, that you could have somehow saved him."

Sandy's words were a shock to Marybeth. Her friend had never said anything so mean before.

"That's not true," she denied hotly. Two people at a nearby table glanced at her. She leaned forward, lowering her voice. "I would have been better prepared if I had known, that's all."

"And where's the danger in Erik's work?" Sandy demanded. "The man raises cattle. I know it's not completely free from risk, but what is?"

Marybeth sat back and closed her eyes. "You don't understand," she muttered, rubbing her temples. "Erik keeps things bottled up inside, important things. He doesn't *trust* me enough to—"

"Is this about Erik's flaws or your own?" Sandy asked suddenly, gaze intent.

Marybeth gaped at the other woman. In the time they'd become friends, she had shared things she'd never told anyone, not even her husband. She suspected that Sandy had been as candid with her.

"What are you getting at?" she asked tightly. If she had known that Sandy was going to turn on her, she would never have asked her to come by.

Sandy shrugged. "You've probably told me things you haven't told Erik." She tore off a piece of her gooey sweet roll and popped it into her mouth, then licked her finger.

"Of course I have," Marybeth admitted.

"Why haven't you told him?" Sandy demanded, tearing off another bite of roll. "Don't you trust him?"

"It's not that!" Why was Sandy doing this? "I just haven't known him as long as I've known you. I haven't had the time—"

"Precisely." Sandy chewed and swallowed the bite of roll. "Maybe that's just what Erik needs." She took another sip of juice. "And maybe you need to cool your jets for a little while. Let him work through this grandparent thing."

Annoyed, Marybeth pulled her own sweet roll into bits, but didn't eat any. "I've given him time," she said shortly. "You don't understand."

Unmindful of the crowd around them, Sandy grabbed her hand where it lay on the Formica tabletop. "But that's just it, sweetie, I do understand." Her voice was earnest, almost pleading. "You've told me yourself how I pick a relationship apart and then convince myself it's not working, just to avoid intimacy."

"You *were* listening," Marybeth commented dryly, failing to hold back a slight grin. She'd lectured her friend more than once about finding flaws in the men she dated, just to give herself an excuse to break things off before they could get serious.

"Of course I was listening. I know I do it, but that doesn't mean I can stop." Sandy sounded grumpy. "Now, we're talking about you, not me."

Marybeth allowed her friend to guide the conversation back to its original topic. "You think all Erik needs is more time?"

Sandy hesitated. "Now, that I don't know," she finally admitted. "All I'm saying is, don't judge him by the problems you had with Mike. He's a different guy."

Marybeth glanced at her watch and shoved a couple of the smaller pieces of her sweet roll into her mouth. "I've gotta go to work." She took a big swallow of coffee, then wished she hadn't.

"Oh, Lord," Sandy exclaimed. "I'm going to be late." She shoved back her chair and drained her juice.

"Thanks for listening," Marybeth told her. Maybe, just maybe, some of what Sandy had said made sense. She didn't have time to analyze it now.

"Why thank me?" Sandy's grin was cheeky. "All I did was tell you stuff you didn't want to hear."

Marybeth smiled as she scooped up both their trays. "Yeah, but at least you cared enough to say it."

Sandy shrugged. "I'll do a lot for a free breakfast. Let me know how things are going." With a careless wave, she turned and hurried away. Several male heads watched her progress. Dumping the trays, Marybeth muttered a protest at the clock on the wall and raced for the elevator.

While Marybeth had been meeting with her friend in the hospital cafeteria, Erik was busy trying to mediate a casual breakfast conversation between his daughter and her new grandparents. The evening before, he had allowed Tina to stay in her room, to give her the night to sleep on the startling news. Perhaps he had handled things badly, but he'd had no idea she would get so upset.

This morning, Erik gave Mrs. O'Reilly the day off, just so the four of them would have some privacy. Tina, who had been reluctant to come out of her room, finally appeared.

"Hi, sweetheart," Erik told her. "How are you this morning?"

She looked at the older couple and said nothing, ducking her head as she slid into her chair at the kitchen table.

For the first time in years, Erik felt out of his depth with her. He'd had to learn parenting by trial and error, but nothing had prepared him for this.

"Are you okay?" he asked her.

She looked up and nodded. Her gaze darted to her grandparents, and then she began fumbling with her napkin.

"Tina?" Erik tried again.

"Excuse me," Sal interrupted. "Maybe I should plead my own case."

Frustrated, Erik took his coffee and retreated to the counter to look out the window. He'd gotten little sleep the night before, partly because he'd been thinking about Tina and trying to decide how best to proceed with the can of worms he'd opened, but also partly because of Marybeth. Her hasty departure had carried with it an air of finality that left a cold, empty hole somewhere near his heart. His instincts had to be wrong; she couldn't be giving up on him now. How could he go on without her?

With a guilty start, Erik swung his attention back to the conversation taking place at the kitchen table. Then, while he listened, he began to grill the French toast he'd prepared.

"You'd like New Orleans," Mr. Bernadetti told Tina with a calm smile. "There are riverboats and beautiful old plantation houses with white columns in front, and we have a wonderful aquarium."

"We have an aquarium in Seattle," Tina said with exaggerated boredom. "Daddy takes me there all the time."

Erik thought he saw the corner of Sal's mouth twitch. "Our aquarium has white alligators," he informed her.

Tina's eyes widened. "Pure white?" she asked.

"With green eyes," he added, straight-faced, as he turned his attention to his coffee.

"We have baby seals," Tina volunteered after a minute. "Don't we, Daddy?"

Erik nodded, fascinated with Sal's progress. "That's right. They aren't white, but they're gray and have spots and big black eyes."

"That sounds exciting," Betty interjected. "Maybe we'll have time to go to your aquarium before we leave for home. I bet they have a lot of neat things we don't have in Louisiana."

Tina's timid smile crumpled. "Daddy," she cried on a panicky note, "am I going to go live with them?"

In a blinding flash of revelation, Erik began to understand her initial reaction to Sal and Betty's sudden appearance. He crossed to the table and pulled her into his arms.

"No, baby," he said, rocking her gently. "Grandma and Grampa Bernadetti wanted to meet you and to see where you live. But they aren't taking you home with them."

"That's right," Sal agreed, when Tina turned a wary face to him. "You're our only grandchild. We'd like to get to know you, but your place is here with your—" his voice faltered for just a moment "—with your dad."

Erik felt her thin body heave with relief. "Oh," she said in a small voice.

As if he understood her need to assimilate what she'd just found out, Sal turned the conversation to Erik's beef cattle and the ranch's operation. While they finished breakfast, they talked about that and about Whidbey Island.

"I'm done," Tina announced during a break in the conversation. "Can I be excused?"

"Sure," Erik said. "Put your dishes into the dishwasher, okay?"

"Okay." She did what she was told, then stopped by her grandma's chair. "If Daddy's taking you for a ride today, could I go, too?" she asked, glancing at Sal, too, as she spoke.

Erik watched while the two elderly people exchanged significant glances. He released the breath he'd been holding.

"We'd like that," Betty said, her voice only slightly shaky. "I think it will be fun."

Erik smiled at her over Tina's head. He had a feeling that everything was going to work out after all. How he wished he could say the same thing about his relationship with Marybeth.

The day went better than Erik had dared hope. The four of them explored the island thoroughly, including the park at abandoned Fort Casey on the outward coast and Deception Pass bridge at the island's northern tip. The view from the span that linked the island with the mainland was Erik's favorite spot in all that he had seen of Washington State. The jagged coastline and rocky beaches far below, divided by swirling green and blue water, the surrounding evergreens clinging tenaciously to the barren cliffs, never failed to awaken a sense of appreciation inside him.

While they all stood on the high bridge, the Bernadettis agreed that the spot was breathtaking. They had brought their camera and took lots of pictures, especially of Tina, who posed willingly.

After a picnic lunch on the beach, followed by a quick tour of the malls near Burlington on the mainland and dinner at a popular seafood restaurant, they drove back down the island toward home. Before they had gotten far, Tina crawled into her grandma's lap and was soon fast asleep.

"I can't tell you what this visit means," she told Erik while Tina slept.

His eyes met hers in the rearview mirror. "I think I understand," he said quietly. Beside him, Sal smiled.

When they got home, Tina woke up, but she was clearly exhausted.

"I'll help you get ready for bed, sweetie," Erik said. "I think you can take your bath in the morning."

"I had a nice time," she told her grandparents. Erik could see that she was beginning to like them, now that the threat of going away had been banished.

"We did, too," her grampa told her. "Sleep well."

"I'm glad we came to visit," Betty added. "Do you think I could tell you a bedtime story?"

Tina glanced at Erik, her expression concerned. "Would you be upset if Grandma tucked me in?" she asked.

Relieved, he shook his head. "Not at all. Give me a kiss, okay?"

She reached up and he lifted her high. When they had exchanged good-nights, she kissed her new grandfather's cheek and took her grandma's hand. Joker followed them down the hall.

Accompanied by the fading sound of her chatter, Erik and Sal exchanged glances.

"It was a good day," Sal said. "I think she's adjusting remarkably well."

"Me, too. I'm just sorry I got things started off so badly," Erik responded. He was glad his poor management hadn't cast a pall on the visit.

The older man waved a dismissive hand. "Not to worry."

Erik glanced at his watch. "Would you and Betty be okay for a little while? There's something I need to take care of."

"Something to do with a certain attractive woman we met last night?" Sal guessed.

Erik nodded. "As you know, we didn't part on the best of terms. I hate to leave things festering."

"Go ahead. If it's all right, we'll make some coffee and watch a little television. I imagine Mother will want to turn in early. Got a lot to see tomorrow before our plane leaves."

"Sure, make yourselves comfortable. And thanks," Erik told him. They were going to Seattle to sightsee on their way to the airport the next day. He almost wished Tina's grandparents could stay longer, but he hadn't known how things would go when he had first invited them. Next time, perhaps.

As he drove to Marybeth's, he wondered what kind of reception he was going to get. She'd been extremely angry when she had left the night before. Perhaps she'd had time to calm down.

By the time he was standing on her front porch, Erik had convinced himself that they would talk, and then everything would be fine. He could hear the dogs barking. Optimistic, he rang the bell.

Marybeth pulled open the front door, and a frown marred her face. "What are you doing here?" Her tone was edged with frost.

Erik's hope that things weren't as bad as he remembered went up like a puff of smoke.

Chapter Thirteen

"We need to talk." Erik pushed by Marybeth without giving her the chance to say no. As always, her appearance in snug jeans and clinging knit top made him want to take her in his arms. Instead, he paused to extend a hand to Annabelle, who stood in the living room, wagging her tail. When Erik scratched behind her ears, her tongue lolled and her brown eyes squeezed shut.

He wished he could get half as enthusiastic a reaction from Marybeth.

"Fine watchdog you are," she grumbled at the dog while she shut the front door. She didn't invite Erik to sit down, so he stood his ground, arms folded across his chest, and watched her carefully for clues. Maybe she wasn't as angry as she had first appeared.

And maybe someday world peace would be a reality.

"We have nothing to say to each other," she told him. There was a hint of sadness in her gray-green eyes, but her mouth was compressed into a grim line. "I wish you'd go."

"Not until we've cleared up a few things." Erik would have liked to kiss her in an attempt to melt some of that icy aloofness. Instead he let the hands that wanted to reach out fall to his sides.

Where to begin?

Marybeth glanced pointedly at her watch. "I have things to do. Perhaps some other time—"

"No." Erik knew that, despite a long history of facing the most dangerous situations with nary an outward qualm, his courage might fail him if he had to postpone this confrontation. How uncomplicated his life had been when he was responsible only for himself, a fortune in espionage equipment, national security and a few other lives.

He cleared his throat.

"You might be interested to know that Tina and her grandparents have been getting along very well, considering their less than ideal first meeting," he began. "So I guess I owe you an apology. You were right about not keeping them apart." If he'd expected the admission to warm her up, he was in for a disappointment. If anything, her frown deepened.

"I don't mind admitting when I'm wrong," he added.

Marybeth's expression was unreadable. "I hate to say 'I told you so,' but perhaps you'll remember all this in the future, the next time you're tempted to clam up around people who care about you."

Erik had been about to ask if they *had* a future. Instead, he exclaimed, "Clam up! I've told you more about myself and my background than anyone else I've ever met. How many people do you think actually know I was a special agent?"

Her accusation incensed him, turning his despair to fury. He'd tried to be open with her, but it wasn't easy to undo the habits of the past thirty-odd years. "This is getting us nowhere." Erik reached out to her, but she ducked away while he struggled to control his impatience.

"I'm glad to hear that Tina's visit with her grandparents has been a success," she said. Her voice was calm enough, but her color was high. "How long are they staying?"

Erik hadn't come here to talk about other people! "They're leaving tomorrow after we show them around Seattle. Why don't you come with us?"

The invitation clearly surprised her. Hell, it surprised him. He hadn't planned to ask, but it wasn't a bad idea. "I'd like you to get to know them," he added, doing his best to be persuasive.

Marybeth watched him through narrowed eyes. "Sorry, but I have to work. Tell them goodbye for me, though."

She didn't look very sorry.

"I'll tell them." He hesitated, unsure what to say next. If there was only some way to get over the wall she'd erected between them. This kind of indecisiveness was new to Erik, but he wasn't sure what she wanted to hear.

Marybeth shifted impatiently. "Was that everything?" Her chin was up, her voice aloof.

Erik could see that he was getting nowhere. Despair came back, as chilling as a Northwest fog. "No, it's *not* everything." What he wanted was to haul her into his arms and show her that she couldn't resist him. "What about us?" he demanded instead.

"What *about* us?" she echoed.

How he wished he could tell what she was feeling! "I don't want to lose you. I want things back the way they were before." Was that open enough for her?

Apparently not. He hadn't gotten the words out before she began shaking her head. "No, not back the way they were."

"What's wrong with that?" he asked. They'd been good together. More than good. His senses began to hum with remembrance. "What we had, uh, have, is special. It's not always that way, you know."

She turned away. "But you still don't trust me, not really," she said in a small voice.

"How can you say that?" he burst out, stung by her accusation. What did she expect? If she really knew him, knew the things he was capable of, she might run the other way. He couldn't risk that.

"It's easy to say. I still don't know very much about you. Oh, sure, you told me a little bit about your father. I understand why those memories are painful. But there are great gaps you're reluctant to fill." She gripped his hand. His fingers curled around hers. "There's a shadow inside you. I can see it in your eyes. Until you confront it, we just won't work."

Her words made Erik go cold. How did she know?

Her hand tightened on his and she began speaking again. "I want to know everything about you. Why you are the way you are. The bad and the good. And I want to share myself with you. No reservations."

He thought of Tina's mother and the way she had died. How would Marybeth react to that? How could he ever risk telling her? He pulled his hand from hers and stuffed it into his hip pocket.

"You don't know what you're asking."

Her gaze compelled him. "Yes, I do know. I told you about Mike, how he never talked about his work. I thought he needed his privacy, so I never asked. Maybe he didn't think I was interested—maybe he really didn't want to bring it home with him." She clasped her hands together in a gesture of entreaty. "I'll never know." Her eyes darkened with remembered pain, making Erik long to comfort her. "I went through hell, and part of it was that his death was so unexpected. Sure, he was a cop. Sure, I knew there was danger. But I didn't know about this particular situation. I didn't know about a threat that could take him away from me at any moment."

Erik wasn't sure what to say. Before he could think of anything, she took a deep breath. "Don't you see? There was a part of Mike I never knew. A part I'll never know now. I can't go through that again with someone else I—"

She stopped abruptly. Erik wondered what she had been about to say. Someone else she loved? If she loved him, why didn't she stop trying to end things between them? He didn't see how all this related to him, anyway.

"*I'm* not in danger," he argued. "Not anymore. I'm not undercover, I'm just a local rancher, with a child." He debated a moment, then decided to tell her. "When I left the agency, they gave me a new identity."

Marybeth looked stunned.

"That's right," he continued. "So my old enemies couldn't look me up and exact a little revenge for deeds past. My last concern was Tina's father, and now I'm sure he's dead. His parents are no threat. I know that now."

"That's another thing," Marybeth interrupted. "Contacting them was something that could have changed your life, endangered everything. You never even *thought* to tell me. You're too used to operating alone, in a vacuum. Erik Snow, superagent."

Her voice was bitter.

"Actually, that's not quite true. Erik Snow wasn't my name when I was an agent," he felt compelled to point out.

She made a sound of utter frustration. "I don't care. That's not what I meant."

He shrugged, confused. "I'm trying to change, but it's not easy. It takes time."

Her face was sad. "We're out of time."

What was he supposed to say to that?

She turned away again, shoulders drooping. "I really wish you'd just go and leave me alone. You have company. Perhaps you'd better get back to them."

"They can manage," Erik said, tone grim. He couldn't admit defeat yet. He *couldn't* lose her. "How's this for sharing my feelings?" he asked, circling to stand in front of her. Tension knotted his stomach. If this last, desperate attempt didn't work, he had nothing left to try.

He tipped back her head with one finger, so his gaze bored into hers. "I love you," he said, and he felt as if he were stripped naked, standing there. "I realize now that I've been falling in love with you for weeks. Can't you give us another chance?"

Surely his declaration would soften her, buy him some time.

To his surprise, she twisted away. "Love!" she exclaimed bitterly. "I love you, too."

For a moment, elation filled him; he reached out. When she held up her hands and backed away, Erik felt his heart crack.

"That's precisely why I can't risk being hurt again." Tears spilled from her eyes and she dashed them away impatiently. "You even kept *that* to yourself. I had no clue as to whether your emotions were involved or not."

He shook his head in denial, trying his damnedest not to panic. "Surely you suspected. I've never—"

"No, of course I didn't suspect! How could I know if you cared, or if I just turned you on? You keep everything bottled up inside.'' She thumped her chest with her fist. ''I suppose that's thanks to your father, too.''

Erik opened his mouth to refute what she'd said, then let it close again. What could he say to convince her? Nothing came to mind. If a declaration of love, something he'd never given any other woman, didn't move her, he was at a dead loss. Maybe the best thing to do would be to retreat and regroup. Surely there was something he could do to sway her. He just had to think about it.

He tried to school his features so they revealed nothing of his inner turmoil. ''I guess I've wasted enough of your time for one day,'' he told her. ''But don't think for one damned minute that I'm giving up.'' Submitting to the urge that had been plaguing him since he'd first walked through her doorway, he reached out and hauled her into his arms. Surprise lit her eyes. With a burst of some primitive male satisfaction he knew he should probably be ashamed of, he held her tighter.

She began to struggle but he ignored her feeble protest. He'd taken enough. If words didn't convey how he felt, he'd damn well show her. Wrapping the fingers of one hand around her chin, he tilted her head back. But even as the heat rushed to his face, he had the sense to say, ''I've never forced a woman. And I'd never hurt you. So don't be afraid. After I kiss you, if you want me to stop, I will.''

Marybeth was afraid, all right. Afraid she couldn't hold out against him.

With deliberate determination, Erik covered her mouth with his. He could feel her body braced against him. Her lips remained still. He gentled his, calling on every skill he knew, pouring his heart into the kiss. He'd give her something to remember him by! Sleep on this, he thought, as passion and need raced through him.

With an effort that had him shaking, he rubbed his lips ever so lightly across hers. When she didn't respond, he did it again. Then he traced his tongue along the firm line of her mouth, back and forth. He thought he felt a shiver run through her. He stroked her again.

She moaned, tried to pull away. He held her fast. Her eyes were screwed shut. When he tipped his head back and waited, they fluttered open. She saw him watching her, and closed them tight.

He bent to her mouth again. With the tip of his tongue, he teased the corners. He heard a soft moan. She shivered again. He nibbled, he rubbed her mouth with his, he trailed his lips to her ear and back. At last, when he was about to give up, he felt her soften just a little bit.

Hope flared through him. He kissed her eyelids, traced her brows with his tongue, snuffled her cheek with his nose. Her body trembled, melted, flowed against him. He let his tongue coax her lips apart.

He heard another groan when she yielded. This one came from him. He wanted to sing, to laugh. To weep with relief.

He wanted—no, needed—to love her.

She reached for him.

"Are you sure?" he asked. If she said no, he would turn away somehow. Even if it killed him, which it might.

"Yes." The word, whispered, sounded like a burst of music to his ears. His intentions to hold back went up, not in smoke, but in a burst of flame so hot it left him smoldering.

Marybeth's hands slipped around him, clutching him close. He thrust his tongue into the dark delights of her mouth. She gasped, curled hers to it. He held her even closer, knowing that she could feel the passion roaring through him. Dimly he was aware of the small sounds of response she made. Her hands slid higher to stroke the short hair at his nape. Her softness cradled him; her curves cushioned and warmed and drew him. Her mouth robbed him of reason.

Vaguely he realized that the lesson he'd meant to teach her had been turned on him with a vengeance.

When he lowered her to the carpet, she didn't protest. She exulted. Settling beside her, he pulled off her shirt. Her eyes, narrowed to slits, watched him, her expression inscrutable. For once, Erik didn't care what she was thinking; he only cared what she felt. He ached to be buried inside her, made welcome by the fit that seemed custom-designed just for him.

Bending his head, he kissed the creamy skin he'd exposed. She moaned and tossed her head. Freeing the catch of her bra, he closed his lips over first one tightly beaded nipple and then the other, as she dragged her fingers through his hair. When he let his tongue curl around one straining bud and then pulled hard with his lips, her fingers tightened and her back arched.

"I want to feel you, too," she gasped.

Erik released her just long enough to rock back onto his heels and undo the buttons of his shirt. When he leaned over her again, her hands flowed toward him. Her nails scraped his chest lightly, drawing a moan of reaction from him when she found his flat nipples.

Driven now, as if by demons, he directed his attention to the snap and zip of her jeans. As she began to shimmy out of them and her panties, he freed himself from the rest of his clothes and stretched full length beside her on the carpet, barely noticing the hardness of the floor beneath them. He skimmed one hand over her breast and down her side, but when he got to the thatch of hair below her stomach, she tossed her head back and forth.

"No," she protested. "No more teasing. I want you now, all of you."

Erik needed no further urging to merge himself with her. He shifted. Beneath him, she opened her legs and imprisoned his hips. When she did, he thrust into her, burying himself to the hilt in an attempt to leave her stamped by his undeniable possession.

She gasped and thrust upward. The world around them dissolved into a red haze as Erik drove hard, desperately. The start of her tiny convulsions rocketed him into a climax more powerful than anything he had ever known. She sobbed out his name. His own hoarse cry was still resounding in his ears when both his breathing and his heart beat began to return to something close to normal.

He let his hold on her gentle and, before he was nearly ready, she started to push at him. He moved to the side and she sat up. Ducking her head, she reached for her clothes.

"Damn you," she muttered fiercely.

"What are you doing?" he asked, a foolish question under the circumstances.

"I hope you're satisfied," she cried, "but this only goes to prove that I can't think straight around you."

She began to pull on her clothes with more haste than care. Erik realized that he felt vulnerable, sitting on her floor as naked as the emperor in the fairy tale, so he dressed, too, even though her change of tune bewildered him. "I think we need to talk," he said.

Together, they stood. He jammed the tail of his shirt into his jeans with frustrated jabs. Marybeth still refused to meet his eyes. Instead, she glanced at the front door. Annabelle was lying there with her head on her paws, watching them.

Marybeth sucked in a deep breath. "No, I think you'd better leave now," she told him through gritted teeth, as if moments before they hadn't been entangled together on her living-room rug.

Still shaken by the way he'd totally lost control of the whole situation, Erik didn't bother to argue. He had done nothing she hadn't wanted or had tried to resist in any way, he told himself. If anything, she had encouraged him. Too overwhelmed and confused to argue, he brushed past her and bounded down the steps, never once looking back.

Let her stew while he planned his next move!

The next day had dawned perfect for sightseeing in Seattle, with blue sky unmarred by clouds and temperature promising to hit the low eighties. If Erik's attention wasn't totally taken up by the panoramic view from the Space Needle and the selection of souvenirs in the shops along the Seattle waterfront, he tried not to show it.

"Come on, Daddy!" Tina hollered, racing ahead to hold open the door to a quaint-looking place that undoubtedly sold more T-shirts, ceramic sea gulls glued onto bits of driftwood, and earrings in the shapes of sand dollars and starfish.

When Erik got inside, he roused himself enough to smile at the three people with him. Neither Sal nor Betty had asked any questions over breakfast that morning, but Erik suspected they guessed that his visit to Marybeth the night before hadn't gone well.

He had tossed and turned through the night, looking for answers. Today, he knew, the lack of sleep showed in his face. "You go ahead," he told Tina and her grandparents, trying to keep the weariness from his voice. "I'll catch up."

Betty gave him a sympathetic look. "Don't hurry."

The Bernadettis purchased the requisite number of presents for friends back home and then Erik treated them to a memorable meal at a seafood bar. It was located at the end of a long pier, surrounded by gulls and salt breezes.

By the time they had checked in at the airport, Tina was obviously wilting. Erik, less noticeably he hoped, was more than ready to go home to brood if not to rest.

"Thank you so much for sharing your home and your daughter with us," Sal Bernadetti told him while his wife said her goodbyes to Tina. "We'll rest easier, knowing that our son's child is in such a nice home, cared for by someone who loves her as we do." He reached out his hand, and Erik clasped it firmly.

"Thank you," he said, surprised by his own sincerity. "Meeting you has meant a lot to both of us." Until recently, he'd been afraid of this couple's very existence. Now he thought of them as family. "I'm glad that Tina has grandparents to love her like you do."

"And I'm glad she has a father like you." Sal's expression was warm with approval. Then he turned to hug Tina as Betty threw her plump arms around Erik's neck and embarrassed him with a hearty kiss on the cheek.

"Come and visit us," she suggested. "We'd love to have you both." There was nothing except loving acceptance in her faded blue eyes.

Erik appreciated his inclusion in her invitation. Neither she nor her husband seemed to resent him in any way. Instead they made him feel loved, a sensation he was still getting used to. Maybe someday he'd tell them how he'd really come into Tina's life, and maybe they'd understand.

"I miss you both already," Tina said, voice starting to waver.

Erik scooped her up and settled her upon his shoulders.

"With school starting soon, you'll be too busy to miss us," her grandmother said quickly. "Perhaps, if your grades are very good, you can convince your dad to bring you for a visit during Mardi Gras sometime."

"What's Mardi Gras?" Tina asked, successfully diverted.

"It's like the whole city having a giant birthday party at the same time," Sal told her. "With parades and wonderful music, and everyone dressing up in costumes."

"Can we, Daddy?" She leaned down to peer at him while Erik held on to her tightly.

"We'll see."

"That's what you always say."

Before anyone could add anything else, the airline representative announced the first boarding call for the Bernadettis' flight. There were hugs and kisses all around again and promises to keep in touch. Then the older people disappeared down the jetway.

"Can we stay and watch their plane take off?" Tina asked.

Erik, grateful she hadn't started to cry, quickly agreed. He wasn't eager to turn his thoughts back to the problems with Marybeth just yet. He and Tina waited at the huge windows while the big 737 taxied away from the gate and rolled slowly out of sight. A few minutes later, the plane raced down the runway and soared into the sky.

Tina insisted on watching until it was only a tiny speck.

"Well, princess," Erik told her when he set her down, "I guess it's time to go home."

When Tina looked up at him, her dark eyes were sparkling. "First I want to thank you, Daddy."

"Thank me for what?"

"For getting me some grandparents. Now I'm like most of the other kids. And when I have a mommy, I'll be *all set.*"

Chapter Fourteen

Over the next few days, whenever Erik's subconscious thrust Marybeth's name or even her likeness in front of the conscious part of his brain, he did his best to ignore the reminders of her existence. Instead, he kept busy. Busy enough that he fell into bed each night, exhausted. If he still couldn't sleep, at least his tired and benumbed brain didn't race in circles, trying to figure out where he'd gone wrong.

At least, not all the time.

During the day, he listened to Tina's endless comments about her grandparents and questions concerning New Orleans and the whole state of Louisiana. He dragged up every bit of knowledge he had about the city where they lived and the festival of Mardi Gras. They even paid a visit to the local library to check out everything they had on Louisiana. Tina's thirst for knowledge seemed insatiable.

A week after the Bernadettis left, a package arrived from them. Inside were New Orleans T-shirts for both Erik and Tina, an elaborate feather mask for her and earrings for Mrs. O'Reilly. With the gifts was a note saying the flight back had been uneventful and they were now settled at home.

"Can I wear this on Halloween?" Tina asked, after she'd donned the shirt and the mask of peacock feathers.

Erik studied her for a moment. "Don't see why not. You might have to wear a coat, though." October evenings in Puget Sound tended to be cool and rainy.

After serious thought and a couple of phone calls, Erik went into Tina's room where she was playing with her dolls a few evenings later. Beside her on the floor, Joker was sprawled on his side, dozing. Tied around his neck was a wide red ribbon.

"Hi," she said, glancing up at Erik briefly before returning her attention to Jennifer, Kim and Heather.

"Hi." Erik sat down on the edge of her bed and watched her while she laid out clothes for each one. "What are you doing?"

"Getting them ready for the first day of school. Kim's scared but Jennifer told her not to be."

Erik couldn't hold back a grin at her grave tone. "I see."

After another moment, Tina stopped playing and stood up. "Is there something I can do for you?" she asked politely.

Erik's grin grew wider. He was sure she'd be pleased at what he was about to ask. "Well, I wondered if you'd like to take a week out of school next spring and go to Mardi Gras?" He was unprepared for her reaction.

Tina launched herself at him and clamped her hands around his neck. She planted a wet kiss on his cheek with a noisy smack. "In New Orleans?" she cried.

"Yeah," he said, hugging her close. "Your grandparents would really like us to go." He didn't tell her that they'd invited Marybeth, too, if Erik cared to bring her. Next spring was a long time away. She would probably be involved with someone else before then.

The unexpected pain the thought brought with it almost doubled him over.

"Wow," Tina exclaimed. "I can see Grandma and Grampa, and miss school, too! And we can go to all the places we read about." For a moment, her arms tightened, then she slid off his lap, where he'd pulled her during the hug.

"How soon is next spring?"

"A while after Christmas," he told her.

For a moment, her smile wavered. "I just hope I can wait that long," she said gravely.

Erik rose and looked down on the little girl who'd come so far since he'd brought her with him from Argentina. "The time will go fast," he said. "Try not to get too impatient."

"Okay." Her attention was immediately taken up with her dolls.

As he left her room, Erik wished ruefully that his own thoughts could be so easily distracted.

That night he found himself thinking of Marybeth's accusation that he kept his feelings locked inside. How could she still think that after he'd told her he loved her?

But she was right, he finally admitted to himself. He hadn't been completely honest. Was it really because he didn't trust her enough to confide in her, or was it the training he'd had, to submerge his own emotions, to mask them at all times, to keep his vulnerable side completely buried? Or was it because he'd learned in childhood not to reveal too much of himself?

Erik shifted uncomfortably in the leather recliner in his den. Such deep self-examination made him uncomfortable. Still, he pondered her accusations. How could he convince her that he was trying to change? How could he persuade her to give him another chance?

He'd become more open with Tina. He'd taken a big risk with uniting her with her grandparents, and it hadn't gone sour. Maybe there was still something he could do to get Marybeth back into his arms, into his bed, and into his heart, where he now knew she belonged. He was no dummy. If he thought about the problem long enough, he was bound to come up with a workable solution.

Marybeth sat on a flat rock and watched the waves as the tide worked its way up the beach. As usual, the dogs were racing up and down the thin strip of wet gray sand, splashing with carefree abandon. First, Arthur would chase Annabelle and then, as if by prearranged signal, they would both wheel around and Annabelle would chase Arthur back past Marybeth. Finally, tongues lolling, the two big dogs loped over to where she sat, shook themselves and collapsed at her feet. Their panting was noisy, and their sides heaved.

Marybeth scooped up a handful of sand and small pebbles, sorting through it idly as her brain continued to whirr along on its own.

Was she trying to make Erik pay for Mike's sins? For her own inability to deal with his death for so long? There were still a lot of questions for which she had no answers.

"It's about time for dinner," she told the expectant dogs.

Immediately recognizing the *d* word, they lunged to their feet. Annabelle began to bark in piercing yips while Arthur ran toward the house and back again, obviously impatient for Marybeth to hurry.

She rose with a sigh. The time she'd spent ruminating over her last meeting with Erik had gotten her nowhere. She had asked herself how she could have permitted him to make love to her that last time under the circumstances, but there had been no easy answer. Because she still loved him. Because she wanted him. Despite his flaws, and undoubtedly hers, too, what they did share was achingly sweet.

This was getting her nowhere. She had loved Mike, too, but that love had ended in pain. Now it was happening again.

Arthur barked sharply, ending her reverie. Marybeth sighed again. She would be better off to stick to her animals and her nursing, at least until she could figure out what weakness drew her so strongly to men who lacked the ability to trust.

Marybeth had no more than made the resolution that it was tested. She was walking back down the beach to her house, the dogs galloping ahead, when she saw Joker racing toward them. Reaching her dogs, he stopped, tail wagging and body wiggling from stem to stern. Eagerly all three animals began the greeting ritual of thorough sniffing.

Marybeth froze.

Not far behind Joker came Erik. He looked so good she wanted to weep. Above the deep tan of his face, his hair shone almost white. His wide shoulders were displayed to perfection by his red tank top and the length of his legs were sheathed, as usual, in worn, snug-fitting jeans.

Marybeth felt exposed by her own white sun top and faded cutoffs.

Erik's expression was serious but not hostile. She looked for Tina behind him but didn't see her, and wondered why he had come back.

"There's something I forgot to say," he announced before she could form a greeting. "I want to tell you about it now, if you have the time." His eyes glittered darkly, and there were lines of tension around his mouth. To Marybeth, he looked like a man who was about to take the biggest gamble of his life.

"What is it?" she asked, her stomach twisting into knots of its own. Had Mike ever worn that particular expression, as if he were about to tell her something she hadn't wanted to know?

Erik took her hand, and she realized that his was cold. Leading her to a driftwood log, he pulled her down beside him.

"Where did the dogs go?" she asked, in a sudden panic to avert whatever it was he meant to tell her. Something she knew she didn't want to hear. A sense of doom weighted the very air surrounding the two of them.

Erik glanced around impatiently. "Never mind the dogs. They'll be okay." He released her hand.

She folded her arms across her chest in what she immediately recognized as a defensive gesture. Taking a deep breath, she clasped them loosely in her lap and made herself wait silently until he was ready to speak. Inside, she was shaking.

"I told you a little about what happened in Argentina, before I brought Tina back to the States," he began haltingly.

"That's right. You did tell me." She tried to smile, but her mouth was trembling.

"But I didn't tell you everything. What I didn't tell you," he continued, "what I've never told anyone except my superiors at the agency, is that I was the one who killed Tina's mother. I shot her."

For a moment, Marybeth remained perfectly still, absorbing the shock of what he had just admitted. Then she looked, really looked, into his face. The guilt and self-condemnation she saw there overwhelmed everything else she was feeling. She slid closer and grasped his hand tightly, wanting only to somehow ease his pain.

"I know it couldn't have been your fault," she said, with utter conviction borne of her love for him. "So why don't you tell me how it happened?"

Her unconditional acceptance of what Erik had thought would be a shocking revelation threw him into confusion. While she sat waiting patiently for him to continue, he studied her face. The love and understanding he saw there warmed him, and he could feel himself start to heal. She hadn't condemned him for the killing of Tina's mother; she assumed it must have been an accident. Her faith in him was more than he had dreamed might be possible.

If she could absolve him so unconditionally, perhaps it was time to forgive himself and let go of the guilt he'd been carrying around for so long.

"Maria's death *was* an accident," he began, confirming her supposition. He narrowed his eyes, allowing his memory to plunge him back into Bernadetti's compound. "Like I already told you, I was in Argentina for only one thing, to gain his trust and lure him back to the States so we could nab him the minute he stepped onto American soil."

Erik glanced at Marybeth, who was watching him with a grave expression. When he hesitated, she gave his hand a reassuring pat. He turned it over and linked his fingers with hers, savoring her warmth.

Inside, he was shaking with fear, still terrified that she might yet turn away when she absorbed what he was telling her.

"After a few weeks, it was clear to me that no amount of persuasion was going to uproot him from his stronghold, so I went to Plan B. I needed to learn as much as I could about his security so a small group of our men could breach it. Meanwhile, Bernadetti's abuse of Maria was getting worse, and I was more and more afraid that he was going to really hurt Tina."

Marybeth's expression became more grim. She looked as if she wanted to say something.

"What is it?" he asked.

"I feel so bad for Maria. Trapped because of her love for her child."

Erik gave Marybeth's hand a squeeze. "When he mistreated her in front of me, I thought he might be testing me in some way. The whole situation made me sick. I'd made a point to befriend Maria, but I had to be extremely careful because Bernadetti was known to be insanely jealous."

Erik took a breath, the memories flooding back as clearly as if the scenes were taking place in front of him. "The worst time, I saw him yank Tina by one arm and then hold her upside down by the ankles. She had accidentally broken a valuable vase. Maria was pleading with him to let Tina go and punish her instead."

He swallowed, remembering the sound of Tina's cries through the open window. He had wanted to burst in and save her. "Bernadetti screamed at Maria, and then let Tina fall to the floor. Luckily she wasn't seriously hurt, but she was terrified. She wouldn't go to him willingly after that, which only infuriated him more."

Marybeth gasped, obviously horrified. Her hands flew to her mouth, and her eyes filled with tears. "What an awful man. It must have been sheer hell for you, not being able to interfere."

Even now, the memory made Erik tremble with suppressed rage. "It was then I knew I had to get them out, but it would have been too suspicious for us to leave before the raid. And then, like I told you, Maria was late meeting me that night. Everything went wrong. I was so sure it was Bernadetti there in the garden. So sure," he repeated.

"I'd seen him moments before in almost the same spot. When I saw that flash of red and the black hair again, I reacted. I saw the gun pointed at me, and I fired." He raked a trembling hand over his face. "I've gone over it a hundred times in my mind, wondering if there was anything I could have done differently. Wondering if there was a split second somewhere that I could have stopped myself, taken another moment to be sure.

"Dammit! I *was* sure." He shook his head, remorse filling him. "How will I ever be able to tell Tina what I did?"

Marybeth reached out to touch his shoulder. Feeling the tension in him, she rubbed his rigid muscles with her hand. So this was the terrible secret that Erik had kept buried inside for so long. No wonder the poor man had been tormented.

"It was an accident," she told him. "You were willing to risk everything, including your own life, to help someone who needed you. You did the best you could. Tragic as it was, Maria's death wasn't your fault. If anything, it was Bernadetti's!"

She searched for the right thing to say, to make Erik realize that he had to let it go. "I can imagine the confusion, the urgency of that night, with the darkness, the shooting, your desperation to get the two of them to safety." She stopped and thought for a moment, picking her words carefully. So much weighed on this, perhaps both their futures.

Beside her, Erik sat tensely and looked out at the water. She hoped he was absorbing some of what she said.

"Sometimes we do our best, and it isn't enough. It happens at the hospital, too. It's all we have to give! Then sometimes all we can do is to let go. To think not that we've failed, but that we did our best and, for some reason, it didn't change things. But we did all we could, and we have to cling to that."

She looked up into Erik's closed face. "Can you understand what I'm telling you? You didn't fail, not really. You didn't turn away—you did all you could. For some reason we can't know, it didn't change the outcome. But you tried. At serious risk to yourself and your mission, you did what you knew was right. That's all any of us can do. When Tina's old enough to be told, she'll understand that. Because you will have raised her to understand and to forgive."

A breeze sprang up, coming off the water. It blew Marybeth's hair across her forehead. She eased closer to Erik, letting the hand that had been massaging his tight muscles rest on his bare shoulder.

"You have to let it go," she continued more urgently. Were her words getting through to him? "You have to forgive yourself. Look what you've accomplished. You've given Tina a loving home. You brought her grandparents out, even though you were afraid you might lose her. If

Maria had made it, I have no doubt that you would have done whatever you could have for her, too."

Erik's shoulders slumped with weariness. "Yeah," he agreed. "I hadn't thought past getting them away from Bernadetti, but I guess I would have had to do more than just that."

"See?" she demanded. "Your intentions were the best. Now give yourself some credit, and then let the pain go. You've been carrying it around for way too long." She watched him carefully, searching for a reaction. "Let it go," she repeated.

He straightened and looked into her eyes. "You're really something, you know that?" In the distance, a lone sea gull cried hauntingly as Erik reached up to touch her cheek. "Thanks." He was smiling but something in his eyes still looked unconvinced.

She knew she had to dig deep, to expose herself totally to make him understand. "After Mike and I were married," she said, fighting the instinct to leave the painful memories buried, "I told myself that it was his fault he didn't share the details of his work with me. I told myself that after he'd been killed. It was his fault."

She took a deep breath of the salt air. "But what I couldn't face was my own guilt. I know now that I made it easy for him to keep it locked inside. I didn't want to know. And somehow I let him see that. I didn't want to share the ugliness, the danger. It was easier to tell myself I was there for him, but I really wasn't."

The confession was a painful one, and she realized she was shaking. Erik turned to face her and took her hand. He stroked it gently. Silently he watched her. His close attention to what she was saying encouraged her to go on.

"In a very elementary way, I failed Mike," Marybeth admitted both to herself and to Erik. "When you kept part of yourself closed off from me, I felt like a failure all over again. I felt that, because I'd shut Mike out, I didn't deserve your trust, that loving you and not sharing everything was somehow my punishment for Mike." As she spoke the words, Marybeth found herself believing them, accepting them.

Erik's eyes had darkened at her admission of love. "No," he said, gripping her hand tighter. "It wasn't your fault. It was never your fault. I'm sure you don't deserve the blame, either. Just like you told me, you did your best at the time."

His expression grew anxious. "I know now that you deserve my trust. But how could I expect you to accept what I'd done to Tina's mother when I couldn't accept it myself?" His smile was ragged around the edges. "I knew how I was starting to feel about you, but I honestly didn't think I deserved any real happiness. I expected Tina to be snatched away from me at any minute. No way could I allow myself to become emotionally involved with someone else I was convinced would somehow be taken from me, too."

Erik raked his hand over his hair, overwhelmed with all the things they'd both said. "Maybe," he mused, "it's time that we both forgive ourselves—and each other. Do you think we could do that?"

Marybeth got to her feet, her expression too complex for him to read. "Sure. I think that's an excellent idea."

Inside her, the small grain of hope was beginning to grow. Then, to her surprise, Erik rose and took both her hands in his. "Will you trust me one more time?" he asked. His face was unreadable, but the pain she'd seen there before had been replaced by something else, a light that seemed to glow from within.

"Come on," he urged. "No questions, okay?"

She nodded, curious. "Okay. We can leave the dogs inside."

Her unconditional acceptance brought a smile to his face. She wouldn't let herself read anything into it. Instead, she shut the dogs in the house and followed him to his pickup. She sat quietly beside him while he drove toward the ranch.

Turning off a side road, he continued on up the hill. Marybeth remembered the last time they'd come this way. Despite her determination to keep her emotions firmly under control, her heart began to soar with hope.

Getting out briefly to unlock the gate, Erik drove the truck through and parked it in the same spot he had before. He got out and extended a hand to Marybeth, who slid across the seat and climbed down. As soon as she had both feet on the ground, he released her.

"Come on," he said.

She followed him without question or comment. When they were standing at the place where they had first made love, Erik took her lightly in his arms.

"I have a lot to tell you." His smile was tender. "I suppose I've been storing it up for years, waiting unconsciously for just the right person to share it all with."

While Marybeth stood in the circle of his arms, he cleared his throat. His eyes were no longer shadowed.

"I love you," he told her, voice rich with emotion. "I meant it when I told you that before, but now my feelings have grown even stronger. I know it's the real thing. Forever. You can't begin to understand how much you mean to me, but I need a lifetime together to show you."

At his words, tears came to Marybeth's eyes. She didn't bother to wipe them away. They ran down her cheeks and she was almost unbearably moved to see that Erik's own blue eyes were wet, too.

Before she could guess what he was going to do, he went down on one knee before her. While he held her hand as if it were a lifeline, his expression became almost bleak, giving her a clear idea of how much of a strain he was under.

"Marry me," he urged, his voice almost breaking with tension. "Now that I've found you, I can't give you up."

She started to answer but he interrupted. "First, I need to make you a promise. I'll share myself and Tina's love with you, if you'll entrust yourself to my care. Just like you entrusted your most painful secrets to me to help me let go of the guilt that had crippled me for so long. In a way, you set me free. Free to love you. I want us to be together forever." He got to his feet, narrowed eyes boring into hers.

"Now you can answer," he said. His smile was brittle with strain.

Tears of happiness rained from Marybeth's eyes while she smiled up at him. Her heart was overflowing. Almost too full of love to speak, she finally threw her arms around his neck. "Yes," she managed to gasp.

Erik wrapped his arms around her as a deep, shuddering breath shook his rigid body. He buried his face in her hair. "Thank God!" he exclaimed. "For a moment, there, I thought I'd really misjudged your feelings. I realize I'm no bargain—"

She pressed her fingers to his mouth, giving him a warning look. "I wasn't looking for a bargain. I was looking for the one man I could love forever, the one man who could give me the love and trust I need." She took a deep breath. "That one man is you."

Erik's face was more alive with emotion than she had ever seen it. He bent to kiss her. His lips were both tender and possessive. Passion began to hum along her veins when he released her and took a ragged breath.

"I never thought I'd be saying this, but I'm damn glad those men tried to rob the bank that day."

"We'll have an interesting answer if anyone asks how we met," Marybeth agreed, remembering how impressed she'd been at the time by his courage.

"Come on," he urged. "Before I fall totally under your spell again, there's a little girl waiting at home to hear the best news we could give her."

"You're right." They began to walk hand in hand back to Erik's truck. "A little girl who dreamed we could be the family she wanted."

Erik's smile, when he looked at Marybeth, was open and loving. Happier than she'd ever thought possible, she reached up on tiptoe to kiss him.

* * * * *

Silhouette Special Edition ®

Linda Lael Miller

Beyond the Threshold

Two stories linked
by centuries, and by love....

There and Now

The story of Elisabeth McCartney, a woman looking for a love she can't find in the 1990s. Only with the mystery of her Aunt Verity's necklace can she discover her true love—Dr. Jonathan Fortner, a country doctor in Washington—in 1892....

There and Now, #754, available in July 1992.

Here and Then

Desperate to find her cousin, Elisabeth, Rue Claridge searched for her in this century . . . and the last. She found Elisabeth, all right. And also found U.S. Marshal Farley Haynes—a nineteenth-century man with a vision for the future....

Here and Then, #762, available in August 1992.

**It's Opening Night in October—
and you're invited!
Take a look at romance with a
brand-new twist, as the stars
of tomorrow make their
debut today!
It's LOVE:
an age-old story—
now, with
*WORLD PREMIERE
APPEARANCES* by:**

Patricia Thayer—Silhouette Romance #895
JUST MAGGIE—Meet the Texas rancher who wins this pretty
teacher's heart...and lose your own heart, too!

Anne Marie Winston—Silhouette Desire #742
BEST KEPT SECRETS—Join old lovers reunited and see what
secret wonders have been hiding...beneath the flames!

Sierra Rydell—Silhouette Special Edition #772
ON MIDDLE GROUND—Drift toward Twilight, Alaska, with this
widowed mother and collide—heart first—into body heat
enough to melt the frozen tundra!

Kate Carlton—Silhouette Intimate Moments #454
KIDNAPPED!—Dare to look on as a timid wallflower blos-
soms and falls in fearless love—with her gruff, mysterious
kidnapper!

**Don't miss the classics of tomorrow—
premiering today—only from**

PREM

Take 4 bestselling love stories FREE

Plus get a FREE surprise gift!

Special Limited-time Offer

Mail to Silhouette Reader Service™

In the U.S.	In Canada
3010 Walden Avenue	P.O. Box 609
P.O. Box 1867	Fort Erie, Ontario
Buffalo, N.Y. 14269-1867	L2A 5X3

YES! Please send me 4 free Silhouette Special Edition® novels and my free surprise gift. Then send me 6 brand-new novels every month, which I will receive months before they appear in bookstores. Bill me at the low price of $2.96* each—a savings of 43¢ apiece off the cover prices. There are no shipping, handling or other hidden costs. I understand that accepting the books and gift places me under no obligation ever to buy any books. I can always return a shipment and cancel at any time. Even if I never buy another book from Silhouette, the 4 free books and the surprise gift are mine to keep forever.

*Offer slightly different in Canada—$2.96 per book plus 69¢ per shipment for delivery. Canadian residents add applicable federal and provincial sales tax. Sales tax applicable in N.Y.

235 BPA ADMC   335 BPA ADMQ

Name	(PLEASE PRINT)
Address	Apt. No.
City	State/Prov. Zip/Postal Code

This offer is limited to one order per household and not valid to present Silhouette Special Edition® subscribers. Terms and prices are subject to change.

SPED-92   © 1990 Harlequin Enterprises Limited

NORA ROBERTS

Love has a language all its own, and for centuries, flowers have symbolized love's finest expression. Discover the language of flowers—and love—in this romantic collection of 48 favorite books by bestselling author Nora Roberts.

Two titles are available each month at your favorite retail outlet.

In August, look for:

Tempting Fate, **Volume #13**
From this Day, **Volume #14**

In September, look for:

All the Possibilities, **Volume #15**
The Heart's Victory, **Volume #16**

THE
LANGUAGE
of LOVE

Collect all 48 titles
and become fluent in

® *Silhouette®*

Back by popular demand...

TELL ME NO LIES

In a world
full of deceit
and manipulation,
truth is a double-
edged sword.

Lindsay Danner is the
only one who can lead the
search for the invaluable
Chinese bronzes. Jacob
Catlin is the only one who
can protect her. They
hadn't planned on
falling in love....

Available in August at
your favorite retail outlet.

ELIZABETH LOWELL

Silhouette Books®

SEL92